Praise for *In the Shadow of Silence . . .*

"A deeply nuanced and emotionally complex novel that explores some of the most challenging aspects of mental health, relationships, and family dynamics."

—David A. Mitnick, M.D., Clinical Assistant Professor of Psychiatry, Weill Medical College of Cornell University

"*In the Shadow of Silence* captures, in beautiful prose, the hardship to the family members of someone who suffers with clinical depression. The author conveys the many truths in loving someone who sinks into mental illness. She clearly knows this terrain. She describes the constant worry, the nuanced relationships, and the resistance to staying in treatment."

—Caleb Mason, author of *Normal Family* and *Thickafog*

"This captivating novel brings the reader into the lives of characters they will cherish forever. It touches on much of what makes us human. It also delivers a powerful message: Even the deepest love may not be capable of rescuing another from the depths of mental illness."

—Lissa Parsonnet, Phd, LCSW, Former Asst. Director, Dept. of Social Work at Memorial-Sloane Kettering

IN THE SHADOW OF SILENCE

IN THE SHADOW OF SILENCE

A Novel

Rae Dumont

SHE WRITES PRESS

Copyright © 2026 Rae Dumont
All rights reserved. No part of this publication may be reproduced, stored in a retrieval system, or transmitted in any form or by any means, electronic, mechanical, photocopying, recording, or otherwise, except for brief quotations in reviews, educational works, or other uses permitted by copyright law.

Published in 2026 by
She Writes Press, an imprint of The Stable Book Group

32 Court Street, Suite 2109
Brooklyn, NY 11201
https://shewritespress.com
Library of Congress Control Number: 2025917170
ISBN: 979-8-89636-072-8
eISBN: 979-8-89636-073-5

Interior Designer: Kiran Spees

Printed in the United States
This is a work of fiction. Names, characters, places, and incidents are either products of the author's imagination or are used fictitiously. Any resemblance to actual persons, living or dead, is purely coincidental.

No part of this publication may be used to train generative artificial intelligence (AI) models. The publisher and author reserve all rights related to the use of this content in machine learning.

All company and product names mentioned in this book may be trademarks or registered trademarks of their respective owners. They are used for identification purposes only and do not imply endorsement or affiliation.

For Laurel and Sylvan

AUTHOR'S NOTE

I am a mother, a widow, and a friend. Life has brought its share of pain, my own and that of loved ones, and I know its ripple effects.

As a pediatrician and as a family therapist I have borne witness to many people's experiences, and I have tried to help. Sometimes, despite my best efforts, I could not ease their suffering. In writing fiction, I hope to bring these many lives to the page, and to share what they have taught me.

When tragedy touches a loved one, a family, or a friend, its effects reach far beyond those it affects directly. Depression and anxiety are on the rise. Suicide leaves behind a storm of sorrow and confusion, guilt, and anger.

I wrote this book for those who struggle with depression. Help is at hand; there are people who love you, and people who care. There is light beyond the darkness.

This book is also for you, if you have loved someone who suffers, and you have felt helpless.

I want you to know you are not alone, and it is not your fault.

Part I
A Family

"Love is the pursuit of shadows."

—Margaret Atwood

Prologue

Summer 2018

Old photographs with curled edges are scattered on the red kilim rug. Barefoot on her knees, in faded denim overalls, Eva sorts them into piles. She pulls a shoulder strap up over her vintage silk shirt, bright purple with tiny daisies.

She tosses the blurriest, most brittle pictures on the discard pile, sits back on her heels, and tucks a loose strand of gray hair behind her ear. Three shoeboxes sit on the floor, filled with still more images.

On the coffee table, Eva carefully fans out the largest black-and-white photos. Uncle Roger spent hours in the dark room creating these crisp prints, full of contrast and shadows, on grainy matte paper. Eva picks up a self-portrait of him with her aunt. He wears enormous furry mittens, like bear paws. Aunt Josie is trapped in his arms, and he looks at her with amusement. She smiles at the camera, coquettish, and nestles into him. How Eva misses them and the delight they took in each other.

Here is a small photograph of young Eva, perhaps two or three years old, perched on top of a huge Belgian draft horse. Uncle Roger stands beside the beast. He looks up, holding the halter. She is just a little girl with a pale full-skirted dress, her legs stretched across the broad back, a wide grin on her face. The sweet smell of the horse made her feel safe. Her love of horses was one of the many lasting gifts from Uncle Roger.

Eva's knees hurt. Serves her right, she thinks, for getting so lost in time. She slowly gets up and makes her way to the kitchen. She fills the kettle, then returns to collect some smaller pictures from the living room floor in the lid of an open shoebox. She straightens, careful with her back, sets the lid on a tray with her tea, and heads out to the patio. She settles into her funky cypress rocking chair. She rests her foot on a stool; her feet cannot reach the ground without it. Gabe, her middle child, laughed when he first saw her sitting in it. "Hello there, Edith Ann!" he said. And it's true, the oversized rocker dwarfs her.

She sits for a while, admiring the fields and tall grasses. A few irises sparkle an impossible blue. She tracks the swallows overhead and listens to the busy red-winged blackbirds. It is too hazy today to see the Green Mountains further away, but she knows that they stand there, steady and familiar.

The venerable northern red oak proudly towers above the white ash and hickory. Over the years, it has become a little easier to look at that tree, but still, almost every time, she relives that awful day again. And then her thoughts spiral to Lyman's terrible note. What if she had not gone on that trip? Maybe he—maybe she could have stopped him . . .

Her mind wanders through the years that followed. Olivia, the youngest, might not have had such a turbulent adolescence with her father around. Maybe Gabriel wouldn't have stepped into the void his father left, to support Olivia—and grown up too fast. Then again, perhaps he became more himself, finding his footing as he supported his stumbling little sister.

And Ezra? Her intense and talented firstborn? He took on challenges at full speed; when he slammed into walls, he bounced back and made it all into music. Would he have dealt with his troubles more wisely if his father had lived? A familiar, sad-angry chill prowls around her heart at the wonder and the tragedy of her marriage.

She is too old to live alone in this big house, but she cannot bear the thought of leaving. She has raised her children here. When she first bought it, it was a tiny, dilapidated cottage, but then she and Lyman improved it and made it bigger over the years. So many memories live in the house. In the fields and in the trees too.

And so here she stays, and she remembers.

Chapter 1
June 1975

Someday, he'll come along, the man I love.

Eva sings at the top of her lungs as she drives north on Interstate 87, leaving Manhattan behind. Her lime-green Subaru is packed with her few belongings, including a medical license and a brand-new Board Certificate in Child Psychiatry. They are safely stowed in a file box on the back seat, next to her growing collection of jazz albums. She is exhausted after the long years of medical school and then these four years at Columbia, training in psychiatry. It was all exhilarating, but she is ready for fresh air and open space, and excited to start her job in the Department of Psychiatry at the University of Vermont.

And he'll be big and strong, the man I love. There could be no better place than Vermont to find him because he will be a man at home in the mountains and on rivers.

She desperately wants to find someone to love, someone who will love her back. Her parents were emotionally absent, so self-absorbed they could not see who she was or what she needed. They were caught up in constant bickering. Too often, try as she might, she got caught between them. She was barely eight the first time she dreamed of taking a train to her Aunt Josie and Uncle Roger. They lived an hour away in Brussels; she wanted to ask whether she could live with them. There was laughter in their apartment high above the city; people talked there and listened to each other. Nobody barked their displeasure, and nobody got ordered around. And there were no secrets lurking.

Much as she adored them both, she also knew she was not their favorite niece. It was her cousin Annie who made them smile, whose bright blue eyes and dimpled cheeks made them happy. Eva, to them, was the capable one, and Uncle Roger expected a lot from her. He scrutinized her grades and expected her to excel, convinced her that she *could* excel; he presented her with tricky questions of logic, and he was pleased when she figured them out. She treasured the way he challenged her to think. But even so, she always longed to be special to them both, in that tender way that they reserved for her younger cousin.

Eva was sixteen when Uncle Roger took her aside for a talk, one day in the yard, at a family gathering. He handed her three boxes of birth control pills. She gaped at him, not at all ready for this. What did he think she was up to? She didn't even have a boyfriend, wasn't interested, really.

"What you do is your own affair," he said that day. "But you should know that Aunt Josie had a wartime abortion. She was nineteen. She survived it—many didn't. She could never have children afterward. She—we—wanted children very much." He gave her that piercing look of his, blue-gray eyes like knives. "So, Eva, don't get yourself pregnant. And if you do, then don't be a fool, ask for help. I have colleagues who could help. Just ask." And he sauntered off, leaving her stunned.

After that talk, Eva understood why they had pulled Annie into their orbit, as much as her parents allowed. It was Annie who filled a void for Aunt Josie.

Uncle Roger has loomed large in Eva's mind and heart over the years. She longs to find someone like him, a man she can admire, and to whom she matters, who makes her feel special.

He'll look at me and smile. I'll understand. And in a little while, he'll take my hand . . .

Spring 1977

Eva has lived in Vermont for two years now. She loves her child psychiatry practice and her colleagues at the hospital. But she is still looking for the man in the song. *The man I love . . .*

She is twenty-nine now, staring at thirty. Vivid fantasies about children intrude more and more often. She loves babies, she knows how to nurture toddlers and bond with surly teenagers. She can guess what they need because she remembers what she did *not* get growing up. She loves her work and connects with young people instinctively, almost immediately. Doesn't that mean she *should* be a mother?

Aunt Josie yearned for children of her own, and now, years later, here Eva is yearning too. She does not want to be condemned to wishing that other people's children were her own. So, she had best do something about it. Methodically, she goes on a few dates. But her heart is never in it. Nobody is quite as brilliant or as fascinating as Uncle Roger was. Or as courageous as he was, risking his life in the Resistance, surviving two years in a Nazi concentration camp.

Besides, she still hurts over Daniel, who promised her the moon only to break her heart. It was just a year ago that he dumped her without explanation. A terrible certainty had washed over her then: I am not lovable. In Uncle Roger's eyes, she only came second, after her cousin. With Daniel, she wanted to believe she came first and that he really loved her. But he did not.

A few months ago, she met Sam. He was kind and steady, and he liked her. She forced herself to spend time with him, reminding herself that kindness is better than charisma and more trustworthy than brilliance. Sam was a gentle soul. He opened doors for her and brought her flowers. After she mentioned Virginia Woolf, he gave her a lovely edition of *Mrs. Dalloway*. And she soon wanted to scream. She got bored and imagined herself trapped in a conventional life like her mother's. She bolted, called it off awkwardly, and fretted about hurting this gentle man who was so easily bruised. And again, her mind turned back to Daniel. She is now much too careful, too skittish, and too picky. She expects—she deserves—another betrayal. She will, without a doubt, only be the next item in the next man's catalog of conquests.

Where did she rank in Daniel's catalog of conquests, she wonders?

Genus:	Woman
Species:	Smart
Identifying characteristic:	Available
Natural habitat:	Summer: shorelines
	Winter: mountains
Name:	Eva

Perhaps she is better off on her own then. She doesn't need the heartbreak again. After Daniel dumped her, she took some horseback riding lessons at the nearby equestrian center to distract herself. It made her think of Uncle Roger, to be around horses, and she loved it. Then someone told Eva about a small horse whose owner could no longer ride. Not a show horse, just for trail riding. And in exchange for mucking out a few stalls, boarding the horse would be free. It was an irresistible offer, so she bought the lovely little mare and named her Tarot. The horse helped, but it still took months for her to claw out of her despair.

And yet there must be *someone* out there for her. Someone passionate and bright. Someone who loves the outdoors as she does. Someone to share adventures with, and whose mind challenges hers. Someone who is sharp and curious, and who will love her. She doesn't want to choose between care and excitement.

But he hasn't come her way. Not yet.

One rainy April evening, she leaves the hospital, walks to the parking lot, and notices a flyer pasted on lamp posts along the path. An ecologist who teaches here at the University of Vermont. He is giving a lecture tonight.

The Greenhouse Effect:
Impact on Natural Habitats in Rivers and Lakes
Dr. Lyman Willis
7 p.m., Rubenstein Auditorium
School of Environment and Natural Resources

That could be interesting. It is a miserable wet evening, and she has nothing urgent to do. Going for a ride is not appealing in tonight's damp chill. She grabs a bite at the pita place and makes her way to the auditorium. Only four people are there when she arrives. That doesn't bode well for the speaker, whoever he is. She fervently hopes he will be interesting enough to sit through this, because it would be rude to leave early if there were only a tiny audience. She takes a seat, not too close to the front, and hangs her fisherman's cardigan over her chair.

A moment later, a tall man walks into the back of the room. He has curly reddish hair and a beard. He carefully drops his slides, one by one, into the projector's carousel. A dozen more people straggle in and find chairs. At seven sharp, the man ambles up the center aisle toward the front. He ignores the steps to the podium and easily leaps up in a single stride of his long legs. He scans the audience while people continue to talk. He checks the remote for the projector. He seems unruffled and unhurried. At five minutes past the hour, he clears his throat.

"Good evening, folks. My name is Lyman Willis. How are you tonight?"

"Hey, Lyman!" someone shouts from the back door. "Can't stay. Sorry. Just wanted to say hi. Make our department proud, man!" With a thumbs up, he disappears.

Lyman smiles, dims the lights, and clicks the remote. A larger-than-life image of him appears on the screen. His shirt and overalls are soaked and filthy. His face and hands are caked with mud, his lips are blue, and his hair and beard drip with icicles. He is squinting at a rack of test tubes.

"I'm here tonight to show you how much fun it is to study rivers and lakes," he says with a grin. He opens his hands toward the audience. "We always welcome volunteers."

There are chuckles from the audience. "Yeah, right!" someone says.

Lyman is a riveting presenter. He is relaxed, but there is a palpable energy in his voice, in his movements. He talks about tracking riverine bird populations and about the decline in fish stock; he describes the spread of dead zones. "You see, pollution raises nutrient levels, so that the water supports more algae and bacteria, until nothing else survives." Eva has heard her share of academics who revel in jargon and dry, needlessly complex explanations. But Lyman doesn't sound like a textbook.

"But that is not all," he continues. "The greenhouse effect makes the water warmer, and then the fish need more oxygen because their metabolism speeds up." He raises his left hand. "And yet warmer water holds *less* oxygen." He lowers his right hand to illustrate the discrepancy. He doesn't seem to need you to know how smart he is. He just wants you to follow what he says. Eva has the fleeting thought that she would gladly follow him into those muddy rivers. He is so comfortably in charge.

Even when he shows them numbers and graphs, Eva is drawn in. She has clearly lost track of time because, all of a sudden, Lyman is wrapping things up. The first slide is on the screen again, the one where he looks happily miserable.

"So, I'm standing there," he says, "thigh-deep in a river that is icing over, as you can see."

A few people in the audience make shivering noises.

"And something punctures one of my waders."

"Oh shit," someone says.

"That's exactly what I yelled," he says, lifting his left foot and pointing to the bottom of it. "A sharp stick, right through here."

There are some *Ooohs* and *Oh nos!*

"My sock is soaked, the water rises over my foot, and then above my ankle." He indicates the rising water with his hand. "I'm shivering, and my teammates are shouting at me to get out. But I'm not done collecting samples! And then, instead of wading in to help, they take this flattering photo of me."

Everyone laughs.

"I probably should have listened to them, instead of standing in the river for another ten minutes," he grins. "It took the rest of the day to stop shivering. But without those last samples, I wouldn't have had much to tell you today." He turns the projector off and flips on the lights. "Thank you for listening."

People stand and clap. A few come forward to ask questions. Eva lingers and takes in how handsome he looks—rugged but strong without that bulked-up look men get from hours in the gym. His face is tanned, but the skin at the neck of his green corduroy shirt is pale. He wears well-used Carhartt pants, and his hiking boots are scuffed.

She notices his unhurried, nimble responses to people's comments. She racks her brain but cannot think of a smart question to ask. She hangs around until she catches his eye, and then she only tells him how much she appreciated his lecture. He shakes her hand. She feels awkward as she leaves, and only then does she come up with intelligent scientific things she might have said. She can't get out of there quickly enough.

When she enters the parking lot, Eva stands a while before walking to her car. It is no longer raining; the air is fresh and clean after the downpour. She feels fluttery and a little silly, wishing she had said something less mundane to Lyman. She shakes it off and gets ready to leave when she hears a voice calling behind her. "Miss! Miss! Is this your sweater?" She turns around and sees Lyman running out of the building, waving her fisherman's cardigan.

"Oh!" she says as she blushes. "How careless of me, thank you!"

"Quite alright," he says. He looks at her for a moment. "Actually, I could use some coffee. Care to join me? There's a place around the corner."

That's a nice surprise, she thinks as she finds herself walking along the sidewalk with him. He asks what drew her to his talk. She tells him about her love of the outdoors, of quiet places, and of snow and water. She says she worries about what climate change might do to the world she loves.

"I hope my talk wasn't too boring . . ."

"No, the opposite actually. A nice change from the ones I'm used to."

"Oh, where?"

"I'm a child psychiatrist, here at the university. Presentations can go on and on. You know, academics—"

"Oh yeah, I do know!"

At the coffee shop, he orders black coffee, and she asks for ginger tea. She sits by the window, and he carries their mugs to the table. He asks her more about her favorite places. She mentions Mad River Glen.

"Really?" he says. I love it there too, but not a lot of people even know about it. Stowe is where they go, or Killington."

"I know," is all she says. An image of Daniel comes to her at Stowe during the department ski weekend. How dashing he looked, flying down on black diamond trails.

Be careful, Camila told her that night. *Daniel is a charmer.*

"Do you go to Mad River Glen for telemark skiing?" Lyman asks. "I do."

That brings Eva back to the present. "Yes," she says. "You too?" Telemark skiers are a tribe all their own, and how lovely that Lyman is a member too! "I love the dance and the grace of it, coming downhill. And I especially love how you can go up anywhere you want, away from the crowds and without waiting in line for the lifts. There is such great backcountry skiing around there."

"It might be the telemark capital of the world," he laughs. "Let the downhill skiers stay at Stowe, right? More room for us at Mad River then. And where else do you like to go, besides skiing?"

She describes the small lake near the Old Pump Road, where she goes to sit when she needs to clear her mind.

"Wow, I know the one," he says, surprised. "You probably take the spur off the main trail to reach it? I can show you another way up there. There is a lovely, unmarked path, really just a deer trail. It's a little hard to find unless you know where to look."

"I'd like that," she smiles. "Do you discover those places while you do field research?"

"Sometimes. But I love being out when I'm not working, too. I like exploring new territory, off the beaten track. I love getting lost and then finding a new way back." He pauses. "I like solitude, to be honest."

Wait, does that mean he doesn't like people? Of course, she doesn't ask. He tells her about long stints alone, doing field research. About backpacking to somewhere remote, with all his supplies, and camping out there for days. He speaks lovingly of the creatures in the habitats he studies and explains why ecosystems fascinate him.

"Enough about me," he says. "What about you? What fascinates you?"

She talks about the youngsters she works with, the way they tug at her heartstrings. She talks about her joy when they learn to trust her and her triumph when they get better. She confesses her anger when parents point fingers at their kids and refuse to understand their point of view. He listens.

"Take this teenager I work with. He didn't say a word the first time, not until I got his parents out of the room. Then I asked him what he was so pissed about, and he looked up, surprised. 'Me? Pissed?' he asked. And he burst out with 'My father is an alcoholic, and my mother is a workaholic, and they fight all the time. Why *wouldn't* I be pissed?'"

Eva doesn't mention that she presented this boy at the weekly team conference. Daniel was there. He had a sharp eye for context; he said this was a perfect situation for family therapy and that he could help her learn how. She thought him brilliant then and terribly handsome. She blushed when he offered to help and hid her face in her files, feeling like a schoolgirl. She doesn't mention that either.

"You're passionate about this, aren't you?" Lyman says. "You sound like you care about these kids."

"I do," she smiles again. "I guess I can get pretty worked up about it. Maybe I identify with them, and I try to be their ally. You know, that kid had *so* much reason to be angry, I had to fight my own rage at his parents. His father was mean and kept blaming the boy, and his mother only whined and hovered weakly. I remember all too well how *that* feels—" She leaves it at that. She is not going to describe her own family.

"Yeah . . ." he says. If he remembers such things too, he doesn't say.

There is a clattering around the coffee shop. Chairs are turned over onto tables. It is suddenly past closing time. "They probably want us out of here!" Eva laughs. They leave a big tip, and he walks her back to her car.

She is ready to exchange phone numbers and meet again, but he merely says, "It was nice to meet you, Eva. Perhaps I'll see you around some time." He turns back toward the science building, and she watches him walk away.

Is this it then? Will he look her up and get in touch? *Some time?* When is that? Will they bump into each other on a trail? Or maybe not until next winter, at Mad River Glen?

Spring turns into summer, and she does not hear from Lyman. She berates herself for getting wrapped up in him so easily, just as she did with Daniel, who swept her off her feet and made her feel smarter, more interesting, and prettier. At the end of the department's ski weekend, he kissed her as she had never been kissed before, tender at first, until she was on fire. They made their way to his apartment and stumbled onto his bed. His touch was electrifying; she lost herself in it and marveled at this erotic version of herself. During the next three months, passers-by had noticed them and whispered, "What a radiant couple." In restaurants, waitresses brought them little treats "for love." She actually began to believe that she *was* lovable. It lasted three months.

Then one afternoon, he announced that his fiancée was coming back next week. Just like that. She rushed out of the restaurant, blind, in a daze. She sank into a deep well of darkness, a terrifying place without words. She thought she wouldn't survive. But of course, she did. One does. She found some solace in the mountains. She explored riding trails. Someone posted a used Yamaha upright piano, free for the cost of moving it. So she pulled out her sheet music in the evenings and practiced. She tried to forget herself in her work. Her grief made her resonate more with her patients' pain, and that made her a better psychiatrist; she tried, without much luck, to be grateful for that.

And now here she is, fantasizing again, this time about Lyman. She knows better than to believe that people are always as they seem; of course, Lyman is not the man she imagines in her dreams. But Gershwin runs through her head again. *And so, all else above, I'm waiting for the man I love.* She hauls an Adirondack chair into the field behind her house and watches the swallows dip and swoop across the tall grass. She often sits out there sipping ginger tea until dusk. A red-tailed hawk circles above, and to her right, the Green Mountains are hazy, green fading into blue.

Surely, Lyman would love this little house? And wouldn't their children love to chase butterflies through this field? *Stop, Eva! Get a grip.*

She hikes to the little lake she told him about, to which he knows another path. She looks for "his" trail but cannot find it. She spends more time at the Green Mountain Equestrian Center near her little cottage. In the evenings, with plenty of light after clinic hours, Eva goes directly to the barn. Tarot, her frisky little mare, is always good company; she prances over as soon as she sees Eva, nostrils flaring in her pretty upturned Arabian nose. Subtle gray spots show through her white coat. They explore more trails together.

On Saturdays, Eva goes to yard sales. She finds a colorful kilim rug, dyed with indigo blue and the earthy red of madder root. She rescues an old rocking chair and paints it bright orange. She buys a cozier couch and splurges on an alpaca blanket to curl up with. It is a handknit work of art in shades of gray and cream, each square a different Faroe Island design. She keeps her mind busy nesting, surrounding herself with beautiful things. Maybe this is all she really needs: her cozy little house with its beautiful view, her quiet evenings, and her music. It is just as well that Lyman hasn't been in touch. But she cannot put him out of her mind either.

Chapter 2
Fall 1977

That summer, when Eva is at loose ends, she often thinks about the Mercado in Washington Heights. She had rented their upstairs studio apartment during her four years at Columbia. She immediately felt at home there. She wishes she could drop in with the owner and his wife like she used to. They were everything her own family wasn't. They cheerfully rescued stray cats, pigeons, and famished dogs. They welcomed any neighborhood children whose parents had gone missing in action. They pulled Eva into their bustling household, always full of laughter, with people coming and going, and the aroma of delicious food wafting from the kitchen. She misses them. An evening with them would cheer her up. She could use some cheering up.

Calling her parents would not help. Her father is a despicable small potentate who dislikes women, especially his wife. Her mother plays the victim and constantly tries to enlist Eva as an ally. They are the last people she would trust for relationship advice. She occasionally picks up the phone to chat with Camila, who was a rock after the debacle with Daniel. They often meet for lunch. Camila gets it, that Eva is fretting about Lyman. And she has a knack for making her laugh at herself.

In late September, at the end of a long clinic day, Eva finds a handwritten note in her hospital mailbox, addressed only to *Eva*. She rips it open—yes!—it is from Lyman. "I'm back from the field. Would you care for coffee?" There is a phone number.

Yes (yes, of course), she would care for coffee! She immediately dials the number, listens to the generic-sounding greeting on his voicemail, composes herself, and says, neutrally, she hopes: "Hi, Lyman, this is Eva. Thanks for your note. Sure, I could meet up for coffee if you like. Leave me a message at . . ." He picks up before she can finish her sentence. There is no chit-chat. Instead of coffee, they schedule a late lunch on Friday at the Italian restaurant.

Thoughts skitter through her mind. Friday is still three days away. To settle herself, she saddles her mare, and they ride through the fields until dusk. A light wind stirs the tall grasses. Asters make dark purple patterns among intense yellow stands of goldenrod. She wants to sing out loud about the glories of nature. In fact, she does sing, and Tarot twitches her ears. For the fun of it, they jump over a ditch or two, lucky that there are no soft spots to trip over where they land.

As Friday approaches, she reminds herself how little she knows about this man. She has probably imagined a version of Lyman, conjured up the idealized man she yearns for. He has, after all, just vanished for several months, without a word. It is silly to put much stock in his return.

Finally, it's Friday; she rushes to the restaurant and arrives a few minutes late. She tells the waitress she is meeting someone, that they have a reservation. But Lyman is not here. Should she wait by the entrance? Take a table? She decides on a seat by the window. She sits looking in one direction, then turns to look in the other direction. She glances at her watch. Should she order something? She'll just have some water for now. She wishes she had brought a book, but knows she couldn't have focused on it in any case. She hates waiting. It's rude to keep someone waiting.

Lyman arrives half an hour late, and her annoyance melts away when she sees him. "Hi, nice to see you, Eva. How are you?" He smiles and sits. They order.

"Oh, I've been busy," she says. "Working. Riding. Exploring. You know?"

"Riding?" he asks. "Horses?"

She tells him about finding Tarot. She asks about his months in the field.

"Yeah, sorry about not being in touch sooner," he says. "I was gone longer than I planned. It was a marsh project, a collaboration with Fish and Wildlife, and . . . well, nothing went quite as planned. I'm glad to be back."

The food arrives, and she forgets to eat. They eventually order coffee and dessert rather than get up and leave. They simply pick up where they left off in spring. It feels as if she has known him for years. She relaxes, not having to perform or be at her best. She feels at ease within the calm that emanates from him. Time slows down. She is startled when she realizes how late it is. People are coming in for dinner already.

They leave, and on the sidewalk, she waits for a hug or a suggestion that they will meet again. "See you around some time," he says.

"When?" she blurts out and wishes she hadn't.

To her relief, he smiles. "How about walking up to that little lake by the Old Pump Road? I can show you that other path, the one I told you about. Maybe we can bring lunch up there on Sunday if you're free."

Am I free? What a question. Of course, she'll be free.

And so, on Sunday, they meet at the trailhead. He is late again. She makes a note of that, not sure what it means, or whether it matters. Maybe she worries about time too much. He has brought apples, some tamari almonds, and a water bottle; she has packed a rustic bread and a block of aged cheese.

The day is glorious. He is careful not to walk too far ahead on his long legs. He stops to point out a northern goshawk overhead, to listen to a phoebe's song. In a boggy area, he shows her pitcher plants and a Venus flytrap. He is attentive to their surroundings, attuned to the life around them. His quiet presence stills her into the moment, and she silently falls into step. At the lake's edge, they find a dry grassy spot to sit. He hears a kingfisher's rattling call and spots it on a nearby tree; she had never seen one before. A ripple in the water catches his eye. "Look, the otter is back!" he whispers.

"Oh, an actual otter!" she says. He is amused at her delight.

Eventually, they make their way back by bushwhacking rather than following any paths at all. One of these explorations leads to a thorny patch. To get around it, they sink into a deep, swampy stretch. She is happily tired and sore by the time they reach their cars.

He hugs her then, their first hug—a long, slow hug that she leans into. She loves the way he smells, both clean and musky. She trembles as he holds her; she cannot stop it. She hopes he won't notice. *Hmmm*, he hums into her hair. When they pull away, he looks at her, and his eyes are like deep water she sinks into.

"I have a leftover casserole in my refrigerator," she offers, feeling brave.

Later, much later, after the food and the wine and the talking have made her drowsy, it occurs to her that they have not touched. Not since the hug. This is so different from the fiery passion that swept her up with Daniel. She feels at ease and unhurried; she hasn't even wondered what might or might not happen next. This time, she trusts that it will unfold in its own time, and it feels just right.

Around eight, he gets up. "I have to be in the field at four a.m. I'd better go," he says. She doesn't need to ask this time: they will see each other again. At the door, he pauses. "Wednesday? Early evening walk?" She nods. "I'll pick you up," he says.

October tries to put a chill in the air, but by Wednesday, it warms up again. The trees have splashes of red and orange among the green.

"I'm taking you to a place nobody knows," Lyman says. "A bird nesting site by the river. It is undisturbed, there are no trails."

"You mean it's a secret place?" She laughs.

But he is serious when he nods. "Yes. And it is very dear to me," he says quietly, and she feels strangely moved.

He leads Eva through the underbrush toward the river. She has no rubber boots and hopes her thick wool socks will provide some protection, so she gamely follows him. She watches his back as he follows an imaginary path. She notices his surprisingly delicate hands, how they firmly pull low-hanging branches out of the way for her. The canopy of trees gives way to shrubs.

They walk over a ridge before reaching a downhill slope. She trips over a log. He catches her, and then all at once, the sky opens out; diffuse light reflects on the water surface. A faint moon rises downriver. "Oh," she whispers. The air vibrates with sound. Crickets chirp frantically, as if warding off the coming winter. Peepers croak their late-season mating calls. The chorus echoes across the water and fills the mild evening.

Lyman points to a rock big enough for two. Flocks of bank swallows chase insects, skimming the water's surface. They tweet and chirp overhead; she can almost hear a fluttering wing. Then the whole flock veers to the opposite bank. Some of them sing from a tree perch over there. "A murmuration," Lyman says. Eva looks up in surprise; how romantic that sounds.

He notices her look and chuckles. "I didn't make that up," he says. "The swallows gather for fall migration now. And look, there are other kinds of birds too. Together, they become a giant mass of birds. See? It's like a cloud that moves through the air." He points. "So many wings, it *does* sound like murmuring, doesn't it?"

"What a lovely word," she says, and smiles.

"Yes. I just hope their nesting places in South America don't keep shrinking." *It is touching how much he cares*, she thinks.

They sit and listen; the sun goes down and takes its warmth away. He reaches over for her hand. At the touch of his fingers, she notices how cold her own have become; she suppresses a shiver. He opens his jacket and wraps them both in it. She leans into their silence. Her mind goes quiet. There is nothing to be on the alert for, nothing to plan. This is all there is, right now, his arm holding away the cold.

The sky darkens; the fuzzy moon shines through a low layer of fog. One by one, stars brighten into an incomplete map of the sky, with silver-fringed clouds here and there. When they finally stand, it is too dark for Eva to see, but Lyman knows the place by instinct. He leads her by the hand, pointing out places she might stumble, and finds the shortcut.

He drops her at her house, puts two fingers on his lips, and blows her a silent kiss. A smile, his head tilted ever so slightly, and he is gone. The thrill she feels lingers all evening.

A week goes by. Her quiet trust begins to crumble. *Will* things unfold in their own time? Should she call him? Should she wait? She leaves a message, and then wishes she could erase it. "Hey, it's Eva, just calling to say hi. Hope you're okay." Ugh. She was definitely *not* just calling to say hi. And she was not wondering whether he was okay either. She was wondering when the hell he was planning to call her! Or was he?

There are no longer rules about men reaching out or women waiting demurely. Women's lib is seeing to that. But still, she knows herself: she could too easily take the initiative. If she makes it that easy for him, she will always wonder whether he really *wants* to see her, or whether he is ambivalent, and merely agreeable. For all she knows, he has shared the secret place by the river with others, too, and she is not special to him at all.

One evening he calls her, but the connection is choppy. His department has a cell phone, she knows, but wherever he is, there isn't much reception. All she can make out is ". . . in the field . . . another . . ."

She tries to put him out of her mind and waits. But her heart jumps when her home phone rings, a week later.

"Hi. It's Lyman. I only have a minute. But . . . ever been to Lake Willoughby?"

"No," she says. "Why?"

"Do you want to check it out in a canoe?" he asks.

"Yes. Yes, of course, I'd love to." She is so relieved to hear from him that she doesn't care where they go.

"I'll pick you up early on Saturday, okay?"

"Perfect. That's great."

There is a pause, some noise in the background: another man's voice. She hears Lyman whisper, "I'll be there in a minute." There are footsteps. Then he is back, sounding rushed. "Okay, one more thing. Have you heard about the Willows Inn? It would be nice not to drive back the same day, if that's okay with you?"

"Sure, good idea . . ." Is he asking her to spend the night with him? Or just being practical?

"Sorry, gotta run. Do you have time to make a reservation?" he asks. And he hangs up.

She has no way to ask him whether she should get two rooms. How awkward. She calls the inn. The main house is fully booked. The only option is a lakeside cottage, with two small bedrooms and a kitchenette. What a relief, she won't have to decide.

It is a sparkling fall day when he picks her up on Saturday. The drive takes them through beautiful rolling hills. There are comfortable silences. Sometimes they chat about nothing in particular.

After two hours, Lyman pulls up to the shore of Lake Willoughby. He swings the canoe down from the rack on his truck. Before Eva can lift a finger, he has carried it to the water's edge. They load their gear, and he hands her several paddles to find the right length for her. His own is a gorgeous bent paddle made of ebony and cherry. She admires its color and the grain of the wood. "I treated myself to this beauty last year," he says. "I was fed up with crappy carbon paddles. They are hard and unresponsive in your hands. Wood feels alive."

She has little experience with canoes, but he easily compensates, steering from the stern, and he provides most of the power. How lovely to be in good hands. It's a treat not to be in charge. At a cove he knows, they let the canoe float along the shore. They sit quietly, on the lookout for an otter to come out and play, for a marten to appear on the rocks, a glimpse of a mink. They hear a loon and watch two pairs of grebes swim and dive. A heron croaks in hoarse protest when they approach and loudly flaps toward a new perch. The silence is alive.

Lyman points to the summit of Mount Hor. Eva looks across the water to the bare granite cliff that towers 1,500 feet above the lake. "There is a trail that starts at the south end of the lake," he says. "Are you game?"

"Let's do it," she says.

They haul the canoe and paddles out of sight into the brush. The trail is so faint that she wonders whether Lyman might actually be lost this time. It is rough and steep. Eventually, they join a path marked with red blazes. When they emerge high above the ledges, her breath catches. The whole lake lies below them, a deep slash of clear blue between the east and west ranges of the Green Mountains. They huddle together against the wind; she feels warm and safe leaning against him.

"Thank you for this," Eva whispers. She rests her head on Lyman's shoulder, and he kisses the top of her head. She breathes in his scent—less clean and more musky after the climb. Eventually, he stands and offers his hand to pull her up. "The path down can be treacherous in the dark. We should be going." The western sky has turned pink.

At the inn, they barely have time to shower before the brass dinner bell rings. The old dining hall glows with original wood trim, lovingly preserved. Lyman points out the exquisite joinery and carved moldings. "I love this place," he says once they're seated. There is no menu. There are two choices for each course. The simple meal is delicious and smells of someone's home. Lyman has brought a lovely young red wine. They linger and talk. Eva imagines that they are like the two halves of a yin-yang circle, making a greater whole together. He connects to nature first, she with people. She feels complete and at rest.

When they retreat to the cabin, there is no longer any question of separate rooms. They simply gravitate to the queen bed. A large window looks out on the lake. The moon is reflected on the water, bringing a magical light into the room. Unhurried, they face each other and sink onto the bed. Slowly, very slowly, they take off each other's clothes, one piece at a time. Their eyes, their touch, and their lips slowly discover each other. Eva feels as if they have known each other always.

"*Oooh,*" she murmurs. It's like sinking into something older than themselves, where it is safe and warm, entirely new and yet deeply familiar. Time loses its meaning. She dismisses a fleeting thought of how different it was with Daniel. With Lyman, it is not a high-wire act. Content, she drifts off to sleep. When morning comes, they linger and rediscover each other all over again.

At the end of the weekend, on the drive home, she asks about other relationships before her.

"Do you really want to know?" he asks.

"Of course I do. Obviously, I'm not the first. I just want to know what went into making you be you."

"Okay then." He tells her about Joan. "We were together in college for two years. She got a job in Switzerland afterward, in Geneva, and she asked me to go with her." He pauses. Eva's hand rests on his shoulder.

"I missed Vermont every day of those four years at Bowdoin. I cared about her, a lot, but I grew up in Vermont. I belong here. I landed a scholarship for a PhD in ecology here at UVM. I could not face turning it down."

"And you regretted it?" She wonders whether she'll have to contend with an idealized image of Joan in his mind.

He shakes his head. "It's complicated, Eva. I don't think I can make my life anywhere else. You should know that."

She understands the warning. She can see his deep connection to the land. They have left the mountains by now. Rolling fields surround proud old farms. "So, what happened to Joan?" she asks. "Did she ever come back?"

"No. I never saw her again. We were young, but I think I loved her. I had two rotten choices: to lose Joan, or to lose some part of myself." He trails off and briefly turns a troubled face toward Eva.

"There is more, isn't there?"

He hesitates. "She attempted the Furggengrat . . ."

“The fur-what?”

“The Furggengrat. You know, the southeast ridge of the Matterhorn. Every serious mountaineer wants to conquer the Matterhorn.” He glances over and notices her blank expression. “I’m sure you’ve seen pictures of it. You must have. A pyramid of rock, snow, and ice. It looms high above the landscape from every direction.”

With an effort, she conjures up the iconic image.

“It stands there,” he explains, “it’s—it’s seductive. Every year, more climbers try it, no matter how many people died there in the last season.”

What a foreign concept. Eva loves hiking, but what would be the point of risking her life?

He sighs. “So, the route she chose, the Furggengrat? Climbers say it is the hardest of all, a knife edge in howling wind. Steep and treacherous.” He swallows. “Most mountaineers take an easier way up. But that is where she went, with three others. It was foolhardy. I heard later, from one of them, that she fell six hundred feet down. Her body was never found.”

Eva gasps and squeezes his shoulder. “How terrible.” She hesitates. “Would you have—I mean, if you were still together—would you have gone with her?”

“No. We climbed a lot together, but not like that. She had a wild streak, and . . .” He keeps his eyes fixed on the road.

Perhaps he wishes he had talked her out of it? They drive in silence for a while.

“Enough of that,” he finally says. “And you?”

So she tells him about Daniel, how he is still everywhere in her department, still charming and brilliant. How Maureen, his fiancée, turns up at seminars. She fights back tears that she thought had dried up by now.

She leans her forehead on the window to her right until her voice comes back. “He made me feel loved, Lyman. It was an illusion, but like a fool, I believed it. And . . .” She pauses. “If I ever open myself up that way again . . .” She stops, starts over. “Perhaps it was my fault, maybe I was too eager, and I drove him back to Maureen. Who knows. But it almost broke me. You should know that.”

Lyman stops the truck at the side of the road and cuts the engine. He reaches over and simply holds her. “I hear you. I do.” He rocks her a little. “I want this to be real, this journey, you know? This isn’t a flash of gold, here and then gone. I’m not flashy. I’m not playing with you.”

She sniffles.

“We’ll take it one step at a time, okay?” he says. She breathes and lets herself settle back into the ease of being with Lyman.

Lyman’s love is a steady burn. No shooting stars, no sparks flying, no spectacular flames. It does not flicker out. Eva is at peace; she discovers what it’s like, learning to trust someone. More and more, they spend evenings at her little house when he is not away in the field. That winter, they often go to Mad River Glen for a day or a weekend. He is an excellent skier and patient with her. He gives her pointers if she asks.

One evening after work, his research is troubling him. Something isn’t working out as he hoped. She doesn’t quite follow the science, and he explains. She asks another question, feeling naive. She wants to understand his work more. He considers what she says, and he takes a fresh look at that section of his study. “Why, thanks, Eva, that part was murky, no wonder you didn’t get it! What if . . .” She loves it when they discuss things this way, partners in thought.

Other nights, she tells him about the joys of her day, the little victories. Or he listens to more of her heartbreaking stories of children who suffer and are misunderstood. One night, he looks at her closely and asks what more she wishes she had done. Surprised, she realizes she wants the impossible for these kids. “I suppose I’d like to rewind the clock and take their pain away. It feels like I’ve never done enough.”

He laughs gently, hugs her, and reminds her how lucky these families are that she cares so much. Gently, he chides her for always driving herself relentlessly. It’s true, she does. It’s a very old story with her. That was always what Uncle Roger expected of her, after all, wasn’t it? And now she has Lyman, who loves her, knows this about her, and helps her look at herself. He balances her. *He came along, the man I love . . .*

Chapter 3
1978

In March, a frown appears on Lyman's forehead and gradually takes up permanent residence there. Their comfort together fades, and Eva can think of no obvious reason for it. He is silent in the evenings when he comes over, preoccupied. When Eva starts a conversation, he gives one-word answers without looking up. Eva asks whether something troubles him. "It's nothing," he shrugs, and she wonders whether he wants to pull away from the relationship. Is he afraid to tell her?

One night, over dinner at her house, she decides to ask. "You say you're fine, Lyman, you say there is nothing wrong. I try to believe you, but something doesn't feel right." He doesn't look at her. "Is it about work? Or is it me?"

He gives her a blank look and gets up from the table. "I told you, there is nothing." He finds his coat in the mudroom. "I have an early day tomorrow. I need to get home. I'll see you."

Stung by how distant he feels, she watches him go. She busies herself in the kitchen, cleaning up. She wipes every counter twice. She rearranges staples in the cabinets, throws out unmarked jars of spices. She has heard that cleaning is soothing. After ten minutes, she throws the rag in the sink. It's not working for her. She hates cleaning. She has always hated cleaning. In fact, the main reason she is such a neatnik is to *avoid* having to clean up later.

She goes to the piano and plays through a couple of ballads. Music always soothes her, but she has trouble concentrating. She tries "All of Me" and gets impatient with it. Then "A Child Is Born"—a terrible choice in her state of mind. Perhaps a Latin beat then: "Corcovado—Quiet Nights"? She plays it through, then does it again. In her mind, she hears Astrud Gilberto's lovely voice. She imagines being Jobim and laying down a dreamy groove on the piano to support the imaginary Astrud. She answers the song with a counter-melody. A dialogue. A relationship. She plays until she feels better, until she gets sleepy.

In the morning, she wonders whether she was overreacting last night. Was she seeing the ghost of Daniel? Shouldn't she give Lyman space when he seems to need it? She mustn't assume it's all about her if he is preoccupied. Or that there is something wrong that she needs to fix. In her office, it *is* her job to diagnose things like depression. But in private life, that is *not* her place; not everything needs a clinical label.

It will take her many years to realize that her hunch had been right.

She doesn't hear from Lyman for a few days, and then it's only a quick phone call, just to say he is leaving for a new project in a marsh habitat.

"Okay," she says uncertainly. *It's about time you called*, she thinks.

"I'm not sure when I'll be back. I'll be in touch." He hangs up. She'd like to yell at him.

Another week goes by. He is back in Burlington.

"Oh good," she says. "Dinner tonight?"

"I can't, Eva, I have a publication deadline and I'm running behind because of the marsh project. I'll call when I'm done." There is noise in the background, people talking. "I promise," he tells her. "Soon, okay?" And he hangs up.

Eva tries to keep her mind from going around and around old fears. After a long day, she becomes certain that he is planning to ditch her, just as Daniel did. In the morning, she thinks that cannot be. She leaves him a voice message. He calls back, sounding rushed, to say he is headed into the field *again*. Sleep eludes her, but her piano playing improves.

In April, she goes to Mad River Glen by herself, but her heart isn't in it, and besides, the snow is too thin and slushy. Her thoughts keep spiraling. *Stop it!* she tells herself. *Why do you take everything so seriously? Lighten up!*

She sits on the ski lift by herself and cries. How stupid she was to fall for Lyman, and to let herself be that vulnerable again. *You're too hungry for love*, she tells herself, *so hungry you can't tell the illusion apart from the real thing.* She is so busy berating herself that she almost falls when it's time to glide off the lift at the top.

She feels like a child again. Miserably lonely. At home, the tension between her parents made her hide upstairs in her room. With Uncle Roger, she was expected to be the smart one, but she never felt enveloped in affection. Lyman made her imagine she might not have to be lonely forever. She finally found where she belonged, she thought, and now . . .

The snow melts from the fields, and she spends more time on the trails with her little mare. At least Tarot is steady and reliable. And at least her patients still need her.

When Lyman finally returns from his research trip, they meet up, but something feels strained. Laughter doesn't come easily. The long silences weigh her down. Yet sometimes he surprises her at the barn in the evening. Tarot pricks her ears at his arrival and trots briskly to the paddock's gate. Lyman makes a game of hiding a carrot or an apple in a pocket of his Carhartt jacket. After Tarot finds it, her lovely head nuzzles against his shoulder, and he stands still with her for a moment.

She watches the easy connection between horse and man. He softens around Tarot, and it makes his recent reticence with her more painful. He silently picks up a pitchfork to help with the barn chores, and she appreciates it but cannot tell what it means. Is it easier than talking? Does he feel guilty for being distant? Is something eating at him? When the barn chores are done, he leaves. "See you later then." He gives her a peck on the cheek. "I have to do more work tonight. Just came by to say hi. Sorry."

In mid-May, he suggests they meet somewhere after work. "How about the Italian on Main Street?"

It is hard to believe, but it's been over a year since Eva came to his lecture about habitat changes. It's been eight months since their first lunch date last September, in this very restaurant. But by now, she has come to expect awkward silences, and she is tense. Tears well up while she looks over the menu. Perhaps she should call this off. The last thing she needs is to get attached to someone with dark demons.

"Nice to be out," he says. "I like this place." He pauses. "Didn't we have lunch here, on our first date?"

She takes in his smile. His voice is at ease, his mood seems light. Has the cloud lifted? Or is this just a lucky evening? Or was it just as he claimed, a crunch with work? Against her better judgment, she asks. She needs to know. "You seem, I don't know, more relaxed tonight. I have been worried about you, Lyman. Was something bothering you? Is it resolved?"

Lyman shrugs, and his face closes. "Oh, I don't know, sometimes I get a little dark for a while, or more absorbed with work. It doesn't mean anything. Don't make more out of it, Eva, please."

She is suddenly annoyed. He is minimizing his mood and is oblivious to what that did to her and to them! "Lyman, hold on a minute. We hardly spoke for weeks. I know you said it was work. But I simply have to ask: Was it me? Something I did?" If it was about her, she'd rather know now.

He interrupts her. "Stop, Eva. I'm here, aren't I? You know? It's been a year, and I'm not going anywhere."

She looks down, frowns, and hesitates. "Easy to say, but I had no way of telling."

"Telling what?" He sounds genuinely puzzled.

"I thought you were done with us, that working was an excuse." She fiddles with her napkin. "I told you, at the Willows Inn. Remember? Don't make me trust you, and then drop me without explanation. It's not okay, Lyman, it's my worst nightmare, and I couldn't help thinking it was happening again."

He looks at her, eyebrows raised. "I know. You told me. But I said I wouldn't do that . . ." His voice trails off. "I meant it, don't you know that?"

She raises her voice, angry now. "You know something else? There is not much point in being in a relationship if you don't share things. It's about being there for each other, even if it's '*only*' about work—that's the way I see it anyway." She folds her napkin. "Besides—if you don't tell me your stuff, I can't very well burden you with mine, can I?" Then she is afraid she went too far. Has she ruined a nice dinner? Ruined everything, just when he came back? A tightness grips her gut.

But he nods, thoughtful. "You have a point there," he says. "You do. But don't push me, please. I have a deeply private side. That's who I am." He looks at her. "I do love you, Eva, you know that, don't you? Isn't that enough?"

He has never said those words, she realizes. Really? He puts his hand on hers. A slow smile appears on his face. The topic is closed. She looks down. Her cheek feels wet. She replays those words. *I love you.* No, in fact, she had not known that, and she anxiously hopes he means it . . .

He comes to her little house that night. They open the big window to let in the May air. They linger on the couch while night falls. Music plays softly. Slowly, her fear lets go, and words no longer matter. Eventually, their bodies take over. It comes back to her now, how good this feels, how right. How they fit together. And just like that, Lyman is back in her life. Reliable. Present. Available. Whatever that cloud was, she hopes it's gone for good.

They spend more and more time together that summer and winter. They meet new friends, attend events together. Most days, they have dinner at her house, but he often retreats to his studio near the university if he has more work to do. She wishes he'd stay and share her little cottage. She hesitates to bring it up. Would it push him too much?

Winter turns into spring again. At lunch with her friend Camila, Eva listens to her as she talks about losing a pregnancy, how awful it was for her and for Cesar. How it feels for them to try for another baby, fearing the passage of time, fearing another loss. They are living through a cycle of hope and fear. Eva feels deeply for her friend. She also knows that at her own age, it gets harder to conceive and harder to give birth. It worries her. She yearns to start a family with Lyman.

After dinner that night, she puts a hand on Lyman's arm. "You could work here, you know. There is room for two in my office." He nods vaguely.

"Wait," she says later when he prepares to leave. "Look, I get it. That you need—you know—your space. That you need to be alone sometimes. But we could . . . well—I mean I could give you that space when you're here. We could both work, and—or—do our own thing sometimes." He is listening, and she takes a breath. "You need solitude sometimes, right? It is part of your make-up." She watches his face. He is still with her. "I'm only saying I'd like you to get that, even—um—even while we're in the house together. Do you know what I mean?" She feels both naked and invisible. Such an old story, she realizes. She is wishing, asking for more commitment, and yet doubting herself, whether she deserves it.

He nods and hugs her. "It's a nice thought, actually," he whispers into her hair. He kisses her at the door. "I left some stuff on my desk tonight. Another time?"

Not long after, on a brisk Sunday morning in April, they hike up to their hideaway lake. It's been two years since they first talked about this little lake, that first time they had coffee. They find their way through the last of the snow, slushy with an icy crust on top. It's too wet for skis, too soft for ice grippers. Gaiters can't keep their boots dry, but they trudge on. They sit together on a boulder by the still-frozen lake. Eva leans against Lyman, and he wraps his coat around her, in that way he does. They listen to the sounds of wild creatures waking up all around.

He pulls something out of his pocket, turns to her, and holds up a thin gold ring with a delicate Celtic knot.

"Can we keep doing this forever?" he asks.

She stares at him, speechless . . . What does he mean? Her heart thumps with hope and excitement. He takes her hand, and she watches him slip the ring on her finger.

He smiles. "I don't like showy gemstones; I hope you don't mind?" Is this a marriage proposal, or something else? Her answer is lost in a long kiss.

She curls up with her head on his shoulder. He holds her tighter. Bits of ice sparkle on the lake, like so many diamonds. The best kind of diamonds. "I love you, Lyman," she whispers.

"I love you, Eva," he says. "I want to be your husband. I want to grow old with you."

He takes her face in his hands. "I know you've—that you've wanted the next step for a while now." He kisses the top of her head. "But sweetie? I couldn't do this before—before I felt certain." She buries her face in his chest.

After a moment, he lifts her chin to look at her. "I'm sorry I couldn't hurry this for you. But I am sure now, very sure." Her lip trembles. "So why wait? Is—uh—is two months too soon?"

She gasps. "Sure, yes! I mean no, it's not too soon! I mean, yes, of course . . ."

Chapter 4
1985

While they were preparing for their wedding, life felt exactly as Eva always dreamt it might someday. They wrote their vows together. They chose a love poem and recited the verses for each other. Then, together, they fixed up the little house. A sunny new kitchen opens onto the living room with a bar counter. A kitchen nook with a large window looks out onto the field. They have breakfast there in the mornings, getting ready for the day. The air in the house is full of promise, and the months and years fly by.

They add a room with cheery wallpaper and soon place a yellow baby crib there. Within two years, a little bed is moved in next to the crib. Now Eva has her hands full with their two boys. She only works half-time, and Lyman has cut down on field research, but there is rarely any quiet time. Ezra turns five; he is adorable and spunky. His young mind is quick and curious; limits are an irresistible challenge. He makes them laugh; he is constantly on the brink of disaster. A rainy fall keeps them inside too much, so last week he decided to use the bookcases as a climbing wall. Yesterday, he wandered far off into the wet field, following a stray cat, while Eva turned her back for a moment with Gabriel.

Gabe is three now. He has his father's red curls. Fortunately, he also has Lyman's quiet temperament. He is a cuddler, and he idolizes his older brother. If Eva berates Ezra for being too rough, Gabriel runs over and frantically tugs at her sleeve to pull her away. "Ez'a is *my* big brother, Mommy," he protests. "Don't be mad."

On family outings in the nearby hills, Gabriel rides in the backpack on Lyman's shoulders. He grabs his daddy's hair. "Giddy-up, Daddy! Giddy-up!" he shrieks. "Faster, Daddy!"

"Way to keep fit," Lyman puffs after Gabe asks to get down. Eva gamely carries a small bucket, which the boys fill with mangled worms and bugs. When Ezra is bored with that, he runs ahead and swings a stick at the trees. Gabriel pokes into hollow tree trunks, runs his fingers through mosses, and examines every living creature he encounters. When they get home, both boys are happy and muddy and ready for lunch.

As time goes by, the boys grow more inseparable. After quiet time, they often play on the living room rug together. Gabriel usually lets Ezra have his way, but this afternoon, he stands his ground about his teddy bear. They argue with mounting conviction and irritation, endless variations on the theme of "who is right and who is wrong." Eva listens and watches while she gets dinner together. From across the counter, she is ready to jump in before they boil over.

"It's mine, Ez'a!" He still can't quite pronounce it . . .

"No, it's mine." Ezra waves the stuffed bear above his head, out of Gabriel's reach.

"You can't take ev'yting."

"I can too, I'm older."

Gabe sounds ready to burst into tears, and Eva can't help herself. She intervenes. She cannot bear to think that either of her boys might ever feel less important than the other in her eyes, so she works overtime to make them both feel special. She kneels on the rug with them, gathers them together to negotiate.

"Ezra, you go first," she says, "and then you'll listen when it's Gabey's turn. Got it? No interrupting." She looks at each of them until she has their full attention. "Don't talk at the same time," she repeats, mostly for Ezra's benefit.

Lyman looks up from what he is reading, a smile in his eyes.

Ezra states his case while Gabriel squirms impatiently, then Gabe gets his turn. She helps them debate what seems like a fair compromise. But this is one of those days when they reach a dead end, so she takes them each by the shoulder and guides them firmly to the mudroom. "Boys," she says, "you'll be stuck with each other forever. You might as well learn how to work things out. So, go outside and figure out what's fair. You can come back inside when you have a solution."

"But Mommy, it's raining," Ezra points out.

"Put on your boots, and don't come back in until you're *both* happy." She smiles as she opens the door for them. "I'll have hot cocoa ready for you."

They protest, but they go. On the way out, she catches a look in Ezra's eyes and holds him back a moment. "Ezra," she says with her hand on his arm, "remember what happened last time? If you trick Gabe into something unfair, he'll probably go along with it. But I'll overrule it. You remember that, right?"

He pouts and goes to catch up with Gabriel.

"You know," says Lyman, "brothers fight. Wilford and I did. It's part of growing up; it's no big deal, they'll work it out."

"I just can't let Ezra be unfair," she says. "Gabriel would let him get away with murder."

"I'm not worried about that," he says, "not if *you* have anything to do with it."

She looks out of the window. The boys are standing on the patio. Ezra's hands underscore something. Gabe stomps his foot. But the rain proves an excellent facilitator. They talk some more and quickly come back in. A few moments later, they are happily slurping hot cocoa on the window seat in the kitchen nook. Eva chuckles at the surprising solution they are both happy with. The toy will be put away for a week, and after that, they will hold a ceremony, and Ezra will donate it to Gabriel. Eva will make cookies for the event.

The days grow short, and the leaves come down. Clouds hang over the fields, and then over Lyman's face too. She tries to remember when it happened before—it was well before their wedding, wasn't it? She has come to believe it was only a passing thing back then, just something to do with events that are long past. Not something about Lyman himself.

Then she notices Lyman is coming home late more often. He mostly misses the boys' bedtime altogether, or he retreats to the study after dinner. He seems distant, and she feels her gut clench, as it did years ago. She waits it out for a couple of weeks, until she cannot ignore the preoccupied look any longer. She reminds herself, once again, that home is not her clinic, that Lyman is not her patient, that nobody requested a treatment plan. Yet troubling images come into her mind.

There was a man Eva treated early in her psychiatry training. His wife had made the appointment for him because she worried that he was depressed. It ran in his family. The man was adamant he was fine, he just had a quiet temperament, he said, and would she please leave him alone already. He was a lot like Lyman. The next time the man appeared in her clinic, a couple of months later, he was recovering from a near-fatal overdose of Tylenol with codeine.

Eva tries, but she cannot put that man out of her mind. One evening, after getting the boys settled, she takes a deep breath and brings it up, when they are both slumped on the couch, exhausted. It's now or never, she figures. "Is something the matter, Lyman? You don't seem happy lately."

"No, nothing, I'm fine," he grumbles.

That was the predictable answer, but she doesn't let it go. "Please look at me. It doesn't feel like nothing, Lyman. You stay away a lot, and you're short with me. You spend less time with the boys, and Ezra sometimes acts out just to get your attention. Gabe greeted you at the door with his latest toy yesterday, hoping you'd play. Did you even notice?"

He looks at his fingernails. "I've told you this before; I get preoccupied sometimes. That's all."

"No, Lyman. I'm sorry, but I have to spell this out. We've been here before, remember? Before we were married? When you pretty much disappeared for weeks on end? I'm getting that feeling again, of something dark hanging over our lives. Only this time, it hangs over our boys too."

He crosses his arms, but she takes his hand and pulls it closer. "Listen to me, please. You always said your dad had irritable and somber moods. Didn't you? And didn't his mother have depression? And maybe your uncle too?"

He shrugs. "So?"

"Could you please look into it this time, Lyman? For us? For our family?" He looks up briefly. "Did you know that children absorb their parents' moods? It's bad for them, this somberness."

He gives a small nod. Then he gets up, turns his back to her, and pours himself a glass of water in the kitchen. "You don't let up, do you?" he mumbles. Then he looks at her. "If it will make you feel better, I'll see someone. But I'm telling you, it's a waste of time. Happy now?" He doesn't sound angry, only sad and weary.

She goes to him and wraps her arms around him. "Thank you for hearing me out. And for doing this for us, even if it's not your thing." She reaches up to kiss him.

She is not sure whether he does see a therapist, or whether he perks up all on his own. He doesn't explain and she doesn't ask. Perhaps whatever hung over him was work-related, as he claimed. Perhaps he has learned to keep his brooding over research at the office, to spare her the worry? Whatever the reason, the man she fell in love with is back, playful, tender, and attentive.

She must have overreacted again. She was always prone to this sort of worrying. She probably imagined the somber mood.

Chapter 5
1986

Lyman's sabbatical is coming up in a few months. He wants to study the impact of climate change in a more vulnerable ecosystem. The boys will be five and seven; it seems like a perfect age to take the family abroad for a year. But where? He is excited about a research team at Lake Malawi, and they welcome him to join their study of the decline of fish stocks.

Eva attends a few lectures at the Global Health department of UVM. At first, she only has a vague notion of what it's about. But the more she learns, the more troubled she is by staggering health care needs. Needs that are worse in poorer countries, where the burden of disease is highest. She begins to wonder whether her skills in psychiatry would be of any use. *Probably not,* she thinks.

Then she learns about a community-led initiative in Uganda that offers training in peer counseling. They focus on remote areas, where the discrepancy between disease and health resources is most stark. The peer support aims to build resilience, and it turns out that together, people do better at coping with hardship. Several teams have shown the same effect: peer counseling improves both health and quality of life. And she finds a program that is trying to bring the idea to new places. That makes great sense to her.

So, she inquires with the regional hospital in Mangochi, near the study team that Lyman will join. The medical director has heard about the resilience idea, and he likes it, but the facility lacks both the staff and the funding. Eva doesn't rest until she gets a small grant through the Global Health program at the university, just enough money to set up a trial program in Malawi.

So, it is settled, they will go to the Warm Heart of Africa, as Malawi is known. And since English is the official language, it will be easy for Ezra and Gabe to attend school.

The family leaves Vermont just as winter arrives. Thirty endless hours later, they land in Lilongwe, the capital of Malawi, in the tropics. A house awaits them in Mangochi, at the southern tip of Lake Malawi. Chifundo, one of Lyman's colleagues on the fisheries project, meets them at the airport. He drives them the rest of the way, a three-hour car ride. Ezra has a meltdown because his shoes feel too tight. Gabriel sobs about his enormous stuffed polar bear, left behind to "watch the house." They are driving in the left lane, and Eva expects to die at every turn in the road. Only Lyman seems unruffled.

They are all sticky with travel sweat when they finally arrive. The boys immediately get into a territorial dispute over beds. Their bodies are beyond exhausted, but their scrambled brains protest that it's only mid-morning in Vermont.

Finally, after they all manage a nap, they go out to explore the neighborhood. The place is beautiful, alive with color. Red dirt roads are lined with concrete houses whose entrance doors recede in the shade of an overhang. Men gather on plastic chairs. Women wear long colorful wraps that have seen better days. People linger in animated conversations in a musical language. That must be Chichewa. Children run around everywhere in playful groups. Noticing the white faces of the newcomers, they stop to stare; a few are bold enough to follow them, smiling and chattering.

When Eva asks a group of women where they can buy food, one of them beckons and walks them to the market, where they find corn, tomatoes, beans, and some dried fish. On the way back to the house with their provisions, they see a general store, where laundry soap jostles for space with canned milk, cans of Raid, and a few loaves of white bread. They buy a jar of peanut butter.

They make sandwiches with the tasteless bread and go out again; they meander to the edge of town, where the concrete houses are spaced further apart. A path winds through impenetrable tangles of trees and shrubs. A boy fills a bucket at a hand pump. Ripe mangoes hang from a tree next to a lush patch of corn. Beans climb on a flimsy stake, intertwined with vines drooping with ripe tomatoes.

By early afternoon, a pitiless sun beats down through the cloud cover. The humidity of the rainy season adds weight to the heat; it takes Eva's breath away. The nearby lake offers no breeze, and relentless plant growth presses in all around. Further up, Lyman gazes toward the hills that slope away from the lake. Up there, the thick forest is pocked with irregular bare patches. There are thin trails of smoke above the hills. He points, then makes an arc with his hand toward the lake below. "See that? They are burning charcoal. It's the only fuel they have—what's left of it. And those smoke particles? I bet much of that drifts right down there, and into the fisheries." Eva stands closer and looks up. She can hear the wheels turning in his mind.

They take a few days to settle in. Ezra and Gabriel get excited for their first day of school. It's just a little way down the dirt road they live on. Lyman and Eva walk them over this first time. The low concrete building is coated with the red dust that settles everywhere. Doors and windows are wide open. A sister greets them and welcomes Ezra into the classroom for grades one to three. She claps her hands once and calls "Children!" There is immediate silence. Smiles play on curious faces. Battered desks stand in disciplined rows. The sister tells them, in English, that Ezra is their new classmate. She says something in Chichewa. On cue, the children sing a welcome song they have rehearsed, and Ezra beams with delight. He happily takes his seat in the front row.

Another sister appears and leads them to Gabriel's kindergarten class. The rows of desks are not quite so straight here. Everything in this room feels looser, more playful. Here, the students intone a welcome song with intricate handclapping. They encourage Gabriel to try it, are amused when he gets mixed up, and cheer when he catches on.

Eva makes sure the sisters know how to find her if one of her boys has a crisis. They nod politely, but of course, everybody already knows where the new white family lives. The week goes by without a glitch. Lyman joins the research team on the Shire River. It is time for Eva to make her way to the hospital.

Mangochi is a small city in Southern Malawi; its regional hospital serves a large area. Long lines of people wait outside every morning to be seen. Some are so feeble they can barely stand. An elderly man leans on his daughter; his breath rattles. Mothers carry limp children with vacant eyes, little heads hanging on their shoulders. A screaming toddler hangs in a wrap on his mother's back and clutches his ear. An impossibly thin woman balances a listless infant on her hip; the baby is all protruding ribs and stick-limbs. With a jolt, Eva notices the brittle yellow hair and realizes this is what kwashiorkor looks like. How is protein malnutrition possible in this lush place, where fish are sold at every corner? Then she remembers how: worms, parasites. Everyone has them.

Eva tries to find Emmanuel, the head nurse in pediatrics, who will show her around. He knows about her small grant for a trial resilience project and will be her contact. She approaches the children's unit when an alarm screams overhead. Nurses start running, and she follows, vaguely thinking she might be of some use. She enters a ward where a crowd of staff surrounds one of the beds. A mother and grandmother stand back, eyes wide as they watch the ambu bag force air into a child's lungs and see the chest compressions. A middle-aged man calls clipped orders; syringes are filled and handed to him.

And then all at once, there is silence. Oxygen stops hissing. The IV stops dripping. In the cavernous nothing, the mother keens. In the other beds, small children gape with terrified expressions. A few have family by their beds, and they reach out to be held. A couple of children stand alone, gripping the bars of their cribs. Suddenly, a wail comes from the far corner, where a little boy clutches the railing of his bed. He wails, and wails, and barely takes a breath. Eva cannot bear the sound of his terror, but nobody pays him any attention. Families turn to their own children. Aides gather discarded syringes and medication bottles; nurses resupply the crash cart used for resuscitations; someone brings a stretcher and wheels the small body away.

Eva aches to pick up the wailing child but realizes her pale face might frighten him even more. It might seem like Death has come for him too . . . She backs away, disheartened and shaken. She is in no shape to seek out Emmanuel. She wanders through the hospital until she finds an exit. What did this look like to the other children in the ward? It must have seemed a brutal assault, a mob battering a child until nothing was left but silence.

Eventually, she goes home. She is relieved to find Lyman and the boys busily engaged. They don't need her; she pleads a headache and goes to bed. Lyman looks at her with a questioning frown, but she shakes her head. She will tell him later. Right now, she can't. She hardly sleeps that night, haunted by the children's frightened eyes. And what is she doing here anyway? A white woman from another culture? What on earth made her think she could be useful?

But the next day, she goes back to the hospital, her heart beating in her chest. Emmanuel introduces her to the staff in the pediatric clinic. He asks whether she'd like to see patients or just observe today. Eva wants to get a feel for things, to figure out where she might be useful. The waiting room is overcrowded; families stand in the hallway and lean against walls. There must be a hundred people here. The pace is dizzying. People file in and out of consultation rooms; their visits take perhaps five minutes, and then they pick up remedies at the pharmacy window and leave. A nurse carries a syringe into a room, and a baby lets out a long, enraged cry. "Quinine," the nurse whispers to Eva when she comes out again. "Very painful." If the baby has malaria, Eva hopes it is not a resistant strain. The mother follows the nurse to the pharmacy; the child is still crying, weak and hoarse in his mother's arms.

Overwhelmed by what she saw in pediatrics, Eva visits several other hospital departments and clinics over the next few days. She must explore where a peer counseling program would fill a need. She cannot squander the small grant from UVM, so she takes her time. And by now, she wonders whether the whole thing was even a good idea.

One day, in an adult clinic, a thin middle-aged woman with graying hair comes in with headaches. Eva notices the staff's annoyance and curt, dismissive treatment of her. The woman's forehead is deeply grooved, her shoulders are stooped, and her *chitenge* wrap is dusty and torn at the edge.

"We all know her," Sister Violet explains. "She is here almost every day, always complaining of a headache. But there is nothing wrong with her. I'll give her some more acetaminophen and send her home, again." She sighs. "Until next time," she mutters.

Eva wonders what might *really* be bringing this worn-out woman back to the hospital, day after day. Clearly, she is not getting what she needs, and cannot articulate it, perhaps. Eva asks Sister Violet for permission to explore a bit further. The sister shrugs and introduces her to Pastor Albert, who can interpret Chichewa for her. If he thinks the white woman has strange whims, he is too polite to show it; he follows Eva into the examining room and translates her questions. The woman answers with a flood of Chichewa. Albert cuts her short and tells Eva what she already knows: her head hurts. The woman points to her temples; then her hands encircle her entire head as if to say "everywhere." Albert's clipped words don't match the woman's body language.

Eva asks him to slow down. "I need you to translate exactly for me, please, word for word."

He is too courteous to do otherwise. They slowly work their way through a much longer story. "You are very helpful, thank you," Eva says. "It can be tedious to repeat every word, but it's just what I need." It becomes clear that the woman has severe migraines. She is not making it up and is not making a big to-do out of nothing.

"Your headaches, this kind of headache that you have," Eva explains, "they get worse if you don't drink enough water." She hopes someone has already offered that advice and waits for the woman's hesitant nod, and goes on. "But they will get *much* better if you drink lots and lots of water. You need to drink much more water than you feel thirsty for," she explains through Albert.

The woman looks away awkwardly. Albert is ready to move on, but Eva prompts with more questions.

"Can you go home in the middle of your day to drink some water?"

The woman vigorously shakes her head no.

"Why not?" Albert translates the question. "*Kulekeranji*?"

A torrent of words comes out. Albert is interested now. He leans slightly toward the woman, listens, and asks more questions. This time, Eva sits by and waits, happy to let the dialogue unfold. *Now we're getting somewhere*, she thinks. The woman sits back and looks at her feet. Eva cannot read the blank look on her face.

Albert summarizes. "She is staying with relatives. A different relative every day. She can't go home to drink water."

"But wouldn't your family give you water?"

Another stream of words. "She feels like a burden already," says Albert.

"She doesn't have a home of her own, is that what she is telling us?"

With body language, hand gestures, eye contact, and patience, Eva slowly learns that the woman is afraid to go home. "Her husband is angry all the time," Albert translates. "He shouts at her over nothing. She stays away from his anger."

Is there domestic abuse in this country that they call the Warm Heart of Africa, hidden behind the smiles? "Was he always like that?" Eva asks, groping for a way to learn more.

More words come pouring out. "My husband fell from a roof on a job. Now he hurts all the time. He cannot work, and it makes him angry. We have no money. I tried to find work, but there isn't much."

Albert looks at Eva. "Thank you, doctor," he says. "I had no idea. They live in my parish, and they are members of my church, but I didn't know. They never told me." He makes a helpless hand gesture. "I will go visit their home tomorrow."

Eva wonders what care the husband got, if any. "Is there a community health worker who can check in about the husband's back?" she asks. "Perhaps his pain could be eased?"

Albert nods. He explains to the woman what they will try to do. She looks straight at Eva. "*Zikomo*," she says. *Thank you.* She reaches a hand in Eva's direction and repeats *Zikomo*. A genuine warmth passes from one woman to the other, a moment of simple human contact. Then she turns and leaves.

The encounter makes Eva just a bit bolder. It is not her medical degree that helped this woman, nor her fancy training in psychiatry. It was only empathy and having enough time to listen. She has time that the overworked staff do not have. This is just the sort of thing that a peer counseling program might help with. Who knows how much distress is out there, waiting to be noticed? There is only the hospital to turn to for help, and it only deals with the ailments of the body. There is nowhere one can say, "I'm scared" or "I'm sad, help me please."

Eva starts to offer a daily case conference. She invites nurses and helpers to bring up some patients they have seen. She is used to teaching through questions and dialogue, but here, the culture requires a numbing respect for her authority. Nobody speaks up at first. She treads lightly, tries not to put anybody on the spot. "I'd love for you to tell me about some of the patients you see," she says. "Nothing formal; I'm only trying to understand what problems come into your clinic. Maybe I can be of some use . . ."

Slowly, the staff warms to her. She listens to their most puzzling stories, tries to engage them all in figuring it out. Again and again, behind an illness, she unearths another theme, a deeper layer. There is a pattern: where the medical story doesn't add up, that is where there is something else, something in the person's life circumstance. Something that needs telling and needs to be heard. Eva begins to imagine simple, common-sense protocols and user-friendly guidelines to identify who might benefit from peer counselling.

She decides to bring her ideas to Clara, an experienced nurse who runs the tuberculosis clinic. The older woman hears her out and asks insightful questions; she is wise and kind. Together, they explore how to build a peer support network. Clara brims with ideas. The TB clinic proves to be a good place to try it out. Clara is deeply respected around the hospital. Her colleagues listen when she explains their ideas at a staff meeting.

"We all have too much work," she begins. There are nods. "And digging deeper into the hardest stories will take even more time, obviously." Someone sucks her teeth. Clara is undaunted. "But if we do this right, we will end up with *less* work. And we won't have all those useless repeat visits, you know? Those never fix anything." There are some careful nods. "And the people in our community are burdened, yes? Life is hard. But with support from each other, it won't be so heavy. I know you all want to help your people."

A couple of people look at each other with arched eyebrows. Then somebody sings out *Amen*!

That evening before dinner, Lyman sits with Eva in the garden patch while the boys run around. He asks about the hospital. She tells him about the resilience project, her ideas, and her hopes. She talks and talks. Could it work? Does it have a chance?

Lyman listens closely. After a while, he puts a hand on her knee. "Sweetie, slow down a minute?" he says. "I know you love your work and how much you care. But you sound a bit frantic. Or maybe overwhelmed? Are you taking on too much?"

She rests her head on his shoulder, and he waits, with that tender patience he can have.

"You're probably right," she says after a bit. "I'm pushing way too hard. I have to let it unfold."

He smiles and pulls her closer.

"I really want this year to matter," she says. "I want to make a difference, but I don't want them to see me as just another white do-gooder who thinks she knows best."

"I want to do something here too," he says. "That is why we came here, isn't it, instead of some posh university? But in the meantime, we are having an amazing experience, each doing something we believe in. The boys are loving it, and hopefully learning not to take all their privilege for granted. It's not a crime to relax and enjoy it . . ."

"I guess not . . ." she chuckles. Then why does it feel like she has never done enough?

They watch the kids throw balls for a while, until the abrupt equatorial sunset surprises them, as it still does, every day. "Mosquitoes are coming out," he says. "Boys? Time to get inside." He takes her hand.

Lyman has delved deep into his own work by now, at the project site along the Shire River. It is the only outflow from Lake Malawi in the Rift Valley. It drains into the Zambezi River 250 miles south, in Mozambique. He had hoped his angle on habitat research would smoothly fit into the team's ongoing work. But one night, after the boys are in bed, he tells Eva how baffled he is. "We hire local people to gather samples. They seem happy to get the work. But they don't always show up."

"Do they give a reason?" she asks, looking into the refrigerator. "Want a beer?"

"I'll take one, thanks." She pops the caps off the bottles. He looks troubled. "They show up sometimes, and other times they just don't. I've heard that several of them have a second job, an unofficial one. Their wages are so low that they grab whatever else will earn a little more to feed their families."

"That's understandable, isn't it?" she says, sitting next to him on the couch. She puts her bare feet in his lap.

"I get it, but it's bloody hard to move ahead this way, you know? Yesterday, someone's elderly cousin was sick and had to be taken to the clinic. Last week, several workers vanished because it was harvesting time on the family plot."

"So, you're having to slow down from what you're used to?" she asks with a smile. Lyman told her to slow down and relax, but he obviously doesn't know how, himself.

"That's not even all of it." He frowns. "Something was off with the results, so Chifundo and I dug in and went over everything all over again." He rubs at the stubble on his chin. "It turns out—we found a design flaw in the main project. The sampling techniques are inconsistent, which could invalidate everything the team has done."

"Oh no! All that work for nothing?"

"I'm not sure. I respect my colleagues; they're dedicated and smart. Who knows how this happened, and I don't want to sound like I'm blaming anyone. But we have to tell the team and get to the bottom of it. Soon . . ."

Eva considers him. He is a quiet man; he has taught for years and led many projects. But she knows he hates confronting differences of opinion. He has his science, his kindness, and his patience. But the distress of his team will hopelessly bog him down.

"I'm afraid it's not working, Eva," he says, his head bent.

She sits up to rub his neck. "Wait, slow down a bit. It's too easy to forget this is a different world. Priorities are different here, but you still have months ahead."

Lyman sighs. "I talked with a colleague who had projects in Indonesia. She suggested I should read *The Ugly American*. If you don't slow right down on arrival, she said, you'll be just another foreigner in their eyes. Someone wanting to impose your western ways, your western urgency."

"Makes sense to me."

"You know what else she said?" He looks at her. "That if I slow down enough, I'll accomplish much more than research; I'll make some amazing friends."

Eva smiles. "I'm learning that myself. Clara, for instance . . ."

He takes a deep breath. His neck begins to relax under her fingers. He explains a notion that is taking shape. "Here is what I'm hoping to get to.

Water quality declines with the flow of material from the neighboring areas, right? We know that."

"I remember it from your lecture, the day I first laid eyes on you!" she chuckles.

"Wow, you do?" he asks. "Well, we know that the flow of material accelerates where there is soil erosion. Things run off instead of seeping in. Make sense?"

She nods.

"And deforestation is a big part of that problem. Are you with me?" he asks.

"*Mm-hmm.*" He is going into his lecture mode, how endearing!

"Get this: it turns out that where there is no electricity, people's only source of fuel is wood-burning and making charcoal. I think I could map water quality in places where electricity has been brought in and compare it to the vast areas where there still isn't a grid."

"Weren't there large international grants for electrification?" she asks, surprised.

"There were, but who knows where those funds went. There are some deep pockets somewhere."

She sighs. "I guess that shouldn't be so surprising."

"And, you know what? If the data are solid, my colleague Chifundo thinks we could use them to push for expanding the grid. To get moving on that again."

"Oh, Lyman, how brilliant!" she beams.

The rainy season begins. It's fun at first. Then January brings heavier downpours. By February, Eva is sick and tired of it. When they first arrived, she was enchanted by the beauty all around them, at everything being so green and lush. She savored *not* freezing through a Vermont winter, for once. But by now, the heat drags at her like a wet weight. The sun comes out every day, at least for a little while, but nothing is ever dry. Her armpits feel disgusting. The boys' clothes are streaked with red mud.

The boys are oblivious to the heavy, wet heat. She hears them in the bedrooms, happily arguing about "multiverse" and superheroes. In a minute, they'll be starving, and then debates can turn into fights. She sets the table. Where the heck is Lyman? She hopes he takes over soon. She needs some alone time to wrestle with the funk she is getting into. The rain cannot last forever. They are almost finished with dinner when Lyman finally bursts through the door. "Hey, everyone! Guess what I have? A whole bag of *Mbatata*!"

"Oh, goodie!" Ezra jumps up to see. They love the heart-shaped sweet potato cookies, which are yummy, moist, and full of raisins. Gabriel asks, "Can I have one right now?"

"Great," Eva complains. "Pump them full of sugar before bedtime. You can get them to settle down then. I'm done for the day."

Lyman turns to Eva, hands her a flimsy plastic bag, and winks. "I have a present for you too," he says.

"Some gift wrap!" she pouts. She takes a bottle out of the bag, and her annoyance vaporizes. "Where did you find *that*? An actual Châteauneuf du Pape, in Malawi? This is fancy stuff!"

"I drove all the way to Lilongwe to get this for you, my love!" He curtsies.

"Sure, you did," she mocks. "Seriously, what makes you so late? And why were you in Lilongwe, anyway?"

"I had to go get more conductivity meters and pH strips. Three hours each way."

"You look awfully chipper," she says. She puts the bottle on the counter. "What's going on?"

"I'll tell you as soon as these monkeys are in bed. Boys! Enough cookies. Off you go. Brush those teeth before they fall out. *Shooosh*, go!"

"Aw, Daddy, not yet!" they whine in unison.

"Yep, now. If you're quick, you get an extra installment in our story."

They race each other to the bathroom. They somehow talk and brush their teeth at the same time. Eva looks up. His radiant good mood is infectious. She throws herself on the couch with a book and wonders what is making Lyman so happy. The boys certainly love it.

After a while, he comes back grinning. His clothes are rumpled, his hair mussed up. He plops down next to her and takes her by the shoulders. "You'll never guess, Eva."

"Tell me."

"Fisheries do decline *downwind* from charcoal burning. And we finally have the data to prove it!"

"You do?" She has uncorked the bottle and hands him a glass. "How?"

They swirl the wondrous liquid around and admire the deep black-currant color.

"*Hmmm*," he inhales appreciatively. "Remember how I first tried to prove the impact of charcoal burning? Well, the numbers I got were all over the place. Useless. I was pretty unhappy about it, as I'm sure you noticed. There are fewer fish everywhere, but I couldn't link it to anything. The data would go one way today, and the other way tomorrow. Nothing panned out."

"Frustrating . . ." He was quiet these last couple of weeks, and she got into a funk. It wasn't just the rain that got to her, she realizes now.

"I decided to look again at the small rivers that flow into the Shire," he says, "but I measured conductivity this time. Not just phosphate and nitrogen."

"Conductivity? What's that?"

"It measures minerals too. The total load of minerals. And you know what? I was right. I found that the rivers have more minerals and fewer fish *downwind* from where they burn charcoal. It's not just what *flows* into the rivers. It also happens where the only possible source is the air itself. The impact of the air on the fishery is *independent* of soil erosion and deforestation. All these factors add up."

"Wow, Lyman, that's impressive."

"The thing is, the water *looks* the same in both areas. There is nothing to see. No cloudiness, no silt. But all that smoke slowly drops tiny particles and minerals into the water."

"And that compromises the fisheries . . ." She takes this in.

"Yes. You know, fisheries are everything here. It's how they earn what little money they can. Lake Malawi takes up almost half the country, and *everything* depends on it."

She shakes her head. "Can anything be done?"

"We simply have to push the government to keep its promises about the grid. We were discussing it at the team meeting. Chifundo figured out the right politicians to talk to."

She hugs him. "This is just great, Lyman!"

"Honey," he adds, "I know you've been worried about me recently."

"You do? I didn't say anything, did I?"

"No. But your eyes were following me. I recognize that look and that frown. Prickly about the rain. Careful with your words. When you start watching what you say, babe, something's up!" He adds, "I should have said that sooner, about work. But my head was lost in the research problems."

"Thank you," she says softly. She worries too much when he is preoccupied. She knows this about herself, but she can't stop imagining that he is going dark again. It feels so different when he acknowledges that he's chewing on something; it's easy to keep her worry in check.

They snuggle with their wine glasses. The best wine she has ever tasted. Before long, Lyman pours her the last of it and scrutinizes the bottom of the bottle, just to be sure.

The weeks go by. Meanwhile, the boys have a fabulous time and make friends. One afternoon after school, Eva hears feet pounding the dirt road and approaching the house. "Mom? Mom, where are you?" Ezra calls as he runs through the door. Over his shoulder, he grandly proclaims, "*Takulandirani*!"

Bare feet come padding in. Three boys and two girls appear, with radiant smiles, faces wide open with expectation. Eva tries a greeting in Chichewa. A girl giggles, quickly shushed by the tallest boy. They look shy suddenly, waiting.

"We have lots of cookies, right, Mom? I told them we can all have cookies." Belatedly, he asks, "It's okay, right, Mommy?"

"Yes, sure, let me see what I have. Where is your brother?"

"Oh, he's coming. I think."

"Ezra! You *think* . . . ? Did you leave him at school? You're *always* supposed to walk home together!"

"But Mom, he's walking with friends too."

Eva lets it go. She points to the backyard. "Have fun," she says. "I'll bring out cookies and drinks in a minute." She tries to remember the word Ezra used. "*Taku-landi-rani*," she adds slowly. She hopes it means welcome. To her relief, the tallest boy smiles brightly and says, "Thank you, ma'am." His English is perfect.

She checks the street and sees Gabriel sauntering home, brightly chatting with two kids his age. Eva hears a mix of English and Chichewa. Gabriel's young brain, like Ezra's, soaks up words and meanings through trial and error, miming and pointing. Soon, nine children are playing outside. She brings out snacks, glasses, and a pitcher of lemonade. Five minutes later, Ezra comes inside asking for peas.

"Peas?" she asks. "Frozen peas?"

"No, no, pigeon peas! You know the ones? Big round, brown peas; the dried ones."

"Honey, you can't eat those like that, they're hard as pebbles, and they take a very long time to cook. Sorry, buddy."

"It's not to eat, it's for a game. They're going to teach us. I saw kids play it at school, and it's really fun."

"Ah. Okay, how many do you need?"

"A bunch. I don't know. A lot."

There is chanting and laughter outside, and through the window, Eva sees a boy and a girl crouching, facing each other. The others point and clap. There is a rhythmic song. A dozen little squares have been scratched into a patch of dirt. A few peas are within the squares; the opponents move them from one square to another, according to mysterious rules. Now it's Gabe's turn to play against the girl; the others cheer and clap.

Then, all at once, the sun sets, and the children leave just as suddenly, around the house and through the gate. Happy voices fade down the street.

Ezra and Gabe come in laughing. They are soon sprawled on the floor playing UNO. They have loud arguments about what "Reverse" means if there are only two players; about whether wild cards are for color alone, or numbers too. She reheats the corn porridge; a big pot of *Ndiwo* peanut sauce simmers on the stove. She bought fresh-caught Chambo fish on the way home, but she can't decide how to prepare it.

Lyman comes in, and she wrinkles her nose when she greets him. "You smell of mud and fish and . . . *hmmm*, something rotten?" She kisses him anyway. "Big field day?"

He checks in on the boys. They don't look up from the UNO cards. He returns to the kitchen.

"Can I help here, maybe make us a fish stew?"

"Great. Glass of white wine?"

"Are we celebrating something?" he asks.

"Maybe, yes. The boys are making friends; they brought a crowd home, and I almost ran out of snacks. The kids taught them some games with lots of hand clapping."

"That's worth toasting to," he says.

When everything is finally quiet, Eva puts on some music, and they curl up with a book each on one end of the sofa. Thank goodness it's Friday. After a while, Lyman looks up. "How about taking the boys on an expedition to Liwonde National Park this weekend? Wouldn't they love to see elephants and rhinos?"

"Great idea!" She plants a kiss on his nose. "Let's hope it lives up to their wild imagination."

"And then, how about an adventure for just the two of us, to celebrate our anniversary. Any thoughts?" he asks.

She smiles and ponders a moment. "You mentioned the Mulanje Massif a while back. It intrigues me. I've been asking people about it. Clara has a cousin who worked for the Forest Reserve at Mulanje."

"What did she say?" Lyman asks.

"Definitely not a place for children. You need a guide and a permit."

"You do?"

"Do you know the name of the tallest peak of the massif? Sapitwa. Clara said it means *Unreachable* in Chichewa."

"*Hm . . .*"

"There are lots of myths around it and—get this—they say Tolkien was here, and he based the Lonely Mountain on it!"

"Now that's tempting!"

"Right?" She laughs. "And Clara heard stories from her cousin about foreigners who come to Malawi and underestimate that mountain. Then the guides wind up risking their lives to rescue them."

Lyman considers, and Eva thinks about the tourists in Vermont. They do things like that too. They go up to places they don't know how to handle. They get lost in blizzards. And then a rescue squad has to go up in a snowstorm to find them.

"Well, I'm game. I hope we can find someone who will take the boys for a few days, then," he says.

Eva wonders whether Clara might be willing. She could stay at the house with her grandchildren, eight-year-old Mercy and five-year-old Moses. Eva recalls a day when Clara had to hurry home after the clinic for them. She told Eva then that her daughter and son-in-law both died from tuberculosis *and* AIDS. That was back when the first cases were being reported in Malawi, before people acknowledged AIDS was a problem. Eva gave a look of concern, and Clara turned her face away. "So I'm raising my daughter's children. I'm one of the lucky ones," she said, busying herself with some papers. "At least I'm healthy enough to raise them. And I have a salary. It's exhausting sometimes, but in many families, it's worse." There was a dignified wall around the woman's sadness, and Eva didn't probe further.

The next time Eva sees Clara at the hospital, she asks her about staying with the boys for three days and tells her there is more than enough room at the house for all of them.

Clara is more than happy to; the four children often have wonderful times together. "It will be fun for them," she says. She waves away the idea of payment.

"I'm not paying *you*," Eva insists. "Think of it as a school fund for Mercy and Moses." She knows money is tight even with the nurse's salary. She hopes offering a school fund won't sound condescending.

"I suppose," Clara hesitates. "Thank you. But wait—remember everything is still too wet right now. You'd find deep mud everywhere. Landslides. Rivers too swollen to cross. You have to wait until the rainy season is over."

Early on a Friday morning in April, Eva lugs her backpack to the car; Lyman checks their safety gear. It has not rained for two weeks, but just in case, they pack warm clothes and good rain gear. They have sleeping bags, water bottles, and food for three days. Clara stands in the dooryard, holding Ezra by one hand and Gabriel by the other. Moses has an arm around Gabriel's shoulders and whispers something in his ear. Mercy stands politely and waves them goodbye. By the time the car rolls away, Ezra is already chasing the two younger boys, and they are all laughing and shouting. Mercy yells, "Tag!"

"Thanks again, Clara!" Eva calls from the car window. "See you Sunday evening."

Before noon, they are at the Forest Reserve's information center. They ask about maps and which routes would be best for a two-night trip. The young man at the desk frowns a little.

"Everything is still very wet," he explains. "It could still rain while you're up there. In two weeks, it will be better for you."

Eva nods. "I wish we could. But we'll have to chance it." Lyman is already poring over a map of the enormous massif.

The young man shakes his head, an eloquent *whatever*. "I suggest going to this hut here," he points. "It has clear views of the whole massif and the Sapitwa peak itself. But first, let's find you a guide."

"Is that really necessary?" Eva asks.

The man's veiled expression and practiced patience suggest that he has gone around this mulberry bush before. He takes a breath. "Sir, madam, the trails are not marked; they shift with the weather and the flow of water. People get lost up there every year." Just then, he sees another young man at the door. "How lucky for you. Here is my friend Steven. He is one of our most experienced guides."

Steven has a great smile and sturdy hiking boots. His khaki pants and shirt are a bit worn but clean and pressed. They all chat; reason wins out over pride, and Steven is free to go immediately. He swings a tiny day pack onto his shoulder.

"Is that all you need? For three days?" Eva asks.

"Yes, it's all I need. My cousin lives up at the rescue station, a little beyond the hut. I can stay with him."

He seems so slight. Eva wonders whether he is as young as he looks. He exudes a calm confidence that inspires trust. Lyman and Eva shoulder their backpacks and follow him.

At first, the trail meanders through tea plantations, bright green shiny leaves as far as the eye reaches; a few taller trees stand here and there. They skirt around a maize field, then the path climbs into the shade of trees. Soon they come to a small river. It is shallow and muddy with runoff, but the current is swift. There is no bridge.

Lyman asks, "Is the way across further up?"

Steven is already taking off his boots.

"It's not very deep," he says. "We can walk across. If you want to keep your shoes on, you could hop on the stones. See here? And there?"

They hop, laughing. This is fun. Under the midday sun, the air is still fresh. On the other side, there is no obvious path; it is a mystery how Steven can tell the way. A bit further up, they come to another river, which runs a little faster. They make it across with dry boots. At the next small stream, Eva slips and lands with both feet in the water. Lyman chuckles and offers a hand. "Not funny," she says and wrings out her socks.

By the fourth rivulet, they give up and decide that since their shoes are already soaked, why bother taking them off? They slosh through and decide to just enjoy it. Steven looks fresh and unruffled; he watches them with amusement.

The path climbs gently from there. "There shouldn't be any more crossings," says Steven. "But you never know for sure where the water will flow, or how much of it."

Soon, the trail starts climbing in earnest, straight up, one steep incline after another. Switchbacks are evidently not a thing here. In many places, the trail is nothing more than a gully where rainwater ran down the mountain a short while ago. Everywhere, the mud is slick, slippery, and deep. Eva hangs on to small trees to pull herself up. Bad hiking form, she knows. When a flimsy trunk bends as she grabs it, she looks down. If it breaks, she'll have a long, muddy slide to reach solid ground. They hoist themselves onto small rocky ledges. *I wish I had Lyman's long legs*, she thinks, as she flops up and over.

It's hard to know where they are or how far they've come. There is nothing to see but trees and more mud. They slog higher and higher until the dense tropical vegetation becomes sparse. Eva is thoroughly out of breath, but Steven dances on ahead. He is limber and at home here. Behind her, Lyman is working hard too. What happened to their excellent conditioning, their mountaineering shape? Another steep hill, and she falls behind. Lyman offers a hand.

Eva waves him off. "I can do it," she huffs.

The next time Lyman looks over his shoulder, Eva is reaching for a ledge that his own long legs had easily stepped onto. He pulls her up and hugs her while she catches her breath. They stand laughing, muddy and panting, on a precarious slippery slope.

"If our hiking buddies in Vermont saw us like this . . ." she breathes.

"They'd laugh at us," Lyman agrees. "We're a sight, I'm sure."

They sip some water and rally, but soon, Steven looks back at Eva with concern and says, "Let me take your pack, madam." He reaches his hand to take it from her.

"No need," she snaps. "And please call me Eva." She realizes how snippy that sounded. "Thank you," she says more gently. "That is very kind, but I'm fine."

But when Eva slips back from yet another ledge that she cannot quite reach, Steven insists. "It will be safer if I take it. For all of us."

She knows he is right. Shamefaced, she hands Steven her pack. He slings it onto his back and carries his own in front.

"I'm used to being up here," he says simply. He points upward. "It gets more level there. See, where those rocks are?"

Eventually, they emerge onto a huge plateau, fifteen miles across. They have climbed over 4,000 feet on bare volcanic rock. In one direction, the rocks and grassy patches stretch out for miles above rolling hills. In the other direction, far into the distance, several tall peaks rise above the plateau. The scale of it all is staggering.

"Which one is Sapitwa?" Lyman asks.

"You can't see it yet," says Steven. "We need to get to the hut for that. Ready to move on?"

They nod and continue over rocky outcroppings and through scrawny grassy patches. There is almost no soil here on the massif and almost no trees. The wind freely sweeps across. They stop to dangle their sore feet in a small rocky pond and munch on some apples. A little further up, they cross another plateau and walk around a hill, and there, the view abruptly opens out.

There is Sapitwa: majestic, massive. Dark and forbidding, it towers above everything as far as they can see. Thin clouds gather around it, and then dissipate. Sapitwa, they know, is the highest point in all of Central Africa, nearly 10,000 feet in altitude. And here it is right before them. It has lured countless people toward its peak. The ascent doesn't seem all that hard, but Steven warns them it is still a long way up from here.

Eva gapes in awe. "Steven, have you gone up the whole way?"

He gives her a puzzled look. "Yes, well . . . I get called up for rescues. We all do."

"Yes, of course, I remember now," she says.

"You have heard what people say, right, that Sapitwa means *Unreachable*?" Steven says. "Well, what it really means in Chichewa is *You don't go there*. It can look okay one moment, like now. And then it changes, just like that. I mean, all of a sudden, you're in a thick cloud. And the wind is howling."

"Really? That quickly?" she asks.

"Sometimes. Last season, a group went up on their own. It was a clear day. At the top, someone moved a few feet away to take pictures. The others told us later . . ." He shakes his head. "Clouds raced in with heavy rain. It was so dense they couldn't see their own feet—that's what they said. And when it cleared, that woman was gone. Just gone." Steven looks at the mountain with a somber face. "Nobody knows whether she fell in a crag, or off a cliff, or what. We searched for four days, the whole team. We never found her body."

Eva puts a hand to her mouth. "Oh, Steven! That must be so hard for you." How typical, she thinks, someone careless and cocky, dragging others into danger. Why don't people listen to reason?

"There are many myths about the mountain," says Steven, looking up. "Stories about the whole massif. They say there is a flying serpent up there that takes people away. Or that there is an old woman who lives in a waterfall. And she creates thick mist so people will get lost when she feels insulted. When the humans don't show her enough respect."

They walk on in silence.

"To celebrate the end of the season," Steven changes the topic in a lighter tone, "every year the guides run a race to the top. All of us."

"How long does it take you?" Lyman asks.

"Oh, just a few hours, up and back."

Eva looks at Lyman. That would seem impossible if they hadn't just seen him climb up without effort, light on his feet.

"We race barefoot, the traditional way," Steven adds with a smile.

"Barefoot? On this?" Eva asks. "Doesn't it hurt your feet?"

"We're used to it," says Steven. "We were always barefoot growing up."

When they fall onto a mattress at the hut that night, Eva nestles into Lyman's shoulder. "Wow," she mumbles into his neck, and starts to drift off.

Lyman spoons her, strokes her neck gently. “You aren’t *really* that sleepy, are you?” he asks, hopefully. “That depends,” she says. “What are you offering?” And then she is wide awake.

By June, the dry season has turned all the mud into hard-packed red earth and dust. The lush trees, shrubs, and garden plots look sad and tired. The grass, where there still is any, turns gold, then brown. Autumn becomes winter, and mornings are downright chilly. The house has no warm water. Cool showers felt lovely before in the stifling heat. Now, it’s hard to convince the boys to bathe at all.

Something else is on Eva’s mind too. Shouldn’t she have had her period by now? She doesn’t really keep track, but it seems an awfully long time. At first, she wrote it off to traveling and the fatigue after the Mulanje Massif. Now she cannot face breakfast. And why is she so tired?

It couldn’t be what she thinks, but there is no harm in making sure. She stops at the pharmacy near the hospital. While dinner simmers on the stove, Lyman and the boys build something elaborate with blocks, and she unpacks the pregnancy test in the bathroom. She stares at the result. Her heart races. She does a second one.

But how could this be? She pauses and remembers the hut on Mulanje. They were so happy and playful, and she was sure the timing was “safe” . . . Wow! She is excited and scared at the same time. This was not in their plans. How will Lyman feel about it?

When the boys are in bed, she calls him to the couch and pats the seat next to her. She says, “I have something to tell you.”

“Oh? Come out with it then. What is it?” he asks.

“I’m pregnant, Lyman.” She searches his face for a reaction. They are forty now. Are they too old for another baby?

“Really? Are you sure?”

“Yes, I’m sure. My body tells me so. And the test does too.”

“Wow.” He takes it in. “How long?”

"Two months," she says and waits for that to register. He looks at her with a puzzled frown, and then he bursts out laughing. "I see, a Mulanje baby? That's going to be one adventurous kid!" He picks her up and swings her around. "Let's toast to that!"

They stay up late, talking. So many thoughts and questions. Where to get prenatal care. Should they return to Vermont sooner, before the end of the year? Where could they set up a baby room? Should they tell the boys yet, or wait? How will *they* react?

"They will be six, and almost eight, when they become big brothers," says Eva.

"Wouldn't it be fun if they had a little sister?" he says. "They'll be so good with her."

"Lyman! They will be great, even if it's a baby brother. Ezra can be wild sometimes, but he is always gentle with little kids. I just love what it brings out in him."

"Yes, me too." Lyman smiles. "He's the same way with puppies too. And even with Gabriel sometimes. He loves to be the big boy, and he'll *really* like another kid to boss around."

"Gabe is such a gentle soul. We'll have to make sure he doesn't fall between the cracks. You know, the proverbial middle child thing?"

"Oh, stop being a psychiatrist," he laughs. "We won't let that happen. And you know what else? I don't have to teach this spring. Perfect timing to have a new baby."

They sit together for a while. Imagining.

Chapter 6
1992

The family welcomes baby Olivia soon after their return to Vermont. The boys are mostly sweet and gentle with their new little sister; Gabe gets fiercely protective whenever he thinks Ezra is too rough with her. They compete over the chance to hold her.

Lyman and his colleagues finish their paper on the effects of charcoal burning at the Shire River. When a leading journal accepts it, Eva takes him out to dinner to celebrate.

Meanwhile, she hears from Clara that the resilience project is thriving. That's not surprising under Clara's leadership! But now she'd like to expand it to other districts. Could Eva come help her with that? What a tempting notion. *Could* she get away for a short stay in Malawi, she wonders, to see what she can do? Maybe a bit later, when the children are older . . .

Their lives are busy, and time flies by. Already, it is Olivia's fourth birthday. It's a cold Saturday afternoon in December. Lyman ties four bright mylar balloons to the mailbox, a big sparkly 4 on each. Then he goes off to get some last-minute things for the party. Ezra and Gabriel are in their room with some friends, building an imaginary world with the Legos they keep in a large storage bin. The boys never tire of them, nor do their friends.

Olivia is in the kitchen with Eva, helping with the traditional triple chocolate cake. She stands on a stool and earnestly whisks everything together; she often tests the batter with her finger.

"You can pour in the chocolate chips now," says Eva.

"Goodie." Olivia tests a few of them too, looking sideways at her mother, a smile and a question mark on her face.

Eva grins. "Just four, okay? One for each year. Save enough for the cake!"

Olivia nods gravely. "Can I lick the pot, Mommy?"

"Sure."

"It's yummy," she announces. She stretches her tongue out toward a big dab of chocolate on the end of her nose. When she can't reach it, she wipes at it with her finger and smears more chocolate all over her face.

"Look at you," Eva laughs. "You need another bath already. You have chocolate all over you, and . . . geez, look at that, chocolate in your hair too!"

Lyman walks in and bursts out laughing. "Yikes, Olivia, can I eat *you* instead of the cake?" He pretends to take a bite out of her nose. She makes a gurgle of protest and pushes his face away with her chocolate-covered hands.

"You two! Now you're both covered in chocolate. Maybe I should hose you both down."

"Let's go, princess!" Lyman says. "Bath time. Have you decided what you want to wear? The blue sparkly dress? Or your new red corduroy romper?"

A month later, on a bitter Sunday in January, there are frost flowers on the windows. It is already getting dark. Holiday decorations still shine their hopeful little lights around the house. Inside, the Christmas tree is still lit. Glass ornaments hang in the windows. Eva can't bear to remove them yet. Hanukkah candles, a chalice, and two glass candlesticks sit on the bar counter between the kitchen and the dining room. Lampshades with animal cut-outs shed warm light into the corners of the living room. The wood stove roars; it has eaten up all the wood Eva carried in this morning. She'll have to go out and get more. Nobody else ever seems to do it.

At the dining room table, she examines a sketch pad and several scrolls of blueprint. She chews on a pencil. "Lyman?" she calls out. Then louder: "Lyman, can you come here please?"

It is weirdly quiet in the house. The boys are out ice skating with friends. Olivia is taking a late nap.

Still no response. "Lyman?!" she shouts.

"What is it?" he asks from the office.

"You said we would go over the blueprints this afternoon. The boys will be back soon, and Olivia could wake up any time. Let's do it now, please?"

"Just a minute, okay? Let me just finish . . ."

She grits her teeth. "No. That's the third time you said that." She bites off the words and goes to the kitchen. She looks in the refrigerator to see what there is for dinner. *Why has Lyman been so unavailable lately?* she thinks.

Lyman walks in and glances at the drawings on the table. "So, what is the question?"

She stands next to him. "What do you mean, what's the question?"

"Well, haven't we gone over this before? Why are we doing it again?"

She takes a breath and rolls out the largest blueprint. She points. "Look at the architect's proposal. He suggests we add another bedroom on the far side of the house."

"Right. And?"

"That puts one of the boys' rooms opposite from everybody else." She traces the distance on the blueprint.

"Why not? Ezra is almost a teenager," he says.

"I'm not too sure. Here's an alternative. We could add a garage with bedrooms above it. All three kids could be upstairs together, on this side." She points at the blueprint and traces out where a garage would go. She shows him her sketch with the garage addition. "See? We'd keep our bedroom above the kitchen, and the office stays down here." She straightens up and walks around the bar counter toward the refrigerator. "Let's get dinner started while we talk. Come to the kitchen with me?"

He shrugs and follows her. "Fine. Pizza night?"

"That was my thought," she agrees. "Sunday tradition." She takes the eggplant out, turns the oven to 450. Lyman finds a large bowl.

"Your idea makes the addition into a much bigger project," he complains.

"I just don't like the rooms far apart like that, Lyman." She chooses a large knife and tests its edge.

He measures a cup of flour. "Why not?" Another cup.

She starts slicing an eggplant. The knife thwacks down on the cutting board. "Come on, Lyman, Ezra is only twelve. One moment he's a know-it-all big brother, and the next moment he's scared of the dark and won't admit it."

"You're exaggerating, Eva. I can't even remember the last time—" A third cup of flour drops into the bowl. He puts the lid on the canister.

She frowns in his direction, cuts the last slice, and her knife clatters down. "It happened three nights ago. You wouldn't know, you weren't home." She faces him.

"Pass me the salt, would you? Do you mean the night I had a late conference?" He finds the yeast and mixes it in.

"Yes. One of your *many* late conferences this past month." She lays the eggplant slices out on a baking sheet, sprinkles them with salt, and slides them into the oven. She turns to him, hand on her hip.

Lyman doesn't look up. He is intent on kneading the pizza dough and sprinkles a little more water. It takes him a beat to register what she just said. He looks up, with the ball of dough in his left hand, a hard look in his eyes.

"*You* may have a half-time position, Eva, but I do not. I have a research team to lead. In case you forgot." He twirls the dough.

She washes the spinach, her back to him. Through clenched teeth, she says, "I know that, Lyman. But darn it, when we agreed on that plan, I never imagined being alone so much."

"Well, that's just the way it is."

She wheels around. "Just the way it is? Whether I like it or not? Look at me! I end up doing eighty percent of the childcare. The kids have barely seen you lately. You're great with them on the weekend, but I am exhausted, and they miss you!"

He tosses the dough in the air, slaps it down again, and tosses and twirls it. Again, toss and twirl. He has gotten good at this, she realizes. He does not answer.

"Lyman!" she shouts. "Are you even listening to me?" She turns to leave the kitchen, tears in her eyes. "It's not fair, it's not what—" she mutters.

"Mommy!" comes a sing-song voice.

Eva goes upstairs to Olivia's little room and wipes her eyes. "Coming, sweetie."

She hears skates clatter onto the tiles by the door. Ezra and Gabriel are being dropped off after hockey practice. Coats, hats, and mittens will make a trail toward the kitchen.

"Can I have a—?" Ezra calls out while he kicks off his shoes.

"Pick up your coats first and hang them up," says Lyman. "You know better."

Eva sits on the floor next to Olivia's small bed and brushes damp hair off the child's forehead. "Hello, sleepy girl! Did you have a nice nap?"

Olivia nods and grabs Eva's fingers. She likes to hold onto Mommy's hand while she wakes up. Her other hand grabs her stuffed baby seal. The toy was once pure white. One of its flippers has been lovingly chewed; stuffing is coming out at the neck. "Up, Mommy?" she asks after a bit; she reaches her arms to be picked up, still holding the seal.

Eva stands and carries sleepy-eyed Olivia downstairs and into the kitchen. "You're getting too big to carry, you know that?" she says. "And you're getting rather big for that thumb, too, aren't you?"

Lyman has brought out milk and snacks. The boys perch at the bar counter. "Go easy with the snacks, everybody, it's pizza night," he says.

"I got really good at skating backwards, Dad!" says Ezra. "And we were practicing fast pivots."

Olivia climbs onto a bar stool next to her brothers and reaches for the fruit. Eva pours her a cup of milk.

"I was working on those special fast starts," Gabriel pipes up. "What are those called again, Ezra?"

"Explosive starts. Duh. And then Josh's dad—"

Gabe finishes his brother's sentence: "Gave us all hockey sticks, and he set up cones and—Dad!—we practiced getting the puck past a goalie. That was awesome."

"Dad, can we join a hockey team?" asks Ezra.

"Josh is on a team, and I want to play too. Please?" Gabriel adds.

Lyman smiles at his sons. Eva breathes out her last bit of anger. Here he is, her handsome, attentive husband. Lyman is right. She has a half-time job, he doesn't. It's just that lately, moods hang over him more often. She reminds herself, yet one more time, that she worries too much. That they have been fine, that *he* has been fine since that time before their wedding. But whenever his mood brightens, she brightens too. Then the next irritable, jarring comment triggers her. Is it just her own winter blues, making her too touchy?

"Let's go skating a couple of times," says Lyman. "Let's do some hockey drills together this week. I can teach you what I know. And then we can decide, okay?"

"Cool!" Gabe pumps his fist. "When?"

"Let's check the weather. Right now, the cook had better get busy on dinner." He turns back to the dough.

Eva hugs her boys. Their cheeks are still rosy and cold. "Go get out of your hockey clothes, please."

They thunder down the hall. She grates a heap of cheese and takes out tomato sauce and pesto. It will be the usual multicolor family pizza: a section with veggies, and a section with cheese only. Three-quarters will be red, the rest green. Feta for Lyman, olive slices for Eva. A happy, normal Sunday evening. Except, is her husband withdrawn lately? He definitely works too many late evenings. She doesn't trust herself to know what's what; it makes her angry at herself.

Later that night, she has trouble falling asleep. When did he start working so late? September? She remembers bringing it up with him. He had been annoyed with her, but afterward, he spent more time with the boys practicing basketball moves outside. And for a while, he kept up a lovely bedtime routine with Olivia.

She turns on her side in the dark and listens to Lyman's even breathing. He can be so present and alive and thoughtful. His kids adore him so much that Eva feels taken for granted sometimes. But since the holidays, Eva has been on the alert for random mood changes. He gets irritable for no reason, and then he is cheerful again, even playful, like tonight. Other times, he is somber and makes himself scarce for days. Does she expect too much?

Then it occurs to her. She is not exactly fun herself these days. During the dark months, she craves light. She feels cooped up in winter. With three children, there hasn't been enough time in the snow. She is often tired and listless. Is she driving Lyman away? Is he staying away because of *her*? Is he irritable because of how *she* is with him? She sits up abruptly and looks at Lyman asleep beside her in the dark. Her heart thumps, and her hands are clammy. She gets up to calm herself and goes downstairs to fill a glass of water in the kitchen. She stares out of the window at the starless night. Perhaps Lyman no longer loves her. That could happen; it *does* happen in some marriages. She paces, picturing her life crumbling and her family falling apart.

She needs to get outside to clear her head, to stomp around where nobody can hear her. She grabs her coat, slips into her boots, and goes out into the field. The icy wind whips at her hair. She shivers, and her hands are numb with cold. Tears freeze on her face. *Stop it, this is only a nightmare*, she tells herself. *It's only my fears that are taking over my imagination. Don't be stupid, Eva*, she thinks, *go back to bed.*

Will she ever grow up, stop going down this worn old path of self-doubt when things are less than idyllic? What a mess she is.

Groundhog Day comes. Eva drives home to meet the carpool from nursery school. It will be dark in less than two hours. The days are not long enough yet to ease Eva's craving for light. She is tired of the biting cold, of wearing a down coat on top of thick sweaters; she loathes hats. Her fingers feel numb on the steering wheel, despite fleece-lined gloves. In the driveway, she gets out of the car, and the wind howls across the field. It burns her face as she carries in an armload of firewood. She kicks off her boots and dumps the logs in the wood-box. The big old window rattles, the glass sucks heat out of the house.

She flings her hat and gloves toward the entrance. Before taking off her coat, she stuffs paper in the wood stove and carefully arranges a layer of kindling. Then the logs: two small ones across, two bigger ones lengthwise. *Please, little fire, don't fail me, I don't want to go out to the shed for more kindling!* She blows little puffs of breath, and soon there is a reassuring glow. Gently, gently, she breathes life into the flames.

The first log catches fire. She stands and admires it and bends down again to blow in just a little more encouragement. When some heat starts to radiate, she carefully closes the glass door. She loves the new Vermont Castings stove, its dark green enamel. It gives her pleasure every day. She holds out her hands to warm them, begins to thaw out, and cheers up.

Olivia's ride is due any minute now. The boys will arrive in an hour. Nobody has sports or music lessons today. She looks forward to these rare quiet times with her children.

She takes off her puffy purple down coat, stuffs her gloves in the pockets, sticks her new lavender angora hat into the hood, and finds a free hook in the mudroom. She drops today's pile of envelopes and magazines on the bar counter. In the kitchen, she sets the kettle on the stove, keeping an eye on the fire. Outside the big window, snow blows across the field in the gray afternoon light. The bird feeder is almost empty; she'll have to get more sunflower seeds tomorrow. She turns on a few lamps in the living room. The light brightens the warm kilim rug.

The kettle whistles. She goes back around the counter and takes out her favorite mug. It is handmade by a local potter; its uneven gray-green glaze soothes her. She savors a quiet moment in the kitchen nook and warms both hands around the steaming mug. Soon, she hears a van in the driveway. A door slams, and Olivia comes running. Her red coat flaps open. Her head is bare, and her brown hair flies in the wind. At the door, Eva picks her up for a big hug.

"Hello, sweetie pie . . ."

Olivia wriggles down. "Hi, Mom, can I have hot chocolate?" She fishes papers out of her backpack. "I painted a horse today! Wanna see?" She shows Eva a very green meadow with a single tree, under a bright blue sky with a huge orange sun. A four-legged animal with a long mane stands with stiff legs.

"Nice painting, honey. Maybe—" But Olivia is already running upstairs to her room. Eva grabs a book and sits near the fire.

After a while, Ezra bursts through the door and leaves it wide open to the wind.

"Close that door a bit, won't you?" Eva says. "It's freezing out there!"

But Gabriel is right behind. "Hi," he calls out. He closes the door, hangs up his coat, and places his boots on the rack. Ezra kicks his boots into a corner and throws his coat over a hook. "Do I smell hot cocoa?" he asks. "Can I have some?"

"Me too," Gabriel chimes in. They each climb onto a bar stool and continue an earlier argument about the coach.

"Ezra, stop griping!" says Gabriel. "You're just mad because you don't get to start at every game."

"I'm on the varsity team! We would win more often if Coach gave his best players more time on the court . . ."

"It's a *team*, Ezra, every—"

"I can't wait to get to middle school," Ezra says. "I'm so tired of sixth grade."

Eva has heard this all before: Ezra being impatient, Gabriel being reasonable. It makes her smile. She cuts some apples, puts out a bowl of nuts, and puts another log on the fire. "Homework? Ezra? Gabe?" she asks.

Ezra takes his mug to the kitchen nook and grabs his pack on the way. "Yeah, some math, not much." He shoves Olivia's pack aside with his foot and spreads his workbook and papers out on the table.

"I have to finish *The Hobbit*." Gabriel gets the book out and climbs back on his stool. "I love that book. Mom, can we watch the movie sometime?"

"Sure," she says. She goes through the mail, standing at the counter. Mostly junk to light a fire with.

Gabriel is deeply absorbed in reading. One elbow on the counter, he munches absently on pieces of apple and a little pile of salted cashews. He hand-combs his tangled red curls. Eva reaches over and ruffles his hair on the way to the stove.

"Don't do that, Mom!" He pulls away.

"Sorry. You're just so adorable. I get carried away."

He sticks his tongue out to hide a smile.

Eva looks at her two wonderful boys, growing up so fast, and so different from each other. She walks upstairs to check on Olivia in her room. "Everything okay here?"

Olivia has a new coloring book, a birthday present filled with detailed stylized birds. She is sitting on the floor of her room, one leg tucked under her. With her new markers, she dresses her birds in fantastic, bright feathers. Eva looks around, remembering she got deeply absorbed like this too, as a child.

"Need anything?"

"*Unh-uh.*"

"Let me know. Snacks are on the counter."

In the kitchen, Ezra sits on the window seat, tapping his foot. His homework is spread all over the table. With headphones on, he is doing math problems while listening to a narration of *Tom Sawyer.*

Eva frowns at the loud voice from his headphones. "Ezra? Hey, Ezra? You have to turn the volume down!" she calls out. "Honestly, it's loud enough that I can actually hear it way over here. You'll go deaf if you keep this up."

No response. She walks over to him, taps his shoulder, and turns the volume down on his Walkman.

"Mom!" he protests.

She gestures for him to take the headphones off. "How can you get any math done while you listen to a story?" This conversation, about doing two things at once, is pointless. They have gone 'round and 'round about this. She reminds herself that multitasking actually calms Ezra's restless mind.

Behind her, Ezra puts his headphones back on and returns to his math. He is very good at it, even if his methods are intuitive and unconventional. To his teachers' dismay, he can never explain how he did it, but his answers are seldom wrong.

She sighs; her firstborn is rapidly growing into a teenager. This morning, she caught sight of him in the bathroom, prodding his first pimple, bent toward the mirror. Right now, he's picking at it again with his right hand, while the left scribbles in the margins of his workbook.

She puts the broccoli in a colander and unwraps the chicken. She goes toward Gabriel at the counter and taps his shoulder. "What?" he asks without looking up from his book.

"Don't you have to finish your rainforest project by tomorrow?" she asks.

No answer from him either. The munching sounds continue. Her children are already old enough to ignore her . . . She tries again. "Gabriel? Sweetie?"

"*Huh*? Did you say something?" he mumbles without lifting his head; his hand continues to fluff up the red halo of his hair. She gives up.

By the time Lyman comes home, three hours later, all three kids are wound up. Typical end-of-day wildness. They have eaten in the dining room because Ezra's homework is still spread out on the kitchen table.

"Come on, Mom," Ezra bickers, standing up. "Do I really *have* to finish all the vegetables? They're *so* overcooked."

"Sit down," she tells him as she goes to kiss Lyman.

"Mom! Why can't I just have half, and move on to dessert?"

Olivia joins in. "Me too, Mommy! I'm full." In her mind, her big brother walks on water. She would follow him, literally and figuratively, onto thin ice with a delighted *Me too*.

Gabe touches his sister's arm. "Shush, sis," he whispers, "if she hears you're full she'll say we don't need *any* dessert."

Lyman takes off his winter coat. Eva meets him by the mudroom. Gabriel whispers to his siblings. "Knock it off! You're being stupid! Just eat the darn vegetables, I want dessert!"

"*Brrr*, your hands are cold," Eva says to Lyman. "Were you rolling in the snow out there?"

He shakes his head and puts on his slippers. He gives Olivia a quick hug, then Gabriel. He pats Ezra on the back where he stands holding the freezer door. "Nah. A student stopped me in the parking lot; she went on and on about something to do with the others in her group." He grimaces. "She seems to think she'll get a better grade if she complains enough about everyone else."

"The worst kind of teacher's pet?" Eva asks. She decides the vegetable and dessert issue is not worth pursuing. She shoos Ezra away and looks through the popsicle supplies. "Is it the same girl that you've mentioned before?" She turns to the kids. "Frozen fruit popsicles, guys? What flavor?"

Lyman fills his plate and goes to the table. "Yep," he says. "If only I could get off the list of faculty advisors . . ." He sits down. "I hate this part of the job."

Eva hands out the popsicles and finds her chair.

Holding her popsicle in one hand, Olivia wants to play rock, paper, scissors. Her brothers are bored with the game. Gabriel gets up. "I have to finish my diorama. Mom? Can you help me?"

"Hey, dude, you can't just walk off," Ezra bursts out, "it's your turn with the dishes!"

Gabe stops and looks over his shoulder. "No, it's not, I did 'em yesterday. Your turn."

Ezra shouts after him. "We traded last week, remember? You owe me a night!"

Lyman shoots Ezra a hard look. Olivia, sticky with blueberry, climbs onto Daddy's lap. She puts her hands on either side of his face. Laughing, she rubs his cheeks and tries to stop him from eating. "Daddy, Daddy, you have to see my coloring book!"

"Hold on, will you?" he says, and frowns.

Down the hall, Ezra and Gabriel are still arguing. Eva sees Ezra grab his brother's sleeve. Gabe shakes him off. "You're a loser!" Ezra shouts.

"Am not! You are!"

Suddenly, Lyman slams his hand on the table. "That's enough. Everybody," he booms. "Get out."

Olivia startles.

"All of you, go to your rooms and calm down. Olivia, get off my lap, *now*."

Eva's jaw drops. Olivia wilts and starts to walk upstairs, crying. Eva fights the urge to jump in and tell her, "It's okay, sweetie, come sit here with me." But they have an unbreakable rule: never, *never* contradict each other in front of the kids. If they disagree, they discuss it later.

"Lyman," she hisses across the table once the kids are gone. "Was that really necessary? For heaven's sake . . ."

He doesn't answer and does not look up. His face is a thundercloud. Eva goes to comfort Olivia upstairs. She sits with her on the edge of the bed, settles the snuffling child's head onto her lap, and silently strokes her hair for a while. Soon, Olivia relaxes and starts absently twirling her hair.

"Honey, your daddy is very tired tonight. He is not mad at you. He just needs to settle in for a bit, and he really needs to eat something, okay?"

"But Mommy, I haven't seen him all day!" Olivia hiccups. "Why does he come home so late all the time?"

"Oh, sweetie, he doesn't . . ." She stops herself. She has been thinking the same thing. And his mood is only getting *more* brittle. She has to comfort her little girl, but she cannot lie to her.

Olivia climbs on her mother's lap, arms around her neck. Eva rocks her gently and replays the last few months in her mind. In the fall, the boys ran to the door when they heard Lyman, excited to throw some baskets or kick a soccer ball with him before coming inside. It is too cold and dark for that now. Instead, they all compete to show him their projects, or a comic book, and Lyman stiffens under the eager assault. Even Olivia cannot always bring a smile to his face when she waves her latest painting. Tonight is not the first time he has been short with the kids. And is it her imagination, or do they act out more, get into more fights, when he comes home late?

She gets up from Olivia's bed and reaches a hand to pull her up. "Come on, bring your coloring book and let's go sit with Daddy. I'm sure he'd love to see what you've done. Come."

Olivia gravely comes back to the table. "Daddy?" she asks shyly.

He looks up and tries to smile. "Yes, sweetie pie?"

"I'm not wild now, see? Can you look at my pictures now?" Eva's heart breaks when she sees her little girl trying so hard to read her daddy's mood and earn his approval.

He sets his plate aside and lifts her onto his lap. She starts turning the pages of her coloring book. Lyman points. "That bird is beautiful," he says. "Look at those pink and red feathers!"

Later, in bed, Eva sits up and turns to Lyman. He is on his back, arm up on his pillow. She *has* to bring up what happened tonight. She reaches for his shoulder and tries not to sound critical.

"Is something the matter, Lyman? Is something bothering you?" Does she sound like a broken record? And how many times has she explained it to him, that she copes better when he *owns* his state of mind, instead of shutting her out . . .

He stares at the ceiling. "Long day. Frustrating undergraduate squabbles. The usual."

"I don't mean just that. It's been happening more lately, you're being short-fused, and—"

He cuts her off. "Here we go again. Can't you just leave it be? Do you always have to analyze everything? I'm sick of—"

"Lyman, stop brushing me off. You had Olivia in tears tonight. Over what?"

"They were all over the place, Eva! All of them at once. Yelling, bickering, wanting attention. Can't I get a few moments of peace and quiet when I get home?"

She bends over and looks at him. "Of course. But they are children, Lyman! And you're their daddy!"

He turns his back to her. "I'm tired. I'm done. Good night."

She is agitated now. She is angry. They *must* be able to talk about these things. And it's been happening more and more, for weeks. There are good stretches, and then there are days on end like this. Little things set him off. He hasn't often been playful with the kids since . . . since fall, some time? Well, he was wonderful at the birthday party. But otherwise . . . And when she brings it up, he shuts down. Then, for days, it goes around and around in her head.

Once again, she tries telling herself it will blow over. It always does. But does it? He wants her to believe that things get better without talking about them. "Not everyone needs to discuss everything all the time, Eva. Or to *work things through*," he says with air quotes. She wants to scream when he mocks her to avoid her questions.

She ruminates, and tears come. There is no point trying to sleep now. She gets up, goes downstairs, and sits at the piano. She softly plays one ballad after another. She improvises until her ear leads her, without thought, into different harmonies. Minor keys mostly, dreamy and a little sad. If the music bothers Lyman, well, she doesn't care tonight. She plays her way into a repetitive, soothing groove. It will elude her by morning, but it settles her enough to go to bed for a few hours. She'll be exhausted tomorrow.

After that night, a dense silence hangs between them. Three days later, before the children arrive home, Eva walks across the fields to collect her thoughts. There are heavy, low clouds; the wind bites her face. The Green Mountains are mere gray outlines. Dull little puffs of snow blow across the field.

Why is the school bus so late? Then she remembers: the boys have basketball practice, and Olivia has a play date. Lyman should be back before the kids today. She goes inside and throws more logs on the fire. Perhaps they will be able to talk, finally. Maybe Lyman himself will break the ice. More likely, she will have to bring it up, as usual. He probably expects it will all just go away . . .

The children have carried on as if the blow-up never happened, but the bitter taste sticks in Eva's mouth. She half-heartedly picks out a new piece on the piano, but she cannot focus. Irritably, she turns on some living room lights. She searches everywhere for her book, which turns out to be hiding in plain sight on the kitchen counter.

Before she has even settled into it, Lyman arrives. She greets him by the door, looking at him carefully.

He tugs at his boots. “I’m glad it’s Friday.” He looks up; his face is relaxed and open. “I can use some downtime. Can’t you?”

She leans against the door jamb. “I need a hug,” she says, trying to smile.

He gets up, wriggles out of his jacket, and finds a hook to hang it. The red wool hat she knitted for him is still on his head as he envelops her in a bear hug. “Are you okay?” he asks.

She buries her face in his chest. Takes in his scent. “*Hmmm*,” she avoids his question. “You smell of fresh air. Were you out in the field today?”

He hangs up the hat and goes to the kitchen. “Yep. Simply gorgeous out there. Cold and crisp, with a thin sprinkling of fresh snow by the river. Like confectioners’ sugar.”

All *she* remembers is cold wind and clouds. Where did he find those gorgeous places while she stood freezing in the field?

He puts the kettle on the stove. “Mint tea?” he asks.

“I’d love some, thanks.” She puts on a CD of Oscar Peterson. “Blues Etude.” She flops onto the couch. She needs this conversation. She’ll be gentle, try not to break the easy mood.

The kettle whistles. She hears tea bags rustling. He calls across the bar counter. “Lemon today? Or honey?”

“A little bit of both?”

He opens the refrigerator, rummages in cabinets, and comes back with both mugs and a few cookies on a small tray. “Here you go.”

She laughs and pats the couch next to her. “Service is not bad in this joint on Fridays,” she winks. They sit in comfortable silence for a while, sipping tea and listening.

“I love what Oscar Peterson does here with the blues,” she says. “Hear how many notes he plays?”

“Maybe he has ten fingers on each hand?”

"Ha, I'm not sure that would help much. But ignore all those notes, just listen to the melody on top and let yourself get dreamy." His outstretched foot rubs her thigh. "Hear how all those notes are like—like a cloud-cushion for the melody to float on? It's almost spiritual." As she talks, she watches him and gauges whether he is ready for what she needs to bring up.

He concentrates and nods. "*Hmm.* You're right, I hadn't thought of it that way."

She is buying time for herself, but everybody is due home in an hour. So she takes a deep breath, sits up straight, and looks at him. "Lyman, we have to talk about the other day. I don't want to spoil a lovely evening. It doesn't have to be right this minute. But if not now, then you need to tell me when."

"What other day?" His lips tighten into a thin, hard line.

"The night you yelled at the kids?"

"Oh, here we go," he sighs. "Let's talk now, let's get this over with, then. What is it?"

She sits back at her end of the couch, and faces him, cross-legged. "Well, you do remember the other night? When you blew up and sent them all to their rooms, and Olivia ended up crying?"

He backs up against the other armrest. He sets his cup down and taps a foot on her thigh. "That was days ago, Eva, and don't exaggerate. I didn't 'blow up,' as you put it. I was just tired after a long day."

"Lyman, please. It's what you always say, and I'd really like to believe you. But hear me out this time. Since the fall—" She reaches her hands toward his foot and starts rubbing it the way he likes.

"I can't be over the moon all the time, Eva." He pulls his foot back.

"I'm not asking that, my love. It's just . . . Well, let's back up. We had a fabulous summer away. We were all relaxed and getting along. The kids loved how you made the big outdoors feel like a playground."

"We did that together, sweetie." He cocks his head. "But after vacation comes real life, in case you didn't notice."

"Of course, it does." She gets up to take out the CD and shows him a Herbie Hancock album, a piano duo with Chick Corea. "Is this okay?"

"Sure." He stretches out on the couch and yawns. She slides the album in and turns the volume down. She walks back and stands close. "The point is, you've been coming home later and later, usually after dark. By then, the kids are desperate for your attention. They get excited, you tense up, and I worry that they'll irritate y—"

"Well, don't! That's *your* problem, Eva," he snaps. He stands, walks around, and carries the empty mugs to the kitchen sink. "I'm not a monster. It's not the kids that have trouble with me, it's *you*."

She follows. He rinses the mugs and opens the dishwasher. She touches his shoulder. "No, it's not about me, Lyman," she pleads. "Please leave those mugs and look at me."

He turns around, crosses his arms, and leans back against the sink.

She puts both hands on his forearms and looks up. "I'm not making this up. Not this time," she says very softly. "You seem unhappy. You don't handle noise well lately. You bristle at little things. You may not notice, but sometimes the kids tiptoe around you. And I catch myself telling them to pipe down." Her voice quivers; she turns her head away. "Lyman, they are just kids, being kids. I catch myself putting a damper on them—you know—just so you won't get upset."

He looks at her in silence, frowning. Then he puts a hand on her shoulder, softer now. "Eva, look at me."

She half turns toward him, looking down.

"I know what you grew up with, what your father was like," he says. "And you've said many times that the tension at home drove you nuts. But don't project that onto our kids. If that's the word for it."

She leans into him to hide her tears and reaches around his middle. "I love you so much, Lyman. And I am grateful that you know how sensitive I am to harsh words or to bad moods. I am. But that is *not* what I am trying to say." She sniffles, and he puts his arms around her, rocking her gently.

"Then what?"

"Like I said, you're not acting like your usual self. You're irritable and gloomy. It looks a lot like depression. Which runs in your family, remember?" Oh dear, she must sound like the psychiatrist she is.

He puts both hands on her shoulders, frowning. “Eva, people don’t have to be happy all the time. And I definitely am not the kind of person who is happy all the time. It’s not who you married.”

She reaches a hand to his face. “I’m not asking you to be happy all the time. I’m trying to tell you that your moods have felt *heavy* lately, and that they’re spreading all over the rest of us. That is what *depression* does, Lyman, don’t you know?” She doesn’t know how to say this any other way. “It spreads, like an oil slick, onto the rest of the family. It’s hard to watch you hurt; I don’t want that for me, or for the kids, for any of us.”

He pulls her closer again and rests his chin on her hair. “Are my moods *that* hard for you?”

“Yes, they are,” she whispers into his sweater. “Not because of my childhood, although that doesn’t help. And not because of the work I do. But we are so connected, Lyman. I can’t stand it, seeing you so somber, it eats at me. If I didn’t love you, then maybe I could ignore it, but certainly not when—well, when it touches the kids. I can’t ignore *that*.”

“Oh.” He turns back to the sink and puts the mugs in the dishwasher.

“Lyman, please,” she reaches for his elbow. “I’m not done. Didn’t you see a therapist a decade ago? I think it’s time for you to go back to the man you saw then. You only went, what was it, two sessions?”

“Yep,” he says vaguely. “Or three.”

“Maybe he wasn’t as good as I thought. Or maybe you didn’t want to get into it. Or maybe it’s actually about me, I don’t know anymore.”

No response.

“I have tried to believe that I overreacted before. It blew over after all. But it keeps coming back, and it stays longer each time, and now it’s been months, Lyman. I can’t—” He looks at her. His face is a mask. “Maybe we should see someone together, if it’s about us?” she asks. “Is it?”

“I’ll think about it,” he says vaguely. He walks through the living room toward the office, a sad look on his face.

Eva goes to the piano and sighs. It’s almost time to pick up the kids. After a while, she pokes her head through the open office door and finds Lyman deeply absorbed in a spreadsheet, dense with data, with rows of numbers in different colors, and some columns highlighted in yellow.

"I'll go get the kids now. But I really don't feel like cooking tonight. I'll pick up some Thai food. Sound good?"

He looks up briefly. "Sure. I can order it. The usual?" he asks.

"Great." She goes to the door, stomps her feet into her boots, and shrugs on her coat. "I can get the food in forty-five minutes, maybe."

"Got it," he answers. She hears his desk chair rolling around and a file drawer clanging. "See you soon," he adds. "And be careful, there was some ice on the roads earlier. Could be worse now."

She closes the door behind her. She is drained. At least she had Lyman's attention. He heard her before he walked away. Whenever she touches a tender spot, he turns into stone. Then minutes later, here he is worrying about her on the icy road. How sweet he can be, and how hard-headed.

She walks to her car and pulls on the fleece-lined deerskin gloves. He loves her, she knows that. But she won't let it go. She can't hope it'll just blow over again, not this time. A smile, a hug, some storm-free days, it's not enough.

Tomorrow is Saturday. She will set up a sitter and make a reservation for an early lunch. Vegan Guevara is quiet at that time, and the food is fabulous. They'll bring cross-country skis, too. There is fresh snow; they'll go up in the hills afterward. The snow, the cold, the fresh air, and hard exercise always bring them back together, to who they are. Out there, away from the rush and the rat race, they always find each other.

The chilaquiles verdes arrive, followed by the white bean chili. The food smells heavenly, and they are ravenous. Eva only had tea this morning; Lyman, a quick cup of coffee.

Lyman sighs a contented sigh and reaches for her hand. "We really should do this more often, shouldn't we?"

"I know," she agrees, "it's stupid to let life get in the way of our time together. Life and work and kids . . . there's always something."

He sips his seltzer. "So, where did you want to ski this afternoon? 'Our' little lake? Toward the river? Someplace new?"

"How about that steep uphill trail we've often hiked? There's a wonderful view at the top, and I love the run down. I'm going soft lately."

"Can't let *that* happen," he chuckles. "Let's try it. We may need Klister; I don't think wax alone will be sticky enough to get us uphill. And I bet there are icy sections. I have purple Klister in my fanny pack."

"Yuck, sticky and messy, but you're right."

He gets ready to go, but she stops him.

"Wait, before we go, I need us to finish what we talked about yesterday. Please bear with me, Lyman, it's important."

He sits back down, half-closes his eyes; she reaches for his hands. He leans forward, looking at her. "I knew this was coming. Shoot then, I'm listening."

She doesn't let go of his hands. "Lyman, I know that you deal with things in your own way. I trust you, but you're not a rock, and you're not alone."

He waits, his face still. His right thumb absently rubs her left hand.

She continues. "When your mood is heavy for so long, it affects us all. And Olivia is the most sensitive to it. Like last week."

He looks down. "Yeah, I know. I've spent extra time with her before bed. She knows I wasn't angry, just grouchy and tired."

"Maybe, but she is only four, Lyman. She is verbal for her age, and she has your tall genes; she looks older, but still, she is only four. It breaks my heart when she tries so hard to please you, to not upset you."

He sits back in his chair, but she reaches for his hand again. "I need you to hold my hand until I've said what I have to say, please?"

He shrugs. "Keep going then. I can tell we may not get on skis after all today."

"Honey, don't get that look as if I'm berating you, I'm not." A pause. If she isn't careful and makes him defensive, the talk will stall out right here. "Do you hear me?"

"I suppose."

"It's the boys, too, Lyman. They shrug you off and turn away when you're in a mood."

"They act like teenagers already, getting rude and talking back."

"Maybe, but they have you on a pedestal, too, Lyman. You're their role model. They struggle with your ups and downs."

Lyman signals for the bill, restless. "Let's walk around. I'm listening, but I need to move."

They meet the waiter at the cash register. Lyman pulls some rumpled bills out of the pocket of his ski jacket. "Keep the change," he says, not looking too closely. "That's enough, right?"

"Sure is, thank you *so* much!" says the young man. He breaks into a huge grin. A university student working weekends, Eva guesses.

They slowly walk toward the car, and she picks up the thread. "There is one more thing," she says, keeping her eyes on the pavement. "The dark moods drive a wedge between us. I'm a grown woman, I can take care of myself, but it drives me away when you're shut down. That's not what you want, is it? To drive me away?" She stops in front of him. "That's not what this is about, is it, pushing me away? Or—or is it?"

He stops and turns to her, surprised and irritated. "Of course not, how can you even think that, Eva?"

She looks up at his startled face. "I wasn't sure. I had to ask."

He pats her shoulder. "I am who I am, you know that."

"And I love who you are. But I don't love these depressed moods. When that cloud rolls in to stay, it hides you from me, and it feels like you're angry at us all. I need you to see someone. I want you to get treatment. Depression is treatable, Lyman." She takes a breath and waits a beat. "Exercise and stoicism are not enough. Please do it for our family, and for me. Do it for *us* if you won't do it for yourself."

They walk on in silence. She gives him time to think. At the car, he slumps into the driver's seat, key in hand. She sits next to him, studying his face.

"Did I ever tell you about my father?" he asks.

"All I know is that he died of Lou Gehrig's, and that your mother took care of him."

"She did, she was amazing, in her reserved way. My brother and I weren't as much help as we should have been. But did I ever tell you about his moods?"

"No." She is surprised. "I heard about your grandmother's depression, and your uncle's, but nobody ever talked about your dad."

"No, because we'd rather not talk about him." He continues in a low voice. "I just didn't want to think about it, Eva. He flew into rages. Long before he got ill, when we were growing up. Wilford and I never knew what would set him off." He shakes his head, swallows. "We often pushed it, just to see where his limit was today. It was a moving target, and we couldn't leave it alone." He strangles a tiny sob, then straightens up.

"Oh . . . that's—I'm so sorry."

He turns the key in the ignition. "It was hard on Mom. She was a stoic. You know how she is. She became hard as a rock when he had a bad spell. She kept us in line and out of Dad's way. His anger seemed to run off her back, and she expected the same from us."

"Wow. Really?"

He pulls out of the parking lot and heads out of town.

"I swore I'd never be like him. I promised myself I'd be better, that my kids would have a better father. That I'd be a better husband too."

He has never mentioned this before, and it moves her to hear it. She reaches over and runs two fingers gently along his neck. His eyes glisten.

Lyman slaps the steering wheel. "Dammit. It turns out that I *am* repeating history. And I thought I was better than that. Stronger." He wipes his face with one finger. "I'm sorry, Eva," he adds, "I don't like any of this. But you're right. Thank you for calling me out on it. You've tried before, I know . . ."

"*Shhh*, don't apologize, my love. I just want my husband back. We can tackle this together."

He drives in silence, lost in thought. She rests a hand on his shoulder. They turn from the main road onto the narrow gravel stretch to the trailhead, but she hardly notices. Her mind's eye remembers the man she fell in love with.

She can't help thinking of the hard times, too, when he withdraws and she can't find him. He stops the car at the trail sign.

"Can we sit for a moment?" she asks. She'd like to hold him; she is fighting back tears.

He shakes his head. "I really need to get outside, in the open air. I have to move."

She blows her nose. "Sure. Let's go skiing."

He leads the way up. The path has been blown over with fresh snow. His long skis break trail through the heavy drifts. From behind, she watches his shoulders; he effortlessly plants his ski poles, and his arms drive him uphill. But she is light and agile, and when he waits for her to catch up, she makes a dash around him. "Race you to the next turn!" she calls over her shoulder.

He is surprised and smiles. "Well, look at you, a snow fox! But you're *not* getting past me that easily!" He grabs her ski pole as she pulls ahead, and he tugs. She falls sideways into his arms. He lifts her up like a doll, skis and all, and kisses her.

In the following weeks, Eva doesn't offer help finding a therapist, and she doesn't inquire whether he has found one. She tries not to eavesdrop on his phone calls. She chastises herself for keeping track of his moods. Lyman seems quiet, but there have been no irritable outbursts. Yet he hasn't been very playful either. Is he sad? Should she ask . . . Shouldn't she . . . ? It is so hard to do nothing.

Finally, one night, she cannot stand it anymore. The kids are asleep, Lyman lies in bed reading, but Eva cannot settle down. She has reread the same page four times now. She turns toward him and stretches out, her right arm folded under her head. Her left hand traces his shoulder.

He looks up. "Yes? Something on your mind?"

"*Ummm*, I probably shouldn't even ask, but . . ."

He cuts in: "—But you'd like to know whether I've done anything about our 'big' conversation?"

What if he hasn't? she worries. How does she handle it if he has done nothing? He sets his book on the side table and rolls over to face her. "I have been seeing Dr. Fishman every week for the last six weeks. I haven't told you yet because I'm still feeling this out." He studies her and makes a face. "I should have guessed you'd fret!"

"Dr. Fishman? Who is he?"

He grins. "*She.* Dr. Rachel. A colleague went to her, and he said she is sharp, kind, and wise. I wanted someone outside your network."

"Is she . . ." She swallows her next words (any good?) and starts again. "Good idea. Do you like her?"

"I do. She doesn't beat around the bush."

"Nice," Eva says quickly. She doesn't want to sound nosy. "You don't have to tell me more than you want to, Lyman. I don't mean to probe. You can tell me to butt out."

She buries her face in his shoulder; he wraps an arm around her.

"To be honest, dearest, I'm impressed that you didn't ask sooner!"

She mumbles something.

"I was building up to ask," he continues. "Would you join our next session? Rachel's suggestion."

She looks up, a little surprised. "Sure. Of course. Any particular reason?"

"You need a reason?"

She laughs. "I'd be more than happy to come. I just wondered: did *she* have a reason?"

"Didn't you *want* to tackle this together?"

She opens her mouth, but he puts a finger on her lips. "*Shhh*, I'm just teasing."

"Ha, you must be in better spirits if you're messing with my head! When?"

The following Thursday afternoon, they are in a small waiting room. Eva admires a delicate pastel landscape of windswept grasses on a marsh. Its soft green and lavender hues are luminous and soothing.

Rachel Fishman appears and invites them in. "Eva," she says warmly. "Please call me Rachel. You don't mind first names, do you?"

Eva smiles. "I prefer it."

"Lyman has told me so much about you. Thanks for coming."

Three armchairs and a small couch are arranged around a low coffee table. Eva takes in the slight older woman. Her eyes are alert, and she moves brightly, with confidence. Her graying hair forms a curly halo around a narrow face. Eva appreciates her whimsical necklace and the red, orange, and purple tunic of Guatemalan cloth. She envies her jeans; the hospital requires more formal attire. All the while, Eva is acutely aware that Rachel, a professional observer of people, is taking in her own green wool dress, her black ankle boots, her black onyx earrings, and her carved ebony pendant. She wonders what Rachel is making of *her*.

Rachel cuts through the pleasantries and comes right to the point. "Do you want to start us off?" she asks Lyman.

He looks at Eva. "The obvious reason for you to join us is that this was your idea. You pushed me until I finally realized something *was* eating at me. Way more than I had wanted to admit. It probably has eaten at me for a long time. You made me see that I couldn't keep ignoring it."

Eva has a lump in her throat. She had been worried she was asking too much, and now he is thanking her for it. Things may turn out okay after all . . .

Rachel looks at her. "It can't have been easy . . ." she says in a low voice.

Lyman continues. "Honestly, Eva, this is hard work. And there are more layers to it than I *ever* wanted to see." He looks down at his hands. "And I struggle with it," he adds after a pause. "So, Rachel thought a stint of medication might help me to face it all; to stay afloat and get through this. I wanted you with me for that conversation."

Eva reaches for a tissue. It takes a moment before she can speak. "Lyman, my love, I—well—I know you never liked the whole idea of therapy. Let alone medication. I—I think you're very brave . . ."

She looks at Rachel. "I'm sure you've heard about Lyman's grandmother, his uncle, and his father?" she asks. "I know it's wrong to 'diagnose' loved ones. But I've been so worried about biological depression." She turns to Lyman and takes his hand in hers. "I mean, *on top of* the layers of childhood stuff. We all have stuff, obviously. It's a relief to see you in capable hands."

They discuss a referral for medication to someone Rachel trusts and often works with. She explains there are other options too. Eva sits back, feeling drained and deeply grateful for Rachel's calm competence. Soon, their time is up. At the door, Rachel offers Lyman an encouraging smile. "There is much to think about. You've made a good start with it. See you next week then?" She turns to Eva. "Call me if you have questions of your own, of course. Will you?"

They stand outside Rachel's office. "I'm washed out," says Lyman. "I'll need to sit with all that for a while. Cup of coffee?"

"Yes, please. And by the way, I promise not to bring this up at home. Not unless *you* want to talk."

Lyman starts Prozac and meets with Rachel weekly. He seems less irritable, less dark. Eva hopes she isn't just imagining that. A few weeks later, Lyman comes home early after his meeting with Rachel. He has a troubled look on his face. The boys are both at soccer practice. Eva, at the bar counter, is folding kids' laundry; Olivia, in the kitchen nook, has paint all over her hands and face; there is even a dab of green on the remnants of her snack. They are listening to an audiobook; Eva turns it off when Lyman enters.

"Hi, Daddy, see what I made?" Olivia waves a page still wet with paint.

He kisses them both and stands next to Olivia. "Nice work, sweet pea. Is that a cow in the field?"

"Daddy, of course not! Can't you tell it's a deer?"

"Oh, sure I can, silly me!" he corrects himself, pretending to look more closely at the generic brown four-footer on the page. He looks toward Eva. "Mind if I go lie down a bit? Not feeling great."

Eva studies him. He looks tired, but not ill. "Of course. Shall I bring up some mint tea?"

"No thanks, I don't need anything. Probably just tired."

He pats Olivia on the head. "When I come back down, we can play a game if you want."

There is an agreeable "Okay, Daddy." Soon, Olivia is ready for a new activity. Eva helps her put the paints away and clean herself up.

"What do you want to do? How about . . . ?" Eva points to the puzzle pieces on the coffee table; they started it last night. Olivia hops over and is soon absorbed in sorting the colors. Eva feels uninspired about dinner, but the boys will be starving. She takes two containers of chili out of the freezer, leaves them in the sink to thaw out, and walks upstairs.

She finds Lyman leaning against the pillows, staring at the ceiling. She sits on his side of the bed and puts a hand on his forearm.

"I'm okay—don't worry," he says without looking up.

"Not worried . . . just wondered. Is something up?"

Lyman inhales, lets out his breath, and inhales again. "Therapy is *bloody hard*."

"Heh. *Yea-ah* . . ." More silence. Should she ask? Or let it be? Was he opening the door for her to ask? "What did you and Rachel—?"

"Got into Mom and Dad stuff today."

"Ah. How did that go?"

He finally looks at her. "I've been so mad at my mother . . . so mad . . . I don't like it. I had pretty much stuffed it, until Rachel . . ."

Of course he is, Eva thinks. After all, his father flew into rages, and his mother didn't protect him or his brother, Wilford. "Of course you're mad," she says. "She expected you to put up with it. You shouldn't have had to . . ."

"Eva, it's worse. I had forgotten about it, but . . . she often *scolded* us for upsetting him. Like *we* were the fucking reason that he was angry." He clenches and unclenches a fist.

"And you were just little boys . . . It was *her* job to—"

He sits up and swings his legs off the bed. She moves over to sit side by side. "I know, but later, when Dad got sick, she was so great with him . . . I dunno, I just feel like a shit, for being mad at her."

Olivia calls from downstairs. "Mommy, I need help!"

"Be there in a minute, honey. Hold on, okay?" Eva yells.

Lyman looks absently toward his dresser. A drawer is slightly open; a single gray sock pokes out. He walks over and starts sorting, folding his socks in matching pairs.

Olivia calls again. "*Mo-o-om!*"

Eva leans over the top of the stairs. "Sweetie? I'll be there in a minute. Why don't you grab another cookie?" She looks at Lyman with a guilty face. "Bribery?"

He smiles a little. "You're the expert on child development in this house." He turns back to the socks. "And speaking of that, when you say my moods aren't good for the kids? I know. I actually get it."

She walks over, turns him to face her, and puts her arms around him. "Hey. It'll be okay. And thanks for telling me. I wish . . ."

"*Hmm* . . ." He rests his cheek on her head. "Actually, there is one more thing that I feel like shit about."

"Oh. What?" she looks up.

"Remember when you told me you felt protective of the kids because of my moods?"

She frowns. "Yes. What about it?"

"Remember how I snapped at you for that? Didn't I say something like *Well, don't*?"

"You did," she sighs into his shirt.

"That was messed up too. I snapped at you because you—Oh, honey. Because *you* were doing what I wished *my mother* had done." He rocks her a little, standing there. He lifts her face. He looks like he might cry. "I'm sorry, Eva."

What can she say? She just stands and holds him a while, silently. *This* silence feels good. They are together in it. She could stay like this with him, saying nothing, forever . . .

Chapter 7
1996

The dark times recede, and the clouds that hung over Lyman begin to fade in Eva's memory. *We can tackle anything together*, she thinks. They have come through; it has brought them closer and made them stronger.

Ezra is almost seventeen, a junior in high school. He has worked hard to become one of the school's best saxophone players. In a competitive jazz program, he leads one of the small ensembles. His bandmates lean on him; they work around his daring and inventive solos. He practices and plays around with his horn all the time. He dreams of becoming a successful musician and writes tunes, usually a tenor line over an intricate percussion part and a catchy bass groove.

Tonight, Eva is stationed in the school's pickup line. It is 9 p.m. She spots Ezra's red windbreaker as he shoves the door open and comes outside, walking backwards. His backpack is slung over one shoulder as he cradles his precious alto saxophone in his arms. The vintage Selmer was his only wish for a birthday gift. He saved up for its shiny molded case, a glittering emerald green. It's typical Ezra, bold and flashy. Tall and lanky, he towers over Eric, a talented bass player who is a year younger and idolizes him. They are deep in conversation. Emily comes out last. She is a slight girl, polite, with long black hair in a neat single braid. She is neatly dressed and unassuming, but Eva has seen her on fire at performances and knows her to be a hell of a drummer.

They all get in Eva's car. Ezra, in front, turns toward the back seat. "Come again, Eric, what were you saying?"

"That the new piece is too hard for us." There is worry in Eric's voice. "The bass line that you said was so simple? Well, it's not. I keep losing the downbeat."

"It's not that hard, man. It *feels* like five-beat measures alternating with three-beat measures. But it's just in four. It's only that the bass line *starts on the first beat* in one measure, and on the *second beat* in the next measure." He hums the melody and taps out the beat on the dashboard. He turns toward Eric and Emily, nodding his head in time. "Get it? It's awesome. Here, listen to Kenny Garrett doing it."

He rummages through his backpack and pulls out the Kenny Garrett CD. "Okay with you, Mom?" He has already popped out her Bill Evans album. She winks. Since they both love jazz, they don't need to argue about what music to play in the car. "Sing a Song of Song" comes on.

"Listen to this. Hear those little pickup notes? That makes it sound like—well—like a polyrhythm." Eva loves hearing him get so technical, serious about music theory.

Eric slaps his thigh and concentrates. "I can see that, sort of. Can you make me a copy of that? I'll have to practice. A lot."

"Sure," Ezra says. "I'll make you both a copy. And one for Davie too. He'll love the piano riffs. Listen, coming up."

"This is incredible," says Emily after a while, "and perfect for Davie too."

"Yep. Now listen, here is Tain Watts's drum solo. Subtle, right? He's not making any great big banging sounds; he's just laying it down light and gentle at first. And then he builds and builds. That's your signature style, Emily, and you've definitely got that Latin beat down."

"I do?" Emily is surprised. "Well, thanks, I worked my butt off on it."

On the recording, between solos, the audience chants the refrain. "Do you think we can get that to happen too?" Eric asks. "You could turn on your charm, Ezra. It could work."

"Hm, maybe," he considers.

Eva stops to let Emily out, and Ezra turns to Eric. "Did you hear my little brother in big band rehearsal this morning?" he says out of the blue. "Who knew he could play clarinet like that. I mean, my kid brother?" It's not often that her sons admire each other . . . "Yo, check this out, man, he auditions as a freshman, and he actually gets into the *first* jazz band! Not the freshman band. I mean . . ."

"Yeah," Eric says. "I've heard him. He—"

Eva stops at the end of a long driveway. "Here you are, Eric."

As Eric walks toward his house, Ezra rolls his window down. "I think we should rehearse this weekend, don't you?"

"Great idea. We sure can use it before the school concert. Let's ask Emily and Davie tomorrow."

Eva drives off. She would love to play in Ezra's band herself, if she were a high school student . . .

"Hey, Mom, if I pass the driver's test, can I drive myself to rehearsals?"

"Ha, let's see you pass that test first! But I imagine you could borrow a car sometimes." She smiles at her son, a young man now. "Do you want to drive the rest of the way home?"

She stops and they switch seats; he is surprisingly focused behind the wheel. It will be nice when Ezra can give Gabe or Olivia some rides. It'll make her life and Lyman's easier.

"If you want to practice parallel parking before the test, Dad said he'd take you."

They arrive home, and Eva offers to help him carry things in. She reaches for the sparkling alto case, but Ezra grabs for it. She protests with a chuckle. "Hey, you! My turn to hold this little gem."

"*Uhhh* . . . alright, I guess." He hovers. She lifts the shiny Kevlar case with one hand. How light it is. He notices. "Isn't that the best? Can't do that with your piano, can you?"

They find Lyman in the cozy chair by the wood stove with a book. He looks up. "There's burritos, son, just the way you like them. Two of them. The way you've been eating . . . anyway, you'll want to reheat them. Salsa is on the table."

Eva takes in the warm lights, the bright rugs, and the glow of the fire. It is good to be home.

The state jazz competition takes place on a Saturday in early May at Colchester High School. Ezra is frantic this morning, and he enlists everybody's help in finding his missing sax cleaning brush.

"I had it a minute ago," he says. "Olivia, did you take it? Somebody did."

"Your what?" asks Olivia.

"Big fluffy orange thing to clean my saxophone. Did you—"

"Pipe down, Ezra," Eva yells suddenly. Her son's anxiety about the day makes her nervous too, and Ezra's disorganized search gets to her. "Why on earth would Olivia take it?"

"It's okay," Lyman whispers in Eva's ear. "I got this. Why don't you see if Gabriel needs anything?"

Gabe's shoulders are rigid, and he barely touches his breakfast. He chews on a cuticle. His clarinet case and music folder sit by the door, ready to go. Olivia dances up and down, chattering to him. "Gabey!" she chants. "I'll be rooting for you. You'll nail this."

"For heaven's sake, Livvie! Leave him alone already," Eva raises her voice again.

Lyman, with a crooked smile, raises an eyebrow. He is right; she is on pins and needles, too irritable. It's been happening too often lately. Could she be menopausal? She makes a half-shrug and gives Lyman a thumbs-up. She should get back to yoga classes.

Hours later, Gabe's band walks onto the stage. Olivia leaps up and waves. "Gabe! Go Gabriel! Knock 'em!" she shouts.

"*Shhh*," says Lyman, with a smile and a finger to his lips.

"Olivia, don't embarrass him!" Eva says sternly.

But Gabriel has heard. He gives his little sister a grin and a wave on his way up to the podium with his clarinet. He has raked his unruly reddish curls into a somewhat contained nest. The director gets their attention and points to each section to tune their instruments. Then he lifts his arms. In the silence, Eva holds her breath. She squeezes Lyman's arm; she feels cold with the stage fright she hopes Gabe is *not* feeling right now, but he looks tense up there.

When it's Gabriel's turn for a solo, he steps forward without sheet music. Eyes closed, he brings the clarinet to his lips and takes a breath. His first run of notes sounds pure and clear. His tension evaporates as soon as he starts playing. He is completely in the zone. To think that reed players call the clarinet a *misery stick*. The audience claps and cheers.

The rest is a blur to Eva. She had no idea Gabe could play like this, and it's only a hobby to him. He rarely practices at home because he is so shy about it. Ezra is the family's acknowledged musician, not Gabe, but it was Ezra who first realized his brother's talent.

When the band files out of the room, Lyman beams with pride. He looks radiant and calm. He steadies her these days, while Eva has been the brittle one.

Late afternoon, it is Ezra's turn. His combo's last number is "Sing a Song of Song," the Kenny Garrett tune he explained in Eva's car a few months ago. They have worked on it, and it has become better each time she hears them at school events.

After their solos, Ezra lets his horn hang from his neck, steps forward, and looks at the audience while Eric and Emily keep the beat going. His long, dark hair swings as he nods his head to the unusual rhythm. He snaps his fingers to the five / three feel. He takes the microphone and softly starts singing the hypnotic refrain. He builds it up; he raises both hands to the audience. "Sing with me!" he shouts. At first, there is only a timid voice here and there. Then there are more. He doesn't stop until nearly every voice has joined, kids and parents snapping their fingers. Then, at Ezra's nodded count-down, Davie bursts into a rousing piano solo. Finally, they slowly bring the energy down, in sync with each other. There is one more simple, dreamy repeat of the melody on saxophone, and they fade out on a chord so unusual, so different from the rest of the tune, that it sounds like an invitation, a question mark.

The applause is wild, and schoolmates call out their names. A petite girl with close-cropped hair runs up to Ezra as he walks off the podium. She flings both arms around him and plants a kiss on his lips. Is this a new girlfriend? He picks the girl up, and she giggles with her arms around his neck.

The next day, Ezra gets up late. He slouches down the stairs. His hair stands up on one side, and there are bags under his eyes. Eva offers him orange juice. Everyone else has already finished breakfast.

"Mom, when are we going to visit colleges? Didn't you say before the end of the school year?"

"Good morning to you too," she says, chuckling. "Sure. Can I finish my tea before we go? I guess you're pumped after last night?"

"Yeah."

"Don't you have to make audition tapes first?"

"*Mm-hmm.* I've started those. And they'd better be good if I want a chance at Oberlin or Juilliard's jazz program."

"Are you sure you want a performance school? Not a liberal arts school with a good music department?"

"I'm not totally sure. I just want to go look and think about it. You know, you keep telling me that teaching—"

"—is a good safety. Yes. Anyway, let's sit down with the brochures this week to plan our trip. It'll be fun."

"Okay."

"Just . . . don't close any doors yet. Music doesn't have to be your *career.* It could be your passion, you know, even if you decide to become—whatever—a mathematician, or . . ."

He shakes his head vigorously. "A mathematician? Why would I want that? Just because I like math?"

"Whoa, sorry, it was just an example. I didn't mean to sound like a broken record, but . . . I only meant that you have lots of options." She worries that for every Cannonball Adderley, there are droves of frustrated musicians who don't make it, whatever *that* means.

He shrugs. "You've said, Mom. A million times."

She has, she knows. It's a stupid habit to repeat herself, as if that would guarantee that she has been heard. Bad habit . . .

Chapter 8
1999

The house feels emptier now that Ezra is at Oberlin. Olivia has become a "tween" with strong flavors of teen. She is smart, willful, and charming. Slim and dark-haired, she looks like a taller version of Eva, and she has her mother's high energy level. She and Gabriel spend more time together, without their big brother to take over.

Gabriel has three college acceptance letters. He wrestles with the choice: the University of Colorado? Bowdoin College? Or the University of Michigan? Each has a good program in environmental science. Stanford was a long shot for him; UVM, his safety school, offers the best scholarship, but that would mean studying in his dad's department. "Too close to home," he said. He goes around his options, over and over again. One day he sounds like he is leaning this way, the next day he leans the other way.

On a Friday evening in April, Olivia is at a sleepover. Lyman, Eva, and Gabriel are finishing dinner. Gabe is lost in thought and chewing his fingernails at the kitchen table. Lyman and Eva exchange a look. She nods. Lyman turns to Gabriel, and she sits back to listen.

"Do you want to talk through your options, son? You still have a couple of weeks to decide, but you look—I don't know—stuck? We're happy to listen."

"We've been making a game of it, you and I," Eva interjects, "pretending that you've picked a school, and I play devil's advocate." Sitting on the sidelines is not her strong suit. "I thought it might clarify things, but . . . And I've heard you debate the choices with Dad too—"

"Right," Lyman jumps back in. "I enjoy the debates. But you'll keep fretting until you've made up your mind, won't you?"

"Yeah, I suppose . . ." says Gabe.

Eva leaves the kitchen nook and goes to the sink.

"So," Lyman says, leaning an elbow on the table, "I have a proposal. Mom and I agree."

"What?" Gabe gives a half-shrug.

"Why don't you and I take a road trip? You've hung out at Bowdoin, but you haven't seen the campus in Colorado or Michigan. I'm done teaching. Wanna go?"

"A road trip? You're kidding . . ."

Eva winks at Lyman from the sink.

"Listen. It's a two-day drive from here to Boulder. Ann Arbor is on the way. Mom and I think you should feel out each campus, take a day, and talk to some students. See if you like it there."

Eva loads the dishwasher. "College isn't just about what you're learning, Gabe," she says over her shoulder. "It's also—actually, maybe it's *mostly* about who you become friends with. Look at Dad. He made lifelong friends at school. I wish it had worked that way for me too . . ."

Lyman carries the pots from the stove to the sink. "Buddy, you'll spend four years there, wherever you go. You might as well like the place and the people. And what's around it."

"Hm, maybe," Gabe says, "but there's no school break before I have to decide."

Lyman puts down the scrubber and turns to Eva with a grin. "Listen to him. Doesn't he know nothing happens at the end of senior year? He would rather be in school than go *skiing*."

Gabe springs up at the mention of skiing. "Wait, what are you talking about? Skiing?"

Eva and Lyman are both laughing now. She puts an arm around the two men. Gabriel is shorter than his dad, but in every other way, they are very much alike.

"Okay," Lyman says with a hand on his shoulder, "here's what we were thinking. Why not have a little fun while you figure this out? The snow is really good out west this season. And I think you're ready for backcountry skiing at the Continental Divide. Take a week off from school. I'd love to show you the Indian Peaks wilderness. Call it—let's say an early graduation present?"

"Whoopie!" Gabe pumps his fist. "Wow, thanks! When are we going?"

"How fast can you pack your bag?" Lyman asks. "I'm kidding. Next weekend?"

"Hey, boys," Eva smiles, "with all that skiing, don't forget to look at campuses too."

Gabe gets up. "Gotta call Aviva!" he yells and runs up the stairs.

"Who?" asks Lyman.

"She's a girl on the ski team," Eva tells him. "I met her on the slopes once."

Gabe comes thundering down the stairs with his car keys.

"Goin' out," he calls as he runs past them.

"Where to?" Lyman asks.

"Aviva's . . ." He grabs a coat.

Lyman looks at Eva. "Are they an item?" he mouths.

Eva shrugs. "Don't know . . ."

"Okay," he says to Gabe. "Don't come home too late."

Gabe steps into his unlaced sneakers. "Dad, come on, it's Friday!"

"Oh well . . . alright then."

Eva goes to the door to plant a kiss on Gabe's cheek before he leaves. "Come tell me when you're home, honey? You know I can't sleep until you're safely back!"

"You'll have to get over that when I'm at college, Mom!" he says.

She watches him get into her old lipstick-red Corolla. She bought herself a new car so that Gabe would have something to drive. He made a joke out of the bright color and covered the doors with silly stickers. He let Olivia paint a black cat on the hood. A clown jiggles in the rear window.

She closes the door and sidles up to Lyman by the kitchen sink. “I’m going to miss these kids so much,” she says in a low voice.

He looks at her. “You’re all misty-eyed, my love! They do grow up . . .” He wraps his arms around her. “On the other hand, I could get into having more time to ourselves, once Olivia leaves. Can’t you?”

“Yes, I suppose. But I get so emotional about them. I don’t know, I feel all weird.”

He rocks her a little. “Let’s leave the rest of those dishes to soak,” he says. “Come on, let’s get on the couch, sip a glass of wine, and practice being without kids for a night. I’ve heard the empty nest is a wonderful thing.” He winks and gets glasses from the kitchen. “Red or white?”

“*Hmm*, red please. Any of that Bordeaux left?” She puts on Brad Mehldau’s new album, a piano trio.

“Lemme see. Yep.” Lyman puts their glasses down and stretches out on the couch. She gets the CD started and snuggles alongside him, her head on his shoulder and her arm across his chest.

“I love you, Lyman,” she whispers.

“Well, that’s a good thing,” he says into her hair. “What with that empty nest coming . . .”

She caresses his neck, dreamily. She finds the buttons on his shirt; her hand slides down, along the graying red hairs on his chest, past the belly button . . .

“Forget that wine,” he mumbles. “It’ll keep.”

He stands, scoops her up, and carries her up the stairs. She giggles. When they reach their room, he drops her on the bed, then bends over with his hands on his knees. “Yikes, I’m not as young as I once was, apparently!”

“Still just as handsome.” She reaches up and pulls him down to her. Clothes fly off the bed with the urgency of earlier days. Their bodies find each other. His arms around her, he rolls onto his back and lifts her above him. She watches the growing pleasure in his eyes. In the last moment, he pulls her toward his chest. She rests there afterward, breathing hard. His heart pounds in her ear. She loves it when he stays inside her like this, unhurried.

He cups her head with one hand and gently strokes her back with the other. They are still and content together. Then she begins moving a little, still straddling him; she slowly stirs him back to life. She sees the delight and surprise register on his face.

Chapter 9
2003

Ezra has managed to keep his quartet together after Oberlin. Vibrations has been on tour for ten months, performing all over the country, in France, and in Great Britain. They just returned from Denmark and landed a gig at the Blue Note in Manhattan in the Up-and-Coming Jazz Artists Series. Eva will drive down from Burlington that Thursday.

"You'll come down with me, won't you?" she asks Lyman.

"And leave Olivia home alone?" he says.

"She has friends she can stay with." She puts her arms around his waist. "Rose's parents are always glad to have her. Rose is here a lot too, after all."

"Nah, I have a project I can't get away from . . ." Lyman turns away.

"Oh, honey, I was looking forward to going down together. Explore the city, and check out my old neighborhood, you know?"

"I don't think so." He heads to the office. "I'm not up for it. You go."

Eva parks at the Mercado in Washington Heights. She lived in the apartment upstairs some twenty-five years ago. The owners are getting old now; they greet her with open arms. There is a spare room, unofficially available for those in the know. In the morning, Eva roams her old neighborhood, reminiscing about her years at Columbia. She was so happy to come to this country and leave Belgium—and her parents—behind. Her years of clinical training were frenetic and sleep-deprived. It was all thrilling, equal parts stress and excitement. She remembers how Uncle Roger sounded proud of her when she called to tell him all about it.

Midday on Friday, she makes her way to Greenwich Village. She'll meet up with Ezra before the performance. She has almost forgotten the grime and the pressing crowds in the city. The noise is unbearable after years in Vermont. She can't recall why the Village ever seemed appealing.

She finds the Blue Note and waits near the musicians' entrance. She hopes Ezra has enough time for a meal before sound checks and last-minute details. She sees his old maroon van pull up. Marlene jumps out, a small woman with a determined face. She pulls her vibraphone out of the back, eighty-five clumsy pounds of instrument in a bulky case. She wheels it to the door and up the step.

Ezra runs to catch up with her. "Why do you always have to do this alone? Show-off." He bumps her shoulder, then notices Eva and bounds over. "Mom! You made it!" He waves for Marlene to come over. "You've met, right?"

"Of course!" Eva laughs. "Each time I visited Oberlin to catch your concerts."

"Right. Duh!" and he is off again.

Marlene greets her, and they go inside together.

Jacob follows, a guitar case over his left shoulder and a bag in his right hand. He has grown some unconvincing dreadlocks this past year. "Hi, Mrs. Eva. It's nice to see you again." He shakes her hand and walks onto the stage. "I wanna check out the setup," he tells Ezra.

Vicky comes last. She carries a long, oddly shaped case with a shoulder strap and several bulging outside pockets. Her black hair is very short on one side, quite long on the other. Bleached streaks have been dyed a vibrant green. She says hello to Eva; Ezra's eyes follow her a moment before he turns to Eva.

"Right-o. I'll get my horns up there and park the van. Bite to eat after that?"

"That's great," she says and looks him over. "You look pretty good, son, for an exhausted touring musician. Can I help carry anything?"

"Nah, I'm good. I'll just be a minute."

* * *

They walk up Third Street to Sixth Avenue. She suggests the little Mediterranean bistro around the corner. "It's just over that way. I used to love the place," she tells him. "I hope it is still there. Their bouillabaisse was as good as any in Marseille."

"I always forget you lived in New York for a while."

They choose a cozy corner table by the window and settle in. They order a salad of baby greens and a bouillabaisse for two.

"So, tell me about the tour? And how is the band doing?" she asks.

"The band is great. Better than ever. You'll see. By the way, did Gabe tell you about skiing in Indian Peaks again? The lucky bastard."

"Nobody tells me anything," she says with mock distress.

He laughs. "And how's my baby sister? Is she a brat yet?"

"Ha, you sound like you miss her."

The waiter interrupts with their salads. "Any drinks?" he asks.

When the bouillabaisse arrives, it smells of Provence, garlic, and saffron. They admire the pretty calamari, the pieces of red snapper, and the pearly scallops. Buttery bread crusts sit on their bowls, rubbed with garlic. The pungent rouille garnish is just the right rust color.

After the first bite, Ezra's eyes widen. "*Mmm*, this is so good! Why did you leave Europe exactly? I hope you had a good reason."

"Honestly, there is nothing to miss about Belgium," she laughs. "At least not since Uncle Roger died. But who knows, if I'd grown up in Provence, I might have stayed, and then you'd never have existed. I could be managing a vineyard and painting blue skies!"

"Ha, funny . . . What *are* you doing with yourself instead, Mom? Anything new and interesting in your life?"

She is touched that he shows an interest. In Olivia's eyes, she is still mostly the parental power that grants and denies things, not quite a person in her own right.

"Do you remember much about Malawi?" she asks.

"Some, why? Are you planning to go back there?"

"There is a community peer support project I worked on there. You were too young to. . . well—it never really went anywhere afterward. I've been talking with Clara. We want to give it another shot."

"Wow, you've been in touch with her? We hung out with her grandchildren a lot. Mercy and Moses, right?"

Mussel shells and fish bones pile up between them. "I'm excited about it," she says. "We have some new ideas for it. I was hoping Dad might go with me to Malawi. He said maybe . . ." She leans back and dabs her lips with the flowery napkin. "Anyway, we'll see. What's next for you?"

He puts down his own napkin. "I don't know, I'm trying to figure it out."

"How so?"

"I think you tried to tell me how hard a musician's life can be. Back when I was deciding about college. I was a kid. I didn't want to hear it, of course."

She studies his face. He turns to look out the window. She leans in. "And?"

"Well, we want to keep the band together. We'll all stay in Brooklyn to record *Space*. But I don't want to spend my whole life on the road. It's not like you make a fortune that way, it turns out."

"So I've heard," she says without irony. She signals for the waiter. "Dessert?" she asks.

He orders a crème brûlée, and she asks for a cappuccino.

"I never thought I'd say this, Mom, but I want to be able to teach too. Don't say you told me so." She smiles. "Vicky and I want to live around here, probably in Brooklyn. And we both want to go to school."

Eva is a little surprised. She always thought there were sparks between Ezra and Marlene. "We?" she asks. "And are you . . . ?"

"You didn't know? I thought I told you."

"Nope, but I'm glad to hear it. I always liked Vicky. And I'm impressed that you survived touring together." She breathes in the scent of cinnamon on her cappuccino and studies his face.

"She's great. She got into the Juilliard jazz performance program. You know, where Wynton Marsalis is? You know who he is?"

"Yes, of course I know." She shakes her head. She is not *that* old and out of it! "That's amazing, good for Vicky."

"Right? She just heard. And I've applied to the Manhattan School of Music."

He glances at his watch. She notices and gestures to the waiter for a bill. "Go on."

"It's a double master's. Performing *and* teaching. Three years. I have a solid shot at it."

"That's fantastic, Ezra! When will you hear?"

"Soon. But I wanted to talk to you first, because . . ." She gets up when he reaches for the jacket slung over his chair; she shrugs into hers.

"I hate to ask," he says, "but I might need a loan for the tuition . . ."

She is incredulous. "Ezra, is that what you've been pussyfooting about? A loan?"

He looks down, frowning. "Well, the deal was you and Dad would pay for college, right? And you did, so . . ."

She takes his arm as they go outside. On the sidewalk, she pauses and looks at him directly. "Here is the deal, the way Dad and I see it, okay? If graduate school offers you a free ride, take it! If your new album makes a fortune, fabulous. *Space*, it's called, right?"

"Yep," he chuckles. "That would be amazing . . ."

"Right, so if *Space* makes you a rich man, then you can feed us in our old age. But for now, if you get into grad school, then we'll help you!"

He hugs her. "Thanks, Mom."

Eva checks out a used bookstore and then finds a quiet corner in a coffee shop. She calls home, and Lyman picks up.

"Hi, sweetie," she says. "Just checking in. I'm in the Village."

"How's Ezra?"

"In a good headspace. I can't wait to hear them play. And guess what . . ."

"What?"

"He wants to do a master's. I said we could give him a hand. Don't you agree?"

"Of course."

"And you? Working hard on that project?"

"Actually, no. I'm not feeling great. I didn't mention it, but I'm trying to taper down the Prozac."

"You—After all this time? Why?" She had no idea. He has been doing so well for so long. Why rock the boat? She takes a deep breath.

"I wanted to try it."

"I see. Well—it might take a bit to . . ."

"Yeah . . ."

"I hope Dr. Grant—"

"Gotta go, Olivia is calling." *That was abrupt*, she thinks. She wonders now if this tapering is the real reason he didn't come to New York with her. She prays he feels better soon. Mostly, she hopes he doesn't fall back into depression.

When Eva returns to the Blue Note later, music stands, microphones, and instruments are all in place. People mill around or stand at the beautiful, well-lit curved bar. Conversations echo through the space. Waiters make their way between the people and the tables, carrying small trays high above their heads. Eva squeezes through. Ezra sees her and jumps down from the stage. He walks her to a table in the first row.

"Mom, meet Josh and Ghana. Guys, this is my mom," Ezra says. "We'll be renting the top floor of their awesome brownstone in Flatbush." There are handshakes and smiles.

Vicky joins up with them, and he puts an arm around her. "They have an adorable Dalmatian that Vicky is in love with," he adds.

She hugs him. "Yep, he's way more obedient than you," she laughs. She turns to Eva. "Sorry for taking him away, but the band needs him up there. We will see you after, right? I hope you enjoy the music."

Ghana tries to explain something, but the chatter around them is too loud for Eva to understand. She makes a helpless hand gesture, pointing to her ears. The band puts the final touches on their setup.

Soon, the announcer requests everyone's attention. "We at the Blue Note are proud to support emerging new artists. We are very excited tonight to present a quartet that has just returned from Europe, where they have received fantastic reviews. Please welcome . . . Vibrations!"

When the clapping dies down, there is a hush, and Eva holds her breath. Ezra counts down. Marlene starts the set on vibraphone, alone. Her tempo dazzles and surprises. An eerie motif builds in the high register. It's like bells ringing, over and over. Below that, a melody dances, while Marlene creates a rich harmony in the lowest range. All that with only four mallets . . .

She breaks abruptly, looks up, and nods to Ezra once. They repeat the initial melody in exact unison. His alto saxophone melds with the resonance of the vibraphone; the light bells still ring above. Vicky comes in on bass and steadies the beat, then Jacob repeats the melody one more time on electric guitar and takes the first solo. It's a frenzy of fast, intense licks. An electric sound with reverb in full force. Then he drops into a gentle, nearly acoustic sound, hinting at Marlene's opening motif again. And Eva is transported.

It's Vicky's turn. She plays a slim, fretless upright electric bass. A fingerboard without a body; only a slim metal arc hints at the shape of a bass. She gives the melody yet another flavor with a full and deeply resonant sound. Then she leaps up and literally drops into an exciting slap bass style; her long hair flies to one side. The bass notes vibrate in Eva's bones.

Ezra plays the melody one more time to end the tune, while Marlene barely hints at the harmony. After this stunning first number, Ezra greets the audience and introduces each band member. "You just heard the title song of our upcoming album *Space*," he says. "We are thrilled to offer its first performance here at the Blue Note. We hope you'll enjoy the evening with us."

That is my kid *up there*, Eva thinks. *All grown up!*

The evening flies by. The title of the new album—*Space*—is perfect for the music's otherworldly flavor. It seems to her that the four musicians are thinking with a single mind. She wipes at a tear. To think that, not so long ago, Ezra was just a boy who had to do everything his own way, and who loved bossing his little brother around . . .

* * *

Eva drives north on Saturday. When she gets home, Olivia is out, and she finds Lyman sitting in the office. A screen saver scrolls on his computer. He is chewing on a pencil. He looks up, a little vacant.

"Hello, babe," she says. There are no papers spread out on the desk. Dusk has settled over the room, but no lamps are turned on. She hugs him. "Still not feeling great?" He obviously isn't. She looks at him carefully.

"I just can't do it, Eva. I can't go off Prozac. I got down to about half, and gloom set in." He leans his head on his hand. "I was so hopeful . . . I really wanted to be—I don't know—cured maybe."

"Oh, my love. How disappointing." She knows this, that some people can stop anti-depressants, and some cannot. It is Grant's job to work with Lyman, not hers. And if Lyman is someone who will always need treatment, then Grant has to help him figure that out. She leans down for a kiss.

"Oh well," he says. He stands and hugs her. "So it goes, I guess."

Part II
The Shadow

"Some moments teach one the price of the human connection: if one can live with one's own pain, then one respects the pain of others, and so, briefly, but transcendentally, we can release each other from pain."

—*James Baldwin*, from *Tell Me How Long the Train's Been Gone*

Chapter 10
Late May 2004

Gabriel graduates from the University of Colorado with a degree in environmental science. He is home for the summer to work on a project at the University of Vermont.

Ezra and Vicky's colorful old van sits in the driveway, filled with band equipment. They will be here all summer too. They have landed a gig at Burlington's outdoor jazz festival in August, and they are writing new music for their next album.

Sixteen-year-old Olivia is beside herself with joy with both of her brothers home. She cancels a mountain trip with the National Outdoor Leadership School, so she doesn't have to miss a single day with them. NOLS can wait. She'll be a junior camp counselor instead, at nearby Crow's Path.

Tomorrow, fifty guests will celebrate Gabriel's graduation. Eva buzzes around all day, fretting about last-minute details. All her babies are home; it could be the last time, and she wants everything to be perfect.

Lyman blocks her path with an extended arm. "Hey," he says. "You'll make yourself sick. Slow down. It's all good, the party will be great."

"I still have to—" she sputters.

"Seriously, Eva. Settle down." His jaw sets.

"I am running ragged, aren't I?"

"Yep. You're making me dizzy."

"But . . ."

"It's all under control, Eva," he snaps. "*Stop* before you get on my nerves." He takes out a mixing bowl. "Play some music, read a book, take a walk. Something. Anything."

She goes to the piano and smiles a small smile. "I hate to admit it, but you're probably right." He mumbles something. She attacks the keys with vigor. She needs some up-tempo stuff first; she needs a hard and hammering beat. She doubles the languid tempo of "Stella by Starlight," creating a different mood. She ignores her fingers' slip-ups and lets herself improvise. Soon, she is lost in an energetic rhythmic variation over a simple bass line; then she tries the same tune in a Latin beat. She changes the beat again, and—now, that's a surprise—it sounds more like a rock tune. Gradually, her playing slows into a mellow version of "Stella." She lingers on all the unexpected notes that make it so special.

The windows are open to a lovely breeze. She sighs and turns around. "I needed that. Thank you."

Four balls of dough rise on pizza stones. Lyman sits on a bar stool, staring out of the window.

"A seltzer with lime?" she asks.

"Sure."

She takes her drink to the patio and stretches out on a recliner. He stands at the edge of the field.

"Come join me," Eva says. He doesn't move.

Eva hears the unmistakable sound of Olivia's Saab. Their youngest has a driver's license now, and she'll soon spread her wings too.

They hear the thud of something dropped by the front door. Olivia appears at the kitchen window, notices them outside, and waves. She joins them, holding an apple. Her long brown hair is tied in a sloppy ponytail. She has her dad's tall frame. She wears no make-up; she has a knack for turning worn-out Salvation Army clothes into an artistic statement. It's all-gray today, from her tight-fitting tank top to her baggy cargo pants. Her whole image screams *I hate consumerism*. She neither hides nor flaunts her athletic figure. Eva thinks, as she often does, *My daughter is gorgeous.*

"Hey, Dad! Hi, Mom! Wassup?"

Eva opens her mouth to answer but remembers. *Wassup* is not a real question. "Glad you're home, sweetie."

Olivia hugs her, walks over to Lyman. "What are you looking at out there?"

"Nothing in particular," he says without moving. Olivia takes a better look at him, leaves it alone, and goes inside.

Ezra and Vicky soon come out too. Vicky has a new haircut: the short left side has grown out. Now the back is shorter than the sides, and one extra-long section of her black hair is dyed bright red.

"When is dinner?" Ezra asks. They are both in shorts and a T-shirt. "Dad, do we have time for a run?"

"Sure."

Back in the kitchen, Eva peruses her to-do list for the party. She overhears Olivia on the phone in her room, raising her voice. Eva glances toward the stairs. Perhaps another fight with her girlfriend? It's happened a lot lately. Hopefully, she and Carla won't last the summer. Eva misses Rose.

Soon, Gabe's Corolla pulls into the driveway. It survived four years in Colorado and several trips back home. The muffler doesn't sound too healthy. He walks in and kicks off his shoes. His curls are longer than usual. His jeans are torn at both knees. A purple T-shirt with snowy mountain peaks reads ESTES PARK.

He pulls out a beer and watches Lyman sprinkle cheese on the pizzas.

"Nobody makes pizza like yours, Dad." He turns to Eva. "Can I bring one more person to the party tomorrow?"

"Why not?" Eva looks up. "Aviva?"

"How'd you guess?"

"Maybe because you've been inseparable since you came home?"

Olivia sets the glasses, napkins, and plates on the patio table. A colorful salad sits in the lovely blue bowl that Eva brought home from the Dedza pottery in Malawi. Four gorgeous pizzas, each perfectly crisp, sit on a side table. This is a family tradition to kick off the summer.

When they are all around the table, Lyman clears his throat. "Here's to a lovely May evening," he says, lifting his beer. "Here's to birds singing all around us, to this field, and to the mountains. And to us all being here together."

Eva smiles, surprised. Usually, *she* is the one asking for a moment of gratitude, not Lyman. An hour ago, his mood seemed flat. And now . . . are his eyes actually glistening? She can't figure him out lately, his ups and downs. He has been so even for years, her rock.

There is a happy hubbub for a while. The salad bowl is passed around. Silverware clatters on plates. An animated debate springs up between Olivia and Ezra about whether adding a singer to a band distracts from instrumental music. Olivia's singing voice has developed a broad range and a rich tone. She has written songs and instigated an *a cappella* group at the high school. But Ezra's position is adamant.

"It's lovely that you are singing, Livvie. But music with a vocalist is simply a different thing. Not less-than, just different. The human voice draws all the attention, and the instruments just become back-up."

"No, they don't," she scoffs.

"They do. It becomes all about the words, about *what it says*. Not what the music itself has to say."

"You're just an instrument snob!" Olivia says. She turns toward Vicky. "Is he still Mr. Opinionated?"

"*So* opinionated . . ." says Vicky. She plants a kiss on his cheek.

"And you're not?" Ezra winks at her, an arm over the back of her chair.

Eva is only half-listening to them while she watches another debate between Lyman and Gabriel. Some detail about Gabe's summer project. He scribbles on a piece of paper, and Lyman bends over it, frowning, chin in hand. "Well, maybe," he says. "You *could* have a point, but—"

"My advisor said that the other method isn't being used much anymore."

Lyman abruptly sits back in his chair. "I hate when people come up with 'new' methods, and then discredit the tried-and-true," he says. He turns away, toward the field, to the horizon.

Gabriel looks at him, unsure of what to say. Ezra notices his father's sudden silence. "Hey, Dad," he says. "When do we go for that hike?"

Lyman shrugs. "Whenever. Ask me after the party."

Eva wonders what this is about. Why so touchy? Is it really about research methods? There must be something else bothering him; she'll ask him later. The sky has turned bright orange over the field; a few wispy little clouds are rimmed in scarlet. "Look at that, everybody!" she points. But the mood has dimmed.

"Let's play a game," says Olivia after an uncomfortable silence. She brings out Charades.

Lyman stands up. "I'll pass," he says, and he goes inside. "I've got some papers to check on. See you all later."

Eva resists an urge to follow him, to check in with him. But an hour later, when she calls it a night, she finds him lying on top of the quilt, fully clothed. He is not reading. His hands are clasped behind his head as he lies there looking up at the ceiling.

"Honey," she says, with a question in her voice.

"Did you have fun?" he asks. He does not turn to her.

She sits at the foot of the bed, leans back on her elbows, and looks at him. "What is it, Lyman?"

"What's what? Nothing."

"Don't play me for a fool, Lyman," she says. "Whatever it is, it can't be nothing. You're way quieter than usual. You've been irritable for over a week. Little things bother you."

"Calm down, Eva!"

"I am perfectly calm," she lies. "But everybody is home, and we've all looked forward to this summer. A few days into it, you become angry with Gabe over some science method. Then you go upstairs instead of joining a game. Don't tell me there's nothing. What *is* it?"

"I don't feel well, is all. Can you not make a fuss, please? Just drop it."

"Sweetheart," she says more gently, a hand on his knee, "what kind of not well? Please tell me."

"Dammit, woman." He sits up and looks straight at her. "If you *must* know, I went off Prozac a month ago. I'm adjusting, and I'm fine."

"You did?" But he had tried that and—was it a year ago? And it didn't work. Why would he do it again, so soon? She searches his face, looks for clues, and waits for more.

"What? What else do you want to know?" He frowns. Crosses his arms.

She stands, walks around the bed, and leans back against her dresser. She chooses her next words carefully. "Last year, when you . . . Um. Did Rachel suggest that you try again?"

"Rachel Fishman? I didn't tell her."

She sits on her side of the bed, kicks off her sandals, and examines her feet so she doesn't stare at him. "You *didn't*?"

"Haven't seen her for a couple of years. I just go to Grant for the prescription, every six months or so. Didn't I tell you?"

Hell no, she thinks. *You don't tell me much lately!* She turns toward him. "No, Lyman, I *did not* realize you stopped therapy. Last I heard, you were checking in with her every few weeks . . ." She takes a deep breath. "So, it's Grant, then, who is helping you taper down? And—uh—more slowly this time, maybe?"

"Haven't told him yet."

She walks out of the room before she says something like "what the fuck" and regrets it. In the bathroom, she takes a long time to brush her teeth. She flosses thoroughly. She gets into her favorite silk nightshirt. When her voice is under control, she goes back and sits against the pillows on her side of the bed.

"Okay, I'm listening." Her profession has taught her how to sound calm, even if she isn't. "Tell me. *Why*? And why now? Did you want to find out if—"

"I got sick and tired of it, is all."

"Any particular reason, or just in general?"

"I hate the side effects," he grumbles.

"You do? You never said . . ."

"Well, now you know."

"What side effects?" She tries to guess what he means.

He stands and pulls off his shirt and pants. "In case you hadn't noticed, it takes the fun out of our sex life." He pads over to the bathroom. She hears the faucet running. Teeth being vigorously brushed. The toilet flushes. *It takes the fun out? Since when?* She is amazed.

When he gets into bed, she turns on her side toward him. "I had *not* noticed, no," she says softly. "I thought our sex life was great. What's wrong with it?"

"It takes forever. It's like—work," he says, turning away from her.

"Lyman! Hold on. Look at me. We are not twenty, we're in our fifties. Dammit, Lyman. It's not news to you, is it, that bodies change? And I, for one, *like* it. I like how we take more time making love!"

He doesn't answer.

"Look at me."

Lying on his back, he sends a quick glance in her direction. "Well, *I don't like it*."

"Are you bored with it? Wouldn't it be fun to be a little more creative?"

"You've said."

"Yes, I have, but not because I'm bored, or because I don't love us just the way we are. I've said it because I want to—to explore together, and—be curious." A hand on his shoulder, she waits. She strokes his neck gently.

"We'll see," he says noncommittally.

"See what?" No answer.

She can't hold back now; she has to make sure he knows this. "Lyman, it's not safe to go off medication on your own, believe me. You need to talk with Grant or with Rachel. Please tell me the plan for monitoring how this goes?"

He sighs. "I'll bring it up with Grant next month."

"Next month?" she blurts out. He is already either flat or irritable. She can see he tries to engage with the family, but he quickly tires of people around him. And that's after just one month. The stuff isn't even all out of his system yet.

"Do me a favor," she asks shakily, "could we discuss it with Rachel together? So that she can help us do this right? She helped you so much ten years ago. She helped us both, actually. I am slipping back into that old worrying place from years ago. I hate that. And I know you hate it when I fret."

He turns his back to her. "Perhaps. Good night."

Eva remembers this mood: the back turned to her, the vague answers, and the irritability just under the surface. It is desperately familiar, and it instantly makes her shaky. She never wanted to feel this way again, ever. She wanted to believe it could never happen again.

She kisses the back of his head and tries sleeping. *One-Mississippi, two-Mississippi, three-Mississippi . . .*

Chapter 11
June 2004

As soon as she learns Lyman has gone off treatment, Eva is off balance. Everything seems precarious. Quiet moments are no longer innocent. Tired and irritable moments are harbingers of doom. She watches each interaction Lyman has with the kids. She knows her vigilance makes Lyman tense, and she tries to stop herself, but she can't. It's exhausting, watching every expression on his face, keeping track, and trying to—redirect. *Is that what I do?*

It's a good thing her clinic hours take her away from her own worries. She is always full of good advice for the family members of her depressed patients. But it is terribly difficult to apply her own advice at home, not to hover and not to nag. At work, she knows what to do. At home, she spins in circles. No doubt she overreacts. Obviously, that's why everybody knows you should never treat your own family.

One day in the clinic, a fifteen-year-old girl sits quietly in her office, picking at her cuticles. Her hair is unkempt and lusterless. It hides much of her face. Every two months, her mother brings her in to talk, and once in a while, they adjust medications. After four years of treatment, Lottie is no longer suicidal, but she is still deeply depressed.

Next to her daughter, Mrs. Monroe drones on: "Now see, Dr. Eva, she just isn't getting any better. That new medicine you added last time makes no difference."

"Can you describe what you see?" Eva asks.

"Well, she wants to be in her room all the time. Those headphones are glued to her. And she just lies there, on her bed. She'd stay there all day if I let her!"

Eva turns to the silent teenager. "Is your mom right, Lottie?" she asks. She expects a rolling of eyes, perhaps an irritated "What does she know?" But Lottie just looks away and bites another cuticle. *That's what Gabe used to do when he was anxious.*

"Mrs. Monroe," she asks, "did she sign up for that dance class she was excited about last time?"

"Yes, Dr. Eva, she sure did. She went maybe—oh maybe twice, and then she quit!" The woman glares at her daughter, who does not look up. "That cost money I don't have . . ." The silence around Lottie suddenly feels heavier, viscous.

"I'm sorry to hear that, Mrs. Monroe—but thank you for trying. Let's figure out what we can do then."

"I don't want her on *more* medication, Dr. Eva. More useless, expensive drugs. She's only fifteen."

"I completely agree with you. We need to keep her safe, right? But I don't want her on anything she doesn't *need*. I hope you know that?"

The woman nods, looking tired and discouraged. She tentatively glances at her daughter. She opens her mouth, then closes it again without speaking.

"How is your son? And the little one?" Eva asks.

"They're struggling too, but not like this." The woman tilts her head toward Lottie, looking grim. "I've been better myself . . ."

Eva leans forward a little. "It was such a big loss. And I know you do everything possible for your children." There is a pause. "How long has it been now?"

The mother looks up. "Since my husband passed, you mean? Two years since he did it."

Eva nods. Lottie was already depressed before the suicide. Of the three children, she was closest to him. He was the one who brought her to appointments. No wonder the girl sank back into despair after her father took his own life.

"Mrs. Monroe, may I speak with Lottie alone? For half an hour, maybe?"

The woman stands stiffly. Her gray sweatsuit sags at the knees, and her sneakers' original red color barely shows through. The toes are scuffed, and the heels are worn down.

Eva sits quietly with Lottie after the door closes. Her heart goes out to this family. "Lottie," she says after a while, "I have known you for what, four years now, right?" The girl sits, expressionless.

"Your mom is very, very worried about you." Nothing. "Tell me, should she be?"

"What do you mean?" Lottie asks, barely audible.

"I don't know, Lottie. What do *you* think she worries about?"

"Who knows. She's on my case all the time. It's always something. Sign up for track, come downstairs, have dinner with us, bring a friend home after school."

Eva nods, and Lottie takes a breath. "And do you know how many times I've heard about the money she wasted on that dance class?"

"I was wondering about that. How did it feel for you to hear her say it?"

Lottie becomes agitated and casts a furtive look toward the door. "She makes me feel so guilty, Dr. Eva, as if I can help it, feeling like this. As if I would make myself miserable just to spite her . . ."

"You know I understand that, don't you?" Eva waits until Lottie looks at her. "We'll try to figure this out. But first, tell me what's going on for *you*."

Lottie picks at her cuticles again, her shoulders slumped.

Eva presses on. "Why do *you* think your mom is so worried when you stay in your room with headphones on?"

Lottie shakes her head. "Ask her."

Eva tilts her head a little. "I could do that. But I need to hear it from you. You know what I mean?"

"Isn't it obvious?" Lottie raises her voice suddenly. "She thinks I'm going to do what my dad did. She is always hinting at it. Asking me whether I want to end up like him! Of course, I don't." She looks at the floor now, her fists clenched. "But she is constantly telling me to fight it. Get up and do something.

Get involved, like my brothers do. Well, I'm not like them! I never was." Her cheeks flush a little.

Eva rolls her chair around the desk, a little closer to Lottie. She leans in with her elbows on her knees. "Let me make a guess: you were always quiet, and it was your dad who understood that about you?"

The girl sighs. "I suppose. Yeah."

"Alright. And there is a kind of being quiet that is okay with you, right? Like just the way you are?" Lottie nods slowly. "And is there a different kind of quiet too? I mean—Do you get what I'm asking? Do you get *too* quiet at other times, maybe too much inside yourself?"

Lottie looks puzzled.

Eva is still leaning forward, looking intently at her. "Let me put this differently. What I am asking is, how does being depressed feel different from just wanting to be quiet?"

"Oh," Lottie brightens. "Sometimes I enjoy listening to music, or being in my room reading, or doodling. When I'm depressed, I can't even really listen, or focus on a book."

"That's very helpful, Lottie. Now tell me, on a scale of one to ten, how depressed were you before that last medication?"

"*Hmmm.*" The girl thinks for a moment. "Probably a six."

"Okay, and can you think back to when we first met? It's a long time ago, but how depressed do you think you were then?"

"Back then? I felt terrible. Everything was dark and murky. At *least* ten out of ten."

Eva wonders what Lyman would say if she asked him the same question, but she shouldn't think of that right now. She holds Lottie's gaze for a beat. "That is how I remember it, too, actually . . . One more question, Lottie. Well, two, really. How would we know that you are where you want to be? And how do we get there?"

Lottie has an immediate answer. She has clearly thought about this. "Well, I'm never going to be a bundle of laughs. I'm not like my brothers. No matter what my mother wants, I'll never be like that."

"Got it. What then?"

"I think about things. I take things kinda hard. That's not gonna change," she continues emphatically. "But I want to feel good enough so I can focus on music, maybe write some poems like I had started to. Pick up my guitar again."

"I hear you." Eva leans back. "That's a great way to look at it. I like that." She taps her fingers on her desk, considering. "So, you're better than you were in the beginning, right?" she sums up. "We need to remind your mom of that. And you're not going to become somebody else. It sounds like you don't want to, either."

"Right," says Lottie. Her eyes are moist, and her face is softer.

"But we are not where we need to be yet, do you agree?"

"Yes," comes a whisper.

"If that new medication does not improve things by next time, let's stop it. We have other options. Make sense?"

"*Mm-hmm.*"

"But *your* job, over the next month, is to find something that you can do, every day, that gets you out of the house. Something that *you* would like to do. You hear me?" Nothing. "It could be a music store, a walk in the park, or hanging out with a friend. You decide."

"Why?"

"Lottie, your mom may not know exactly what it is you need, but about this, I agree with her. Staying in your room too much will pull you down more. You'll be better off if you find something that gets you outside, out of your own head." Pause. "Will you try?"

"Yeah, but I'm not going back to dancing."

"No reason to. You thought that would be great, and it wasn't. So, not dancing. I'll speak to your mom about that."

"Okay."

"Can you agree that you shouldn't be sitting at home all summer?" Eva stands. They have gone well over time. *Worth it*, she thinks.

Lottie stands too and hesitates. "There is a gardening business down the road."

"And you—?"

"They take care of people's gardens. I love flowers. It would be quiet."

"Great idea, Lottie. That sounds perfect." Eva admires Lottie's grit. *What would perk Lyman up?* she wonders fleetingly.

"I'm pretty sure my mom won't like it, though," the girl mumbles as they walk out.

"We'll see." Eva leads her toward the waiting area, a hand on her shoulder. "Let's go tell your mom our plan, shall we?" Lottie nods. Her shoulders slump again.

Lottie is still on Eva's mind when she drives home that evening. Her family had walled off the father's despair for years. And it looks as if the mother is pulling away from Lottie too. Eva's heart aches for the kid. She doesn't want to go home until she collects herself; she feels way too off center. She just might fall apart if Lyman isn't upbeat when she gets there.

She drives to the barn where, years ago, she kept her pretty white mare. Lovely Tarot. She watches the horses in the pasture. A bay gelding notices her and trots over with pricked ears. She reaches an open hand across the fence, and he searches it for a treat.

"Sorry, boy, I don't have anything for you," she tells him. She strokes the white blaze on his nose. She rubs him behind the ears and slides her hand along the muscular neck. He bends his head down, half closing his eyes. His ears relax, and Eva begins to relax too. She has tears in her eyes, but the knot in her stomach loosens. A barn door slides open, and the gelding trots off, suddenly alert and eager.

When she gets home, Eva finds Olivia and Carla in the kitchen, rummaging for snacks. Olivia has grooves in her forehead. Carla is mute. Eva wonders whether they've had yet another fight. The girls take their snacks out to the patio. Carla is muscular, and she moves with graceful determination. She has curly, close-cropped hair and hazelnut skin. Olivia stands a head taller. Normally graceful herself, she stomps out today. At the far side of the patio, they resume an intense conversation. Eva sighs and fills the water kettle.

Lyman walks into the kitchen from his office. "How was clinic?" he asks.

"It was," she answers vaguely. She doesn't want to talk about Lottie. Depression is a loaded topic, dangerous territory right now. He doesn't notice and doesn't ask.

"Tea?" she offers.

"No thanks."

She studies his expression. He seems alright tonight. Gravel crunches in the driveway. A car door slams, and there is Gabe's hearty laugh. He comes in, telling an animated story while Aviva smiles up at him.

"Aviva," Eva says warmly. "We didn't really get to catch up at the party. Welcome. How does it feel to be done with college?"

"It's great. Finally some time to chill," says Aviva.

"Congratulations," says Lyman. Is he just making an effort to be sociable?

"Thank you. That senior thesis was *so* stressful. Stupid me, I picked a tougher topic than I should have."

"What about?" Eva asks from the kitchen.

Aviva sits at the bar counter, and Gabe joins her with two tall glasses of lemonade.

"Redlining," she says. "You know, lending policies that kept Black people stuck where the worst schools were." Eva nods. She knows. "How was that somehow made legal?" Aviva asks.

"It was outlawed finally, right? In 1977, I think? But—"

Gabriel stands up and takes Aviva by the arm. "Hey," he says. "Enough of that. It's summer. Come and sit outside. Need us to take anything out there, Mom?"

Eva waves them away. "I'll call you if I need help. Go!" She asks Lyman whether he needs anything. He shakes his head, and she goes upstairs to shower.

At dinner, Vicky and Aviva enter into a lively debate about music education.

Eva, across the table from Vicky, puts in two cents; Lyman, next to Eva, keeps quiet. Carla is at the far end of the table with Olivia. Gabriel leans across to tell Carla about the superiority of soccer over field hockey; Carla argues and sounds annoyed. Meanwhile, Olivia is talking with Ezra: once again, they are both heated up.

"Ezra," Olivia complains, "really, you're such a snob about music, and you're getting worse about it."

"Come on, sis. Be honest, when was the last time you listened to, say, Ella Fitzgerald, and noticed an unusual harmony behind her voice?"

"Ella is the whole *point* of that performance, Ezra! Her singing is *about* the words. She is great *because* she puts her whole self into those words."

"Olivia," he slaps the table. "Are you implying instrumental music is pointless?"

Olivia raises her hands. "Whoa, Ezra, chill!"

Eva is startled. "Ezra, easy honey," she says softly. He purses his lips.

"Stay out of it, Mom," Olivia snarls. "I can fend for myself." She crosses her arms and turns to her brother. "Geez, Ezra, I just like singing, okay? I love singing. That doesn't mean I don't like *your* music. Did I *say* I don't?"

Vicky, still talking to Aviva, reaches over to pat Ezra's thigh. He squeezes her hand, takes a breath, and leans back.

"Sorry," he says. "No, you didn't. I got carried away . . . Have I told you that your voice is lovely?" He makes a clown face and waves jazz hands.

Olivia grimaces and makes a peace sign. Eva breathes. These two can be so intense with each other. She never likes tension, but especially not this summer, when Lyman's mood seems precarious.

"Tell you what," Ezra offers, "let's do your favorite song together after dinner. Will you pull out your bass, Vicky?" He looks at Eva. "You'll play too, right, Mom?"

"Who wants dessert first?" Gabriel asks.

Several voices pipe up. "Me!" and "Me too" and "Any pistachio left?"

Olivia stacks the empty plates and casts a furtive look at Lyman, who hasn't said a word all evening. He has nodded once or twice, but there is a faraway look in his eyes. Eva watches him track the red-wing blackbirds, busy carrying food to their nests along the edge of the field. He looks her way and notices how she watches him. Was she staring?

"What?" he asks.

She shrugs and shakes her head. She is definitely too touchy tonight. First, about Olivia and Carla, then about Ezra blowing up at his sister, and now about Lyman withdrawing. She gathers the silverware and carries it inside. Olivia follows with the plates, and they bump shoulders, their private affectionate gesture.

"Hi, little mommy!" says Olivia. "You're getting littler all the time, you know that?"

Eva laughs and sticks out her tongue.

Gabe brings out the ice cream cartons on a tray, with a stack of bowls, a scoop, and some spoons. "Who the hell finished all the fudge I bought yesterday?" he asks. There is no answer.

Everybody scoops ice cream into their bowl. Chocolate, blueberry, peach, coffee, and pistachio. Everybody except Lyman, that is. He gets up. "Have fun, everybody," he says.

"You're not staying out with us?" Eva asks.

"Nah. I have a book to review."

"Kiss then?" she asks. He bends down, but his lips barely graze hers.

Carla turns to Olivia. "We were going to watch a show at my house, remember?" she whispers, loud enough that they can all hear.

Olivia has a puzzled frown. "But I told you," she says. "I'm spending time with my brothers while they're home."

"Yes, Carla," Gabe says pointedly. "And *we* want some time with our baby sister."

Carla startles and goes inside.

As soon as she is out of earshot, Olivia turns on Gabe. "What do you have against my girlfriend?" she hisses. "You've been antagonizing her all evening!"

"Well, since you ask, what I have against her is that she constantly wants something from you, and then something more, until you cave in. That's not like you. Why do you let her manipulate you, Olivia? It's been like that since I got here."

Olivia leans over. "She's had some rough times, okay? Cut her some slack," she whispers.

"You deserve better, sis!" says Gabe, more gently. "I really liked your last girlfriend—Rose, wasn't it? She was smart and kind. Why don't you go back to *her*? Or find someone else and dump Carla. Or just enjoy being free for a while."

Olivia opens her mouth just as Carla comes back out. Eva, too, thinks that Olivia deserves better, but saying it would only make her daughter dig in her heels.

Olivia turns to Eva and changes the topic. "What is wrong with Dad?" she asks. "He's been grumpy ever since everybody came home. Is something the matter?"

There is a silence. Eva had hoped nobody else would notice. That her fear over the way he stopped Prozac made her imagine things.

"Dad never liked chaos much," Gabe says. "It always made him go quiet." Eva is surprised to hear him say it, but he is right. Lyman was always at his best in calmer moments and never liked crowds.

Eventually, Olivia drives Carla home. Eva goes upstairs and wonders what she will find there, but Lyman is asleep. Or at least, he is breathing evenly. He doesn't look up when she sits on the bed. She kisses his forehead. She brushes her teeth quietly, slips into bed next to him, and spoons him. The knot of fear in her gut softens a little, and she remembers how they used to be quiet together, in the beginning. Their shared silences were filled with wordless electric connection, back then. Surely, it will come back; she just needs to be a little patient.

The next Sunday, Gabriel turns to Eva after lunch. "Hey Mom, you always want some one-on-one time when I'm here. Today is as good a time as any."

"Yep," Eva smiles, "I do. I like to keep up with my grown kids. Otherwise, I'd be a dinosaur before you can say *endangered*!"

Gabe laughs. "How about a hike? Everyone else has stuff to do. Dad said he has a paper to revise."

"Did he?" *Again?* Eva thinks. "Well, let's go then. You can drive *me* this time."

She pokes her head into Lyman's office. "Gabe and I are going for a hike. You have his cell number, right?"

Lyman swivels his chair a little. "Yep. Have fun."

In the old red Corolla, Eva thinks of all the years driving her kids around in it.

"So, where to, Mom?"

She bends over to lace her boots. "How about Underhill State Park? It's only half an hour away. I haven't gone up Mount Mansfield in a while."

"Sounds good," he says. "I vaguely remember. Sunset trail or something?"

"Sunset Ridge trail." She traces the steep-looking path on the map. "See, there's The Chin."

"Okay." He starts the car and selects a cassette tape. "Remember this mix? Wanna hear it?"

"Sure," she says. "You made that for me in high school. Stuff we both like, you said."

They drive in companionable silence for a while, going past the Green Mountain Equestrian Center.

"I've been dreaming about riding again," Eva says. "Putting my old saddle to use, you know?"

"Do it, Mom!" He glances over. "You always said you missed it. So just do it."

"Yeah, I should. Once I get somewhere with the Malawi project."

"Oh, right, you mentioned that. The resilience project, isn't it? But either way, it's high time for Livvie to fend for herself. You're spoiling her!"

"Are you jealous?" She chuckles. "There's the trailhead." She points to a parking spot.

Gabe reaches for the day pack. "Set the pace, Mom." He falls into step behind her, then pauses. "Is there bug juice in here?"

"In a Ziploc somewhere."

He follows behind until the trail widens enough to go side by side. She looks up at him fondly. "It's so nice to have you home this summer, Gabe!"

"Yeah. I just hope that internship works out."

"Of course it will. Are you worried it might not? Any glitches at the lab?"

"No glitches. But I'm not sure what I want next."

"What are you thinking of?"

"Maybe I'll get some clues from working on this project." The trail gets steeper, and they walk single file again.

"What kind of clues?" Eva asks over her shoulder.

"Whether I like research enough to consider a PhD. All that time on a computer . . ."

She stops to turn around, a great opportunity to catch her breath. "Have you discussed it with Dad?" she asks. "It's his field after all."

Gabe walks past her up the trail. "I know what he'll say, so what's the point?" he says.

Eva follows. To her left, a view opens up briefly, and then they're among trees again. She catches up. "Hold on," she says. "What do you mean?"

He turns his head and scowls.

"Are you annoyed for some reason?"

"Not annoyed with *you*. Just frustrated with myself for going around in circles about it."

"I see . . ."

"And besides, we both know that Dad would say, *Just get a PhD, you'll love it. I loved it*. Or something like that."

"Oh, come now, Gabe, that isn't really fair, is it? He advises students all the time on what's next for them."

"Those students aren't his *son*. He is so thrilled I've gone into environmental sciences. It drips off him, can't you see?"

"But—"

"I don't need the pressure. It's hard enough to think clearly without *that* to deal with."

"So, that's why you made a point of doing your internship in a different lab? For him to stay out of your work?"

"You just figured that out?" He laughs. "I thought it was obvious." He looks over his shoulder and notices she is breathing hard and falling behind a little. "Sorry, Mom," he says. "I forget my legs are way longer than yours. Why don't you walk in front again?"

She reaches up to kiss his cheek. "Thanks, son."

They have reached the steep switchback section of the trail. Eva finds her stride, walking easily now that she is not trying to match his pace. They overtake a couple who were ahead of them. They sit and sip some water at an appealing outcropping with a partial viewpoint.

"It's good to be back east," says Gabe. "The mountains in Colorado are huge and spectacular. I loved it, but I almost forgot how different the mountains feel in Vermont. Just . . . I don't know—"

"Like home?" she smiles.

He chuckles. "Something like that."

"Glad to hear it, honey."

"Yeah, just don't expect I'll live here forever, okay?"

"Oh, come on, give me a little credit here," she says.

"Just teasing."

"Good. But tell me more about that decision you're trying to make. Option one is you apply for a PhD somewhere? And option two?"

"There are jobs as project manager, or research coordinator, or field researcher. Out in the field doing the actual work."

"I see. You'd get to be outdoors, in the field. But on someone else's project?" She reaches for the pack and puts her water bottle back in.

"Exactly. I wouldn't be the one to worry about grants or administration. You know, the stuff Dad says he hates."

He puts his water bottle away, stands, and reaches for Eva's hand. She takes it, and he pulls her up. The trail is wide enough for them to walk together again.

"What about teaching?" She stops and shields her eyes. "Gabe, look at that hawk, circling overhead," she points. "Red-tailed, I think?"

"Where? Oh, I see it!" He turns to her again. "Yeah, teaching. Isn't that another thing Dad complains about?"

On the next steep section, loose rocks make walking tricky. She breathes in the air, thinking. "Gabe? Can I make a suggestion?" she asks over her shoulder.

"Sure. It looks like you're going to anyway." He smirks.

"Smart aleck! So, you *don't* want to discuss this with Dad, because he might tell you to apply to grad school. Right?"

"I guess."

"And *his* gripes lately, about academics, are pushing you away from a PhD?"

"Pretty much."

"It seems to me your *guesses* about Dad have a lot of power . . ."

"I suppose. Fair enough."

"How about ignoring what he thinks for a couple of weeks? Put it out of your mind. Could you?"

He snorts. "I can try, but you know me."

"I know, it will go around in your mind anyway. But just remember, you and Dad are not the same, Gabe."

For the next hour, they climb steadily until they reach the spectacular vista on Cantilever Rock. After a few moments, Gabe looks at his watch. "Do you mind turning around?" he asks. "I'd like to catch up with Aviva later tonight. Is that okay with you?"

"Of course," she says, standing up. "And are you and Aviva—"

He interrupts her. "You're not being nosy now, are you, Mommy dear?"

She almost blushes. "Sorry. A little, I suppose. You don't have to answer me."

"Well, the answer is, I don't know. She is a good friend, and we don't want to ruin that. So, we're taking it slow. One small step at a time." He shoulders the pack and turns toward the trail.

"That's wise. Good for you. You kids are so much wiser than I was at your age."

He walks ahead for a while, his long legs carrying him down at a fast clip.

She is more careful where she steps, not interested in turning an ankle. At a bend in the trail, he stops to wait and appraises her as she approaches.

“Not doing too badly for an old lady,” he teases.

“Hey,” she protests. “Have a little respect. I’m not *that* old yet.”

Chapter 12
Early July 2004

When Eva gets home one afternoon, Olivia is already there. There is some music on. Something Eva hasn't heard before. Something loud. When she comes out of the shower with a towel wrapped around her head, the music still plays full blast. A woman's voice and a guitar.

"What is this?" she asks.

"It's called 'Imperfectly,' by Ani DiFranco. Heard of her?"

Lyman walks out of his office and surveys the kitchen. "Anything I can do about dinner?" he asks.

"Haven't thought about it yet," Eva answers. "Any inspiration you have is better than mine!"

She turns to Olivia, who is sprawled out on the couch. "Never heard of this Ani," she says. "Pretty intense."

"Yeah," Livvie agrees. "She's a badass feminist."

"Does she sing *and* play?"

"Yep. Writes her own songs. It's her own record label, too, Righteous Babe."

Eva notices Lyman scowling at the stereo speakers. She walks around the counter to hug him. He surveys the vegetable drawer.

"Took a short walk after work," she tells him. "Beautiful day."

"Yeah." He turns to Olivia. "Can you turn the volume down?"

"What?" she yells back.

"*Turn—the—volume—down,*" he repeats, clipping his words.

Olivia sits up. "But Dad, it's *meant* to be loud. That's her whole point."

"It's *supposed* to make me deaf?"

Eva can see where this is going. She intervenes. "Turn it down just a little, okay, sweetie?" Olivia does, *just* a little.

Lyman frowns. "What *is* this anyway? Do you call that music?" A few minutes later, he wheels on Olivia, who sits at the bar counter, munching on almonds. "It's still too loud. Turn the bloody volume down!"

"Okay," she says, going through the motions with the knob. "But Dad, give it a minute. Listen to this song. It's how she told the world she's bisexual. That was really brave when she did it. She's a feminist icon, actually."

"I don't care if she is an icon, Olivia! Turn it down before I do! *Now!*"

Eva doesn't like the heat, so she gets out of the kitchen. She takes plates, napkins, and silverware outside. Olivia turns the stereo off and stomps upstairs. Eva would have liked to hear more about this singer. She wonders what her message means to Livvie.

Outside, later, Lyman turns kebabs on the grill. "Almost ready," he says.

Eva walks to the bottom of the stairs. "Livvie?" she calls. She can hear Ani DiFranco, still blasting in Olivia's room. Eva trudges halfway up and tries again. "*Livvie!?*" She sighs, goes the rest of the way up, and knocks on her daughter's door. She opens it a crack. "Livvie? Come down for dinner, please?"

"Sure, in a minute," says Olivia. She is typing something on her laptop.

After much more than a minute, the three of them sit around the patio table. Eva breathes in the aroma of rosemary. "Smells great, Lyman!" she says.

"Tastes good too," says Olivia, but she doesn't look at him.

Eva asks about Olivia's job at the day camp. Lyman has long been involved with the nature program there. "Do they still have their native herbs garden?" he asks. The earlier tension is pushed aside. A breeze picks up, and shadow patterns ripple through the grasses in the field. He asks about the age of the campers and the activities planned.

Eventually, Eva turns to Olivia. "I was curious about this Ani DiFranco," she says, glancing toward Lyman. Maybe he'll take an interest too, for Olivia's sake. "Why is she an icon?"

Olivia perks up. "All her songs have a message, see? She's been speaking up for gay rights. For women's rights. And that song earlier, coming out as bisexual, that was before anybody thought bisexual was a thing."

"How'd you hear about her?"

"Carla told me about her. She wants us to go to her concert."

Lyman is stacking empty plates. "A concert where?"

"In Burlington. At Higher Ground."

"Wait, doesn't that place have several bars in it? Are you even allowed in at sixteen?"

"Of course, we're allowed in. We just can't buy alcohol. At least not without a fake ID," she smirks.

"Olivia—are you telling us—" And just like that, the irritation is back.

"Just kidding, Dad!"

"Last I heard, you can get all kinds of drugs at those concerts too," he says. "I don't—"

"Dad, stop. What do you think, I'm going to take Ecstasy and then drive into Lake Champlain?"

"Don't be rude." He stands up.

Eva carries the leftover kebabs inside. "I'll do the dishes," she says.

Olivia follows with the glasses. "I'll help."

Their evening together is over. Lyman retreats to the office.

"So, the concert?" Eva asks while cleaning up. "When is it?"

"In two weeks, Thursday night. Can Carla sleep over after?" Livvie asks.

"Sure, just check with your father too, won't you?"

"Yeah, I guess. Unless he's in a bad mood again." She opens the dishwasher.

"Olivia, don't . . ." Eva runs more hot water into the sink.

"Mom. He's had nothing positive to say lately. Geez, did you hear how he got irritated over the CD earlier? And then, going on about drugs!" Olivia clatters the plates into the dishwasher.

"Hey, don't break those, please. He just wants you safe."

"Yeah, right, sure, that's it. He is irritated at everything, all the time, because he just wants us all to be safe."

"He isn't feeling great right now, please let it be," says Eva. She tries to sound less worried than she feels. She has friends to chat with. Olivia doesn't need to be burdened with the details.

"If you say so."

The following Saturday, everybody gathers to spend the day at Thayer Beach. Ezra, Vicky, and Olivia will squeeze into Gabe's Toyota. Eva will take her sporty Mazda, and Lyman joins her. *It will give us a chance to connect a little*, she thinks.

"Gabe? Ezra?" she asks. "You all have my new cell phone number, right? In case we need to find each other?"

"Yep," says Gabriel. "Sending you a text right now. D'you get it?"

She checks. "Yep." She gets behind the wheel.

Ezra folds his long legs into the Corolla's back seat next to Vicky and rolls his window down. "Try not to get a speeding ticket, Mom . . ."

She waves and pulls out of the driveway. "I love this little car," she says for the hundredth time. "I deserve a speeding ticket, sometimes . . ."

"Yeah," says Lyman. "But women get away with things that men don't."

"I'm not complaining," she says. "Why don't you pick some music?"

"Nah, I don't feel like having music."

"Oh. Okay." She enjoys this winding stretch of road from Jericho toward Colchester. It's a beautiful day for a family outing. "How about opening the moon roof?"

"Sure."

When Eva has had about all the silence she can handle, she pats his knee. "How was your week?" she asks. "We've hardly had time to chat."

"Fine," he says, facing the window. She can barely hear him. After a moment, he makes a visible effort and turns to her. "I'm glad I'm done with students. And I'm making some progress with that paper I've struggled with."

"Good," Eva says. "Maybe we can all get away on an adventure soon?"

She veers left onto the straighter stretch of road and checks her rearview mirror. There is no red car behind her. She slows down and hands Lyman her flip phone: "Why don't you text them and make sure everything is okay?"

"They're adults, Eva." He doesn't take it from her. "Leave them be."

It's not worth an argument. But she crawls along for a mile or two, until Gabe's car comes into view. She turns to Lyman and tries again. "Isn't it great to have everybody home?"

"Yeah, you like that sort of thing," he says.

"What do you mean, *I* like that sort of thing? *You* don't?"

"Well, you do."

Her foot hits the accelerator; she grips the steering wheel with both hands. She takes a breath. "Lyman, I *hate* when you do that!" she says, managing not to raise her voice too much, even if she is boiling over inside. She treads very carefully these days. *He needs support, doesn't he?* she reminds herself. *Even if he makes it hard sometimes.*

"Do what?" he asks.

"That noncommittal stuff, as if you're not involved. Or you don't care. Or as if it's not *your* family too."

"There you go, making a big to-do out of nothing. All I said was 'You like that sort of thing.' What do you want me to do? Jump for joy?" he stares straight ahead. "You want me to coo over how wonderful it is to have the kids home? And be cheerful all the time?"

He points to the sign for Colchester. She has already turned onto 2A.

"I just imagined you'd enjoy your kids, Lyman."

"Who says I don't. Dammit, leave me be. I'm not a Pollyanna like you."

This is going nowhere good, she knows. Hopefully, once they are on the beach, Lyman will get swept up in the general summer mood. She does not speak again. She finds a shady spot in the parking lot and gets out of the car.

He takes a duffel out of the trunk. "Is this the bag?"

"Yes. I stuffed in some towels and water bottles. And the bathing suits." She needs to walk a little. "I'll just check out the nature trail while we wait."

She really needs to move if she doesn't want to get into a fight about his attitude.

The water is still a bit chilly so early in July. The beach is not crowded; they play Frisbee to warm up after swimming. When Eva tires of the games, she finds a tree to lean against. She reads half-heartedly. Olivia shouts, and Eva rests her chin on her knees to watch them. Gabriel sends the Frisbee toward his sister with a hard overhand. It spins out of her reach. Ezra leaps and barely catches it, then flicks it toward Vicky.

"Back atcha," Vicky yells and sends a thumber his way.

Ezra stops after a low backhand. "Lunch, everybody?" He pants.

Eva stands. "There's a deli on the road, nearby," she says. "I can go get some stuff."

"Oh, I've been there," says Gabriel. "They have great sandwiches."

They find a scrap of paper and a pen. Ezra scribbles down requests.

"I don't want anything," says Lyman. "I'll go get it. I'm done swimming anyway."

"Thanks," Eva says and hands him the keys. "I'd like a veggie sandwich, please," she tells Ezra. "Avocado, no mayo."

An hour goes by. "Geez, Dad, what took you so long?" Olivia teases when Lyman reappears.

"You're welcome for the sandwiches," he says gruffly. He takes a newspaper out of the bag and finds a place in the shade, a few feet away from everybody.

"Sorry, Dad!" Olivia calls after him. "Thank you. I didn't mean . . ." He isn't listening.

The sandwiches disappear in record time. They play catch for a bit afterward.

"Wanna join us?" Gabriel asks Lyman.

Lyman shakes his head. Eva debates joining him but realizes that it would only emphasize the gathering clouds.

On the way home, Eva gives Olivia the keys to the Mazda.

"Mom, can I really? Awesome."

"Sure. You can handle stick shift. I'll sit in back. Okay with you, Lyman?"

He gets in the front passenger seat without a word. In the back, Eva sits brooding. Baffled, strategizing. Things are not getting any better; to the contrary, they are getting worse. Every day confirms that something is very wrong. Olivia asks a question Eva can't quite hear, and Lyman gives a monosyllabic answer. Olivia tries again. Eva can tell her daughter is frustrated when she stops talking and jabs the CD player on.

"What is this?" she asks Eva over her shoulder.

"Keep your eyes on the road," Lyman warns.

"It's a mix of jazz vocalists, I think," says Eva, leaning forward between the seats.

Olivia is grim-faced, heavy on the accelerator. Eva gently taps her shoulder. "We just entered a thirty-five miles per hour zone, Livvie. Did you notice?" she whispers, and Olivia brakes abruptly.

"For God's sake, pay attention. Or else let me drive!" Lyman groans.

Eva leans back and closes her eyes, defeated.

The next morning, everyone under twenty-five is sleeping in. It's Sunday after all. Eva goes to the kitchen, brews a cup of coffee for Lyman and a mug of tea for herself. She carries both upstairs. Lyman is awake; she puts the coffee on his bedside table, carefully closes the bedroom door, and sits beside him with her tea. After a moment, she turns to face him.

"Lyman, we have to talk."

"Again? What now?"

She puts a hand gently on his arm. "Honey, you stopped your meds a little over two months ago, right?" He sighs. "And you have an appointment coming up with the psychiatrist soon?"

"I can't remember. Maybe."

How can he not remember? Is he just avoiding her question? The knot in her stomach tightens. "Listen, I can't seem to stop worrying about you. I know you hate that, and then you pull away more. And then I worry even more."

"Yep," he snaps.

"But the thing is, I *know* too much not to worry. It's what I do for a living. And I'm too close to see clearly, but—" He gives her a piercing look. "Well, I want to have a conversation with your psychologist. Both of us together." He says nothing. "Rachel was fabulous years ago, when you got depressed. If I knew you were in good hands, then I *could* step back."

Silence. Eva looks up, pleading. "She knows you so well, she could help you take stock, see how you're *really* doing off medication."

He turns to her, his face closed. "I can see for myself, Eva . . . And I haven't met with Rachel in a long while."

"I know, you told me. But things are not going well lately."

"Things are fine. You're making a mountain out of a mole's heap again. All because I'm not chipper and playful all the time. Everybody is milling around, and everything is loud and busy all the time, and I am a quiet person, remember?"

She puts her mug down, reaches both hands to hold his. "Please look at me," she asks gently. "I suppose you could phrase it that way. But you're not just quiet. You're so withdrawn, and irritable, and somber. I can't cope with it. Even if you don't think *you* need help, I do, so I don't make it worse. I need someone like Rachel to help and to address my alarm bells."

"Have it your way. Schedule something. I'll make it if I can."

"Lyman! *If you can?* But it's *your* well-being we're talking about here."

"Actually, Eva, it is *your* anxiety, not mine!"

She wants to scream, knows it would only escalate things. She stands abruptly, grabs her robe from the bathroom hook, and leaves. She slams the bedroom door behind her. Fighting tears, she runs downstairs and takes her tea outside where she can cry in peace. She feels out of control. Her world is shaking. And her partner, her teammate, her best friend refuses to see it.

She looks toward the silhouette of the Green Mountains. There are birds all around her, flitting about, doing the business of spring. A few wild irises are coming up in the field. She wipes at her eyes with her sleeve and breathes deeply.

* * *

After a while, Eva goes back inside and finds a sleepy-eyed Olivia in the kitchen. Eva gives her a hug. "Morning, sunshine!"

"What's for breakfast?" Olivia asks.

"You mean brunch?" Eva laughs, glancing at the clock.

Lyman comes down the stairs too. "I'm going for a long run. Not hungry," he says. He ties his shoes in the mudroom and leaves.

Olivia frowns. "Seriously, Mom, what *is* the matter with him?" she bursts out.

"Watch that tone . . ." Eva warns.

"Dammit, Mom, he makes it feel like we all get on his nerves. We're only together for a little while, and it feels like he wants us *gone*. And in case you hadn't noticed, he's rude to you too." She sits on a bar stool.

"Olivia, take it easy. I don't think he's feeling well, I've already told you."

"Yeah, Mom, you did. But if one of us acted like that and gave you a lame-ass reason like 'I'm not feeling well,' you would never let us get away with it." She has an elbow on the counter, and she is not done. "You're making excuses for him. I catch you doing it all the time lately, no matter *how* rude he is to you."

"Livvie, that is not your place—"

"Well, you are *not standing up for yourself*, I just hate it! That's a hell of a role model for your daughter . . . You—I thought of you as a feminist, Mom."

Eva freezes and sternly looks at Olivia. "And now you've decided I'm not? Watch what you say."

Livvie raises her voice another notch and turns away. "Come on, Mother, how can you let a man treat you the way Dad has lately? And to think everyone is on my case about letting Carla get away with things. Well, guess who I learned *that* from?"

"Look at me, Livvie!"

"What?"

"First of all, I can take care of myself."

"Sure," Livvie snarls. "That's obvious . . ."

"Olivia, *that—is—enough!*" Eva steps closer to her daughter, who startles and looks up. "Come on," Eva says in a gentler voice. "Is that *really* what you're upset about? Him getting away with something?"

Olivia stands and walks to the window in the kitchen nook. "I guess that's not all of it. It's just—we could be having a fabulous family summer. It might never happen again, and he's ruining it." She sniffles.

Eva goes over and puts an arm around her. "Sweetie, listen. I am worried about your dad, really worried, and I'm trying to figure out what to do. Picking fights is not going to help. Understand?"

"Why are you worried? You should be mad. He's just being a dick."

"*Olivia* . . . watch—your—language."

Livvie backs down. "Alright, alright. But can't you see? *Why* are you worried instead of telling him to knock it off?"

Eva sighs. "Did you know your dad got very depressed, years ago? You might not remember, actually, you were so little."

"Nope, I don't. News to me," says Olivia, barely interested.

"Well, maybe it's better that you don't. Anyway, he did. He worked hard to get better. It worked. And *that* is the wonderful, vibrant dad that you remember." She swallows.

"Yeah. I never saw anything wrong. He was fun to be with. He cared. So, what happened?"

"His treatment changed," Eva says vaguely.

"Oh, what do you mean? Is the old stuff not working anymore?"

"Sweetie, *something* sure isn't working. And I promise you, I'm doing what I can to help him figure it out. Get it?" *Is that a promise she can deliver on?* she wonders.

"I guess," Olivia says uncertainly. She stands to pour herself some orange juice.

"And, Olivia, listen? Sometimes, loving someone means you cut them some slack. You have to be a big enough person to be able to do that. Taking battle stances is easy."

"Oh." Olivia considers, then flares up again. "So, are you telling me to cut Carla more slack, too, then? Or does that only apply to Dad?" she asks, hand on her hip.

Eva decides to ignore that. "And sometimes, Olivia, things are not so clear-cut. It would be easier if they were, if we had a manual with rules for such things. But for now—are you listening?—what I'm telling you is that I'm worried about him. I'm trying to make sense of it." She squeezes her daughter's shoulder. "Focus on having a fabulous summer with Ezra and Gabe. I'll deal with Dad. Got it?"

Olivia drains her glass and sets it in the sink. She looks at her mother, a little softened and sad. "You were keeping everything all nicey-nice. I thought you were in total denial."

"I'm sorry. I wasn't. And I'm glad you brought it up, instead of stewing."

Olivia looks around the kitchen. "Do I just grab something to eat, or are we doing a family brunch? I could help?"

Eva hugs her. "How about a pile of French toast and a big fruit salad?"

"Awesome. First, I'll go tell my lazy-ass brothers to get down here."

Two weeks later, midday on a Friday, Eva sits in Rachel Fishman's waiting room. *Where is Lyman?* She looks toward the entrance. *He said he'd be here.* She checks her watch.

Just as Rachel comes to invite them in, Eva notices a voice message and listens to it. Crestfallen, she looks up. "He's not coming. Busy at work, he said." She clenches her teeth. "He promised . . ."

"Oh, I'm sorry . . . Do you want to reschedule? Or . . ."

Eva bites her lip, uncertain. It turns out that Rachel is taking the month of August off. So many therapists do. Eva wishes *she* had that luxury. "I'd better use the session then, because I'm at a loss."

They enter the office. Eva sits in the nearest armchair. She cannot settle herself; she leans her elbows on her knees and looks at the carpet. Rachel offers a box of tissues. Eva waves it off.

"Tell me," Rachel asks softly. "Take your time."

Eva wipes at her face with her wrist. "You probably don't know that Lyman stopped Prozac, do you?" she asks. "He hasn't discussed it with Dr. Grant either."

"Well, no, I don't, I haven't seen him in—let me check—" She pulls out a folder. She frowns. "It's been a long time. He was doing well, and he stopped coming."

"You mean without wrapping things up with you?"

"Right." Rachel hesitates. "Perhaps I should have been more persistent . . ."

"Rachel, he's an adult. And you know him well enough to see that pushing—"

"—doesn't work." Rachel completes Eva's sentence. They both nod.

Eva tells her how Lyman tried tapering down the Prozac last year, without any luck. He was disappointed at first, but then he seemed fine . . . until now.

Rachel studies Eva. "You look worried . . . Why exactly did you schedule this appointment? Did something more happen?"

Eva sighs, looks at her hands, and launches into a jumbled account of the summer. "The three kids are all home, you see. Since May. Those 'boys' are men now, but—"

Rachel chuckles. "The kids will always be kids in our minds, right?"

"Yeah . . . and these past weeks . . . I don't know where to begin. He's been remote, irritable." She studies her fingernails. "It's only when I asked what . . . well, that's when I found out he stopped the Prozac in late April, or early May. All at once. And now every little thing seems—I don't know—ominous to me . . ." She looks up to see if Rachel is following.

"Of course. So, you worried, *and* you doubted yourself, I imagine." Rachel leans in a little. "Go on?"

Eva tears up with relief. *Rachel gets it* . . . "Yes, exactly! I've been so anxious. And I know how much that annoys him. It must feel like I'm scrutinizing him. I try not to, you know, but it's awful and it's getting worse. And—and now Olivia is pissed at me for not confronting him . . ."

Rachel raises an eyebrow. "Teenager, right? She still thinks you should be able to fix everything. Even when she also thinks she knows better than you . . ."

Eva throws up her hands. "Exactly. Lyman's mood affects her, a lot. And now I can't do anything right." Eva reaches for the tissue box after all.

"Did she have any suggestions?"

"Yep. *Tell him to stop being a dick.* That's a quote." She manages a wry chuckle. "I guess she imagined that he would say, *Am I? Oh, so sorry!* And that he'd become his normal self again, just like that." Rachel smiles a little. "So, I told her that I am worried. I mentioned he had been depressed before, all those years ago . . ." She shakes her head. "A kid shouldn't have to carry all that."

Rachel shrugs. "I guess, but it might also help her—well—to make sense out of things."

"Who knows. Anyway, then I asked Lyman to meet with you here, together . . ." She pauses. Outside, the day is insultingly gorgeous, with bright blue skies and tiny wisps of pure white clouds.

"And he agreed?"

Eva turns back toward Rachel. "Only with an annoyed sigh, like *If you really want to, and then maybe you'll get off my back.*"

"Ah. And . . . are you scared you'll never have him back the way he was?" she guesses.

"Pretty much. It's not rational—"

"Don't beat yourself up, Eva." Rachel grabs a pen and a notepad and jots a few things down. She taps at her teeth with her pen, thoughtful, before she looks up. "I have to agree with you, a joint session with Lyman would be a good thing. Unless he prefers to come alone."

"Sure, but I'm pretty sure he won't. He is deep inside this dark mood, can't see beyond it. He doesn't seem to *want* to change it, or even think he should." She glances at the clock and gets up, feeling wiped out. "I know my time is up. Thank you, Rachel. I couldn't bear it alone anymore."

Rachel nods. "Do you think you could both come in early next Friday, at eight?"

* * *

On the way back to campus, Eva hesitates. She only has administrative stuff to do; she has no patients this afternoon. On impulse, she parks at the Environmental Sciences building. In the lobby, she studies the directory; she hasn't been here in a long time. She hopes Lyman is not teaching a class right now, but she is prepared to wait for him, as long as it takes.

She knocks at his office door, enters without waiting. Lyman sits at his desk. He chews on a pencil while he scrolls through data. She closes the door behind her, crosses her arms, and stands looking at him.

"What?" he looks up, surprised and not pleased.

"This won't fly, Lyman."

"What are you talking about?" He does not indicate the empty chair across his desk. She is much too agitated to sit anyway. She doesn't answer; she takes stock of him. He tilts his desk chair back. He is good at waiting, she remembers. Better than she is.

"I made another appointment for us with Rachel," she says. "Next week, and I need you to be there. She created a time especially for us. *I need you to come.*"

He swivels his chair away from her, toward the window. "I don't want therapy, Eva," he says through gritted teeth. "I don't want it, and I don't need it. I did my stint and I'm done."

"I have no idea what you need right now, Lyman. No idea at all. But I know that *I need you to be there*, because I can't go on worrying about you like this."

"Bloody hell, like what? If you're feeling so bad, get your own therapist. Don't drag me into it."

"*Listen* to me, I *will not* go on tracking your moods by myself. First of all, as you know, your withdrawal triggers my own childhood stuff. I know you sense it, and then we get into one of those old cycles. Rachel helped us to break that pattern years ago, but now . . ." He doesn't react, so she goes on. "On top of that, I can't just wait around and watch you withdraw from the kids, from everybody, and from me too. You're annoyed with everything, even with the family having fun and being noisy."

Her voice catches. She notices two people outside, crossing the campus, talking and holding hands. She suppresses a sob and faces him. "I won't just stand by, knowing that you suddenly stopped the Prozac, with no tapering, and on your own. It's not safe, and it's not looking good, Lyman!" She bites off each word. "I'm sorry to repeat myself, but I *have* to know that someone qualified helps you look into what's going on. Someone on your side, helping you. Someone who is not your wife."

"If that's what it takes for you to stop nagging me, fine, I'll go. But if this is leading up to another serotonin-whatever again, or some other miracle drug, you can save yourself the trouble. I won't." He turns a dark look on her.

She plops onto the empty chair and reaches for his hand across the desk. "You owe it to your family as much as to yourself, Lyman." She holds his fingers before he pulls back. "We're in this together, and you mean the world to me. You know that, don't you?"

"So you've said. I'm not sure why lately. You sure complain enough . . ."

She interrupts. "If you hear it as complaints, I'm sorry. All I can do is repeat, again, that I am *worried* about you. For you. Not complaining."

He leans way back and swivels toward the window.

"You've been in a somber place before, and you got help, and you came out of it. Remember, when Olivia was little?" She pauses, hoping he'll respond. "How you grappled with your own childhood, your father's depressions? You said that you didn't want to be like him—"

"That was ages ago, Eva. What's your point?"

She is perilously close to tears. "You can come out of this one, too, Lyman. We have a wonderful life together, our kids are amazing, each in their own way. Come back to us."

"You're being dramatic, Eva. Who cares if I am less bubbly than you imagined I should be, with our house full of people? Let everybody have fun, do their thing, and let me be."

"Be what?"

"Be quiet. Be myself. I'm not as gregarious as you. And I'm tired of being expected to play the part!"

She walks around his desk to stand behind his chair. She rests her cheek on his head, arms around his chest. “Were you playing a part these past years, Lyman?” She chokes on the words. “Were you only playing at being happy, pretending all this time?”

He moves her arms aside and stands. From the window, he faces her. “People change. We all change. All I know is that I hate being on medication. I need to be myself. If that is not good enough for you, I can’t help you.” His hands grip the windowsill.

“But you *tried* to taper it, a year ago, and—”

He cuts her off. “That was then. This is now. And I have things to do.” He walks toward the door and opens it. “Are you coming out? You can sit here if you need to.” And he is gone.

She sits, stunned. *Why won’t he hear me?* she thinks. *What have I done wrong?* When she can compose herself, she leaves his office, shuts the door, and heads out.

Chapter 13
Late July 2004

It is the last Friday of the month. Rachel waves them both into her office. Eva hesitates, asks Lyman if he wants to meet alone first.

"I don't care," he shrugs. Inside, Lyman chooses the armchair, so Eva sits in the love seat by herself. Rachel looks from one to the other. She is wearing a faded blue sleeveless dress and sandals, ready for vacation. She tilts her head toward Lyman. "I'm glad to see you," she says. "How are you?"

He glances toward Eva and takes a breath, shoulders tense. "Things would have gone better if I had warned her about stopping Prozac," he says, coming right to the point. "I realize that. But I didn't. Maybe I didn't want to hear her disagree . . ." His jaw is working. "But I never did sign on to take it forever. A year ago, I couldn't do it, but this time—I thought she wouldn't even notice." *That can't be true*, Eva thinks. *Me? Not notice?*

Rachel nods and recalls that they had hoped he might not need medications forever, and Lyman's shoulders relax a little. "Did you consider," she says, "and I'm not implying you should have—I'm just asking. Did you consider running it by anybody? Or—"

"Oh, it wasn't exactly planned out. My prescription ran out. I felt fine. I had to see Grant to get a refill, and I put it off. Or kept forgetting, or . . ."

"Or?"

Lyman sighs. "Once I had been off for a couple of weeks, I started feeling,

I don't know, more *myself.* As I told *her,* as if I had been artificially cheerful all that time."

Eva opens her mouth. She swallows.

"And . . . ?" Rachel asks.

"That's it. Or—" he looks at Eva. "Did you tell Rachel?" he asks.

"Tell her what?"

So, he explains about sex being different. Rachel asks some clinical questions. Eva jumps in, her voice rising an octave. "It looks to me like sex plummeted *after* you stopped, Lyman, not *while* you were taking it!"

He frowns and turns to Rachel. "I felt more alive off Prozac. And for me, alive isn't all a bed of roses." He looks at Eva with a steely glint in his eyes. "I don't want to be dulled anymore. You'll have to take me as I am, or not at all . . ."

Rachel lets that sink in; Eva is crying now, her face averted. She speaks into her hands. "Were you secretly unhappy all these years? Did we *not* have a deep connection?"

"I did not say that, now did I?" he snaps. "Did *you* hear me say that, Rachel? All I said is that I felt more like myself once I came off."

Rachel leans back and speaks carefully and slowly. "I hear you," she says. "And yet Eva thinks you are withdrawn, not just from her, but from the family. That you don't seem to enjoy having everybody around. That you've been—irritable."

Eva studies her shoes; her hands hang limply between her knees.

"Well, maybe I'm just older," he says after a pause. "And I want life a little quieter."

Eva can't stop herself. "But Lyman, the kids are wondering—"

"Now you're discussing me with our kids? Great!" he snaps.

"Lyman, no, of course not. But . . . well, Oliva was upset and angry, after that drive back from the beach. And she asked what . . ." She examines the painting behind Rachel. "I told her you weren't feeling well."

He stands, a fist clenched, and walks toward the window, his back to them. "I—am—feeling—just—fine. Leave—me—alone!"

Eva hesitates. She wants to hold him, but she stays where she is. She reminds him again how, years ago, when he was depressed, she had just wanted her husband back. "Do you remember? How *together* we were while you fought your way out of depression?" She feels like a broken record.

"A long time ago," he mumbles and returns to the armchair.

Eva reaches toward him. "Please?" She leans way over to take Lyman's nearest hand. "My love, listen, it feels—like I am losing you again. I'm so afraid."

Vacantly, he looks at her. "Afraid of what?"

"Of losing—the way we are together." Her voice shakes. "Of losing my partner."

He pulls his hand back brusquely. "I'm here, aren't I? I'm not going anywhere. Are you?"

"Of course not," she nearly shouts. "I am losing you right in front of my eyes. You are here, I can see you, and *I can't find you*." Lyman looks toward the door. "It feels awful!" Eva glances toward Rachel, and then spells it out, articulating every word. "Lyman, if this *is* depression, then would you rather let it destroy our marriage than go into treatment again?"

He waits a moment. "Yes," he says somberly.

Eva has never doubted that their shared life means as much to him as it does to her. Her breath catches. She cannot believe her plea doesn't reach him.

Rachel gives her a look of concern, then turns to Lyman. "Maybe it *is* depression, or maybe something bothers you that we could address. Or both." She pauses. "Would you come and see me, so we can look into things, figure out what to do?"

"Probably not," he admits. "I am willing to exercise more, and maybe meditate some."

Eva accepts that. It's not much, but it's better than nothing. At least it means he knows he's off-kilter. She asks him to meet with Rachel again in September, together.

He sighs. "I don't guess you'll give me a choice, will you?"

Rachel watches them both for a moment and suggests they set up a time as soon as she comes back. They fumble with schedules. "And Lyman," Rachel adds, "if I may say so, I do think you should see Dr. Grant before then. Soon. He might have suggestions." She waits.

He turns to go. "Maybe. I'll think about it."

They leave the building in silence. Eva puts an arm around his waist; he gives her a stiff little hug. Then they go their separate ways.

Eva has a department meeting in a couple of hours. She had best pull herself together before that. She is a mess. She parks her car on campus and walks to Centennial Woods. There is a network of nature trails, and except for a couple of runners, it will be quiet at this time. At Centennial Brook, she sits on the boardwalk. She dangles her legs above the water and leans her forehead on the railing. She lets herself cry for a while. Blue dragonflies dart over the surface of the slow-moving water. Red-wing blackbirds flit through the reeds. Chickadees call to each other, all around her.

She has to talk to someone and unload a little, or her fears will leak all over the family, and that is the last thing she wants. Could she find a therapist for herself? It is so hard to find anybody who is really good and who is not in her professional network. Or perhaps she is only telling herself that to avoid what she needs to do. She certainly can't dump this all on anyone she works with.

She stands and walks on into the shade among the trees. Light plays through the leaves on the ground below. Squirrels run from her, dart up trees, and angrily *kuk-kuk* their alarm. She smiles a little. She stoops where a chipmunk disappeared into a hollow trunk.

She imagines herself meeting a new therapist, explaining all over again about the loveless, dysfunctional home she grew up in. She doesn't need any platitudes about that; she is well aware of her confusion about what she can or should expect from the man who loves her, if anything. She conjures the face of her therapist in Manhattan, during training. He was kind and wise. And he retired long ago.

Rehashing it all with someone new won't make a bit of difference. She kicks at a pebble. Right now, all she wants is for Lyman to get help. Whatever he says, she is alarmed by what she sees, and Rachel is concerned too. Eva has pleaded and tried to convince him. But if she keeps pushing, she will only drive him further away. It's maddening.

Eva's old friend Camila pops into her mind. They were colleagues when Eva was new on the faculty. Camila was her closest friend for many years; her daughter Isabella was the ring-bearer at her wedding. They wore bright matching campesino dresses, Eva recalls. Then, about a decade ago, Camila and her family moved to Arizona, and Eva wishes her friend were still nearby. Camila would understand, as no one else would.

She stops in her tracks; she has an idea. She'll shoot Camila an email. They'll find a time to talk soon. She is so relieved she practically runs the rest of the way. Yes, she will talk with Camila. And it won't compromise Lyman's privacy. Eva has no wish to undermine him in *anybody*'s eyes. She just needs a little support for herself, or else she might sink too.

She sends Camila an email before she goes to the department meeting. By the time she returns to her desk, there is a message. "Eva dearest, we haven't had a good, long talk in a couple of months. I want to hear what's troubling you. Tomorrow? Let's try that new thing, Skype, so I can see your face."

Eva gets home before anybody else; she makes herself iced tea and sips it in the rocker on the patio. She closes her eyes and listens to the chirps and twitters all around. The day is languorous and lovely. A lazy breeze stirs the grasses in the field. She remembers her first evening at the ramshackle little cottage. She had found an old Adirondack chair and dragged it to this very spot. It immediately felt like home. And then she and Lyman built their life here, and their family. They will—they must get through this.

After dinner, when the kitchen sparkles and the dishwasher purrs, Lyman takes a book to the couch. Gabriel lingers on the patio with Eva.

"So, Mom?" he starts.

"Yes?" she looks up.

"I think I will stick around Burlington for the year. The lab offered me an internship."

"How exciting. I'll have you around for a whole year?"

"Well, hold on. Let me explain. Shall I bring us a glass of wine first?"

"Sure, why not. That's worth celebrating."

He returns with the chilled white wine, finds a comfortable chair near her rocker. "So, the lab offered me a paid internship for one year. I get to expand on the project I started in June."

She turns to smile at him. "I knew it," she says, "I knew they'd love the way you work!"

He chuckles. "You don't count, Mom, you're biased!"

She can't deny that. "*Hmm*," she says, "I love this Chardonnay. Go on then?"

"If I take the job, that gives me plenty of time to apply to grad school, and the project will strengthen my application."

"Good point. You've decided on a PhD, then? Where?"

"I want to get into environmental policy. I want to *do* something with all that knowledge, you know? I found a dual master's program at George Washington in applied economics *and* environmental resource policy. What a combination, don't you think? It's about using economic data to design policies. Showing that policies that go against climate change also improve the 'bottom line.' That should get more folks on board than just because it's 'the right thing' to do."

"That sounds right up your alley, actually. Have you told Dad?"

"No, not yet. I want to run something else by you first." He examines the patio stones.

"Go ahead. What?" She studies him. Why is he so hesitant? Is something wrong?

"Well." He takes a breath and looks up. "Don't take this the wrong way, okay?"

"For God's sake, Gabe, come out with it. What?"

"Mom, I'm worried about Dad. He hasn't been himself. He seems, I don't know, angry? Faraway? Not enjoying us all milling around, that's for sure!" Gabe looks sad.

"Sweetie. Don't . . ."

"Let me finish. I'm also worried about you. I see you trying to keep things positive all the time. It doesn't help. You just look stressed and frazzled."

She stands and walks around a moment before she stops in front of him. Her voice catches. "I'm sorry, Gabe. You don't need to worry about *me*. I'm fine. It's just—Dad is going through a bit of a hard time."

"Yeah. Whatever you call it. But I don't want to leave you here on your own with Olivia, with all that tension in the air. It doesn't feel right. I'd rather stick around."

"Wait!" She sits and turns her chair toward him. "Wait, you need to do what's right for *you*. That does not involve hanging around at home because you are worried about *us*. That's just wrong."

"Too late," he says, "I've already decided. I declined the other job offer in Colorado. I'm staying in Burlington, but I won't be living at home."

She feels disoriented. *What is happening to us?* she wonders. *What happened to our happy, close-knit family?* She stares into the slowly darkening sky. "Of course. You deserve your space." She *would* love it if he lived at home, obviously, but . . .

"Mom, it's *Dad* who needs his space, more than me. I could go either way, really. But he can't handle the hullabaloo. Can't you see? And like I said, your efforts at smoothing it over aren't helping."

"Aren't you exaggerating?" she asks weakly. But she knows he is right. She rubs her forehead and tries to ward off a fresh onslaught of anguish.

He puts his glass down. "I found a small apartment close to the campus. Pretty affordable. Aviva will share it with me. We've talked to the landlord already."

"That's nice, sharing with Aviva. Does that mean the two of you are giving it a go?"

"Who knows? Not really. We'll be housemates. I trust her. She is a really good friend. And besides, she wants to spend a year around here for her own reasons." Eva gathers the napkins left on the table. It's getting buggy outside. Gabe gets up too.

"Aviva wants to spend lots of time outdoors after Dartmouth," he says, "and she wants to get back to her painting."

Eva remembers Aviva's striking artwork. "That's great. You'll be in Burlington for a year and have your own space." He nods and opens the door for her to go in.

"I don't even have to say this," she adds, "but we'll feed you any time you swing by. Is that a deal? Aviva, too, naturally."

He gives her a crooked smile. "I figured that! Besides, Olivia would skin me alive if I didn't spend enough time here, with her!"

"Okay then. But you're sure it is what you want? Not just fretting over the old folks?"

He hugs her. "Yep, I'm sure. Told you. That's what feels right." He finds his car keys, tells her he's going out and not to wait up for him.

She is both moved and shaken. "Have fun, sweetie!" she manages. "And thank you, for . . . well, for . . . you are so kind, and mature, and I love you so much, Gabriel. Thank you for being you."

He rolls his eyes, mocking her gently. She shuts the door behind him.

It's dark when she goes upstairs. Lyman is already in bed, reading. She slides under the covers and kisses his cheek. "I love you," she whispers.

He looks up briefly. "You too," he says. She snuggles next to him. At least he doesn't pull away.

She tosses and turns for half the night. Her mind is going in circles. Pretty soon, her arms and legs start twitching. Eventually, ants are burrowing under her skin. She gives up, goes downstairs, and pulls out the sheet music for Oscar Peterson's "Love Ballade." She plays through it slowly, very softly. Then she plays it again, more freely, dreamily. She tries to improvise on the simple chord sequence. A peaceful, repetitive motif emerges. When she gets sleepy, she goes back to bed. It is three in the morning. But at least it's a weekend, so there will be no need to get up early.

* * *

Eva jolts awake at the crack of dawn, when the front door slams shut. Someone stomps around in the kitchen; it must be Olivia. Lyman's side of the bed is already empty, but she doesn't hear his voice. She pulls on a robe and finds Olivia sobbing at the bar counter, slumped on a stool, head on her forearms. Eva approaches and hugs her daughter. Olivia leans in and wraps her arms around Eva's neck, holding on tight. Eva rocks her gently until Olivia has cried herself out and rests her head on her mother's shoulder. She sniffles and then finally goes quiet.

Eva pulls back a little, a hand on each side of Olivia's face. "What happened, baby?"

"I broke up with Carla, Mom . . ."

Eva sits next to her. "You did?"

"I had to. I couldn't take it anymore. Everything was always all about her! And if I didn't do what she wanted, there'd be a guilt trip or a tantrum . . ."

"You know, I didn't want to bring it up, but—"

Olivia turns away. "Yeah, I know. Gabriel went on and on about it too. So last night I blew up at her. And . . ." her voice breaks. "I've explained it to her so many times. Like a fool, I thought she'd—that she'd get it. That if I just said it the right way, she'd change."

"Oh, boy," Eva sighs, "it's really tempting to believe that your love can change a person, isn't it? And meanwhile, it looked like you were trying extra hard to accommodate."

"And who did I learn that from, Mom?" Olivia explodes and glares at her mother.

"Guilty as charged, I'm afraid." There is no use denying it. Eva wants to dig a hole and disappear. But she can't. She straightens and takes a breath.

"Coffee? Tea? Hot cocoa?" she asks.

"Hot cocoa. Thanks," Olivia sniffles, and goes to the CD player. "Can I put on the Ani DiFranco album?"

"Sure." Eva fills the kettle, mixes the cocoa powder with a little milk, and measures loose black tea for herself. "That reminds me. Did you go to that concert yet? How was it?"

Olivia sits at the counter and taps her foot to the music. "Not yet. That's next week. I got two tickets, but now I don't want to take Carla with me."

Lyman walks briskly into the living room. "Can you turn the bloody volume down on this *caterwauling*?" He doesn't wait for a response; he turns the power off on the stereo. Olivia moves into the kitchen nook and starts crying again. Eva puts a finger to her lips and signals for Lyman to go easy. He doesn't notice. He starts the coffee maker. "What's wrong with her?" he asks, grimly.

"Lyman, talk to her and ask. She's upset, can't you see?"

He's not in the mood. He stands waiting for the coffee. Eva walks to her daughter: "Sweetie, you were saying, about the concert?"

"What concert?" Lyman asks, his voice a notch gentler.

"Ani DiFranco. Next week," Olivia answers dully.

"Oh, that woman again?"

"Whatever, Dad!" she cries out and runs upstairs.

"What's gotten into you?" Eva hisses at Lyman. She pours hot water over her tea, fills the mug of cocoa, and adds a lump of sugar. She grabs a teaspoon and goes up to Olivia's room. She knocks before entering. Her daughter has headphones on. She accepts the mug and nods her thanks. Eva plants a kiss on her forehead and leaves. Best give the girl some time.

In the kitchen, she takes out the tea egg and pours some milk. She leaves the carton next to the coffee maker and wheels on Lyman. "I am sick and tired of this, Lyman! I have all the sympathy in the world for the tough time you're going through. But *you—will—not—take—it—out—on—my—children*! Do you hear me!?"

"Don't shout," he growls.

"Listen carefully. *I want you to see Dr. Grant soon.* And if he is away, then you can see whoever is covering for him." No response. "Do it for your children, Lyman, if you won't do it for yourself, or for us. But I will not stand by and let you hurt them. I hope that's clear."

He does not answer. A cloak of sadness hangs over him. She wraps her arms around his waist and looks up into his face. "Please tell me you'll go?"

"I will go if you insist. But I won't go back on any medication. Got it?"

She sighs and takes her tea to the armchair by the living room window. "I hope you didn't mean what you said in Rachel's office?" she asks.

"What did I say?"

"Let me ask again: if it turns out that your depression has relapsed . . . well, I hope it hasn't, but *if* it has, would you rather let it destroy our family, and our marriage, than restart treatment?" She waits, her head down.

He stirs milk into his coffee and walks toward his office. Over his shoulder, he says, "You heard what I told you."

Eva slumps in the armchair. Ezra finds her there a moment later, on his way to the kitchen. "Mom?" he stops to look at her. "Are you okay?"

She shrugs. He takes two mugs out and pours coffee into both. "You and Dad did not *sound* okay just now."

"It will pass," she says, still staring out. "Any plans today?"

Ezra puts one mug on the side table by the other armchair. He carries the second mug toward the stairs. "Be right back, I'll just bring Vicky her coffee. Don't leave."

Eva hears muffled voices, then Ezra's door closes again. He comes back, sits opposite Eva, and leans toward her, both hands around his mug, elbows on his knees. "Are you going to tell me?" he prompts.

Eva looks up. Her eyes water. Her emotions must be all over her face, as usual. "How does Dad seem to you?" she asks, stalling.

He tries a sip, but the coffee is too hot. He sits back. "Well, not good, obviously. Everything seems to bother him. Or everybody. He won't go for a hike. I don't know how many times I've asked him. I can't even talk him into shooting baskets." He hesitates, his eyes fixed on her. "So? What is that all about, Mom? Why are you fighting? Are you getting a divorce?"

"Ezra! Oh my god, no. That is *not* what's going on . . ."

"Well then, what is it, Mom? I was so excited about a summer at home, about Vicky sharing it with us . . ." He looks troubled. He trails off and tries the coffee again.

Then all three of them have noticed, she thinks. Whatever normalcy and buoyancy she tried to preserve, she has failed. A hot wave of anger floods her. She stands and says "*Shh*," pointing toward the office. "Why don't you come outside, Ezra. Bring your coffee." He nods and follows her. They walk toward the edge of the field.

"You knew that Dad had been depressed before, right?"

"Yeah. I vaguely remember that, but he's been fine since—well, for a long time. Hasn't he?"

"Yes, for years. He did therapy, and he went on medication."

"I think I knew that, sort of."

"His own father had depression too. And his grandmother," Eva adds.

"You mean it's in the family?"

"Yes, so it seems." She wonders whether he will worry about himself, too, now. She files that for another time. "It turns out he thought he didn't need treatment anymore. So, he stopped, in late April . . ."

Ezra turns to her, aghast. "Like just before we all came home?"

"Yes."

"That's rich. Thanks, Dad!" He walks a few paces, calms himself before facing her again. "Sorry. Go on. Is that why it's getting worse and worse?"

"Do you think it is? Getting worse, I mean?"

"Well, don't you?" he asks.

"Let's walk a little further into the field," she suggests.

He looks down at his flip-flops and at her slippers. "Why not?"

She bends to pick a sprig of evening primrose. She might as well tell him the rest; Ezra always picks up on more than he lets on. "So, I insisted we go see his old therapist together. Last week. Because I am worried."

"Good move. And?"

"And he didn't show up. Not the first time. Yesterday, he did come." She glances his way. "But he refuses to go back on Prozac, and he probably won't go back to talk with his therapist either. Now you know. He agreed for us to check in with the therapist again in September, but that's it."

"Oh, Mom. I'm sorry." He fidgets. He looks at her. "You know . . ." he hesitates. He paces. He looks away.

"What?"

"Vicky feels like she's in the way. All that tension, and it's not *her* family, you know?"

"Ezra, honey, she is *so* not in the way. You know that, right? She is more than welcome here! I simply love having her around. Please tell her?"

"I realize that. And she does too. But Dad's moods—she doesn't know what to do with herself when they happen." The ground shifts under Eva's feet. Everything is crumbling. "One of my old friends is spending the summer at his parents' house, by himself. To take care of their dog." She picks another primrose and turns toward the house so he can't see her face. "We can stay with him for a couple of weeks and give Dad a break," he says.

"I understand," she says very carefully, when she *can* speak. "I hate it, but I get it. I hope you'll come for dinner often?" Her anger quickly gives way to tears. Lyman's foolish decision is hurting all of her babies, and now it is costing her this precious time with them.

Ezra puts an arm around her and pulls her closer. "Of course, we'll come often. And I'll be here lickety-split any time you need me, or even if you just think you *might* need me. For *any* reason."

She steps out of his hug. "Thanks," she says hoarsely. "You're the best. All of you." She hurries toward the house. "Let's go in, I need a shower. Breakfast in a bit?" He nods.

Eva walks upstairs; halfway up, she remembers the call with Camila. Dang, that was half an hour ago! She lunges for her phone by the bed and texts. "Camila, dearest, I am so sorry. Stormy weather here. Can we reschedule? A little later today?" She gets ready to shower. Her phone pings almost immediately. "Of course, darling. Text when you come up for air. I'm around."

In the shower, Eva wonders how she will tell Camila about all this. She lets the water run for a long time, washes her hair, and massages her scalp.

She slips into a comfortable, no-fuss summer dress. She knocks at Olivia's door. No answer. Of course, those headsets . . . She gently opens the door and mouths *Breakfast?* Olivia nods and gets up.

She knocks at Ezra's door too. "Coming down?" she asks.

Vicky answers. "Be right there, Eva."

She knocks at the office door. "Lyman? Breakfast if you want to join?" she says. She doesn't wait for his response.

She pads into the kitchen barefoot, but she has no energy to make a production out of another meal. She pulls out cereal and granola. She sets milk, yogurt, and leftover fruit salad on the counter. There: self-service breakfast. They all know where to find bowls and silverware. She scans the spread one more time, then sets a fresh loaf of oatmeal bread next to the toaster, with butter and jam.

She is too restless to hang around. What she needs, right now, is enough privacy to talk with Camila. She'll have to go to the office for that; her family can fend for themselves. She scribbles a note. "Gone to the hospital. Back soon." She grabs a slice of bread, slathers plum preserves on it. At the front door, she slips into her Tevas, grabs her car keys and her pocketbook, balances the bread in her other hand, and heads out to her car. She texts Camila. "Half an hour?"

The answer comes immediately. "Yes!"

The psychiatry wing of the hospital is nearly empty. The residents' room is ajar; someone is on the phone. She walks past, fumbles with her key, enters her office, and locks the door behind her. She sinks into her chair. What a relief. She reminds herself not to flood her friend with everything all at once. She starts her computer and opens Skype, but it won't load. She dials Camila's phone number.

"There you are!" says Camila on the second ring.

"So glad to hear your voice," says Eva, "and thanks for making the time! How are you? And—"

Camila cuts her off. "If you think I'm willing to chit-chat and to tell you all about Isabella before I hear what's up with you, then you've forgotten who I am!"

"*Uhhh* . . ."

"Come out with it. Yesterday, you wrote you're a mess. That's not like you. What's going on?"

"I'm not sure where to begin. It's about Lyman. When did you see him last?"

"Let me think. Five years? The summer we visited you in Vermont?"

"That sounds about right. How did he seem to you then?"

"Gosh, you're making me nervous, Eva. Did something happen to him?"

"Not exactly *to* him. I'll get to it. But first, please tell me how he seemed to you then?"

"Well, let's see . . . he was excited about our visit, and he cooked fantastic meals on that grill. He pulled out all his maps to help us plan our camping trip. And he showed Isabella all about—what was it?—the right and the wrong kinds of milkweed to attract monarchs?"

"Oh, yes, now that you mention it. What else?"

"I remember the night Gabriel asked him which colleges have good programs in environmental studies. I remember them laughing together. The rest of us were playing bocce."

"Ha, I don't remember that. But you know, a few months later, Lyman took Gabe on a ski trip to Colorado, to check out the campus in Boulder." Eva ponders. "Did he seem depressed to you, or dark in any way, back then?"

"What? No, of course not. But don't I remember something from years ago? He did have a bout of depression way back, right?"

Eva is grateful her friend remembers. She wipes her eyes before she continues. "Yes, he did. You had left for Arizona by then, so you probably never *saw* it. Anyway, he agreed to treatment once he realized it was upsetting the kids. And, Camila? You and I know what treatment can do, but I tell you, it was a miracle. Not instantly, but once it took hold. He started Prozac, and he came to grips with lots of old stuff. He worked hard at it. It brought us closer too."

Camila is silent for a moment. "Right. It sure can do that. Go on?"

"We've had ten wonderful years since. Of course, we had issues sometimes, like everybody else. But he was *so* present, so engaged whenever we needed to address something. He listened, and he offered creative solutions. You know?"

"I remember how warm and close you and Lyman seemed to be during our visit. I admit I got jealous for about thirty seconds when I saw you two steal a kiss by the barbecue grill!" Camila laughs a little, then quickly sobers. "But what the hell, Eva, will you finally tell me?"

"Yes, I'm sorry." Eva swallows. "I needed to hear whether I made up all those good times, before telling you the rest. Thanks." She sniffles and reaches for a tissue.

"You did not make it up. Go on . . ."

"He stopped his meds. In late April." She starts crying.

"Honey, people do," says Camila in a soothing tone, "as you well know. Sometimes their instinct is right on target too. My patients often know it before I do. That they have healed, and they can come off. So, did he taper slowly, or . . ."

Through hiccups, in bits and pieces, Eva tells the rest about Lyman's unplanned, abrupt stopping. She blows her nose. "And the only reason I even found out was because he didn't seem right. I pushed him about what was going on, and then he told me."

"Oh, dear. Weren't the boys planning to visit this summer?"

"That's part of the problem. Everybody is here. It's a busy family. And now Olivia is mad at me. And Gabe decided he has to stick around home because he's worried. And he's *renting an apartment* to be out of the way!"

"He's *that* worried?"

"Yes, and on top of that, Ezra and Vicky—you know about his girlfriend, right? They have a concert in late August; they were going to be with us until then. But they're moving out too; they found friends to stay with. It got awkward for Vicky, being around us." Eva is hoarse suddenly. "There goes our precious family time, all of us together!"

"That's . . . Oh, Eva, I'm so sorry. Have you talked to him? Would he listen?"

Eva fills Camila in on the session with Rachel and on Lyman's hardening position. “He claims he is not himself on Prozac, too flat. Or too happy. That he needs to be the real Lyman, and that is *not* the cheerful happy guy . . .”

“I see,” says Camila. “Will he go back to Rachel?”

“No. He won’t. He said—I can’t believe this—that I could take it or leave it, but he won’t. And he will absolutely not take meds again.”

There is a silence before Camila speaks. “Eva, listen. We see people sink into depression in our clinics all the time. They come to us for help because they *want* to get better. But once in a while, I see someone get so lost inside their feelings that they stop caring about others, or about what this does to the people who love them. Is that what you’re telling me?”

“That’s it exactly. He wants us to leave him alone. He says this dark person is his true self, whether we like it or not.”

“Do you want to hear what I think?”

“Of course I do! What?”

“That kind of depression, Eva? When they buy into it as their *true self*? You know what I mean?” Eva does. “You know, self-absorbed? Isolated, irrational, and stuck? It’s not a good sign, is it?”

Eva sits bolt upright. “What do you mean? Suicide? No, no, it’s not—it *couldn’t* be that bad.” It has not even occurred to her. Or did she block it out?

“I’m sorry, Eva. But yes, I mean it’s possible. I’m not saying that’s where he is at. How would I know . . . I’m only reminding you that you need to ask, because he wouldn’t come out and tell you, would he?”

“Oh my god!” Eva sobs. She blows her nose again. “I didn’t *want* to think about it, Camila,” she whispers. “I stuffed that right down when it tugged at me. But you’re right. And that risk is higher if they stop suddenly, right? And nobody is monitoring him! Oh Camila, it *is* freaking me out, no matter what he says. But then I tell myself he would never do that to the kids . . .”

“It is the hardest thing,” says Camila, “wanting to help someone you love, when he doesn’t want your help, isn’t it?”

“Yes . . .”

“You’re kind of stuck, it seems to me. It’s not bad enough to call 911, and you can’t *make* him see someone.”

"Right! He can look okay, go to work, and sit through a short bit of family time." She tells Camila her dread of another scenario, in which he gets no better, and not much worse, and goes on like this for a long time. She sniffles. "You and I know what depression costs people in the long run. It is a miserable way of aging, with life shrinking down."

"I hear you," Camila sighs. "But he'll never believe you, will he?"

Eva leans her head on one hand. "It wasn't like that ten years ago. He *wanted* to be better then. I'm *trying* to see it his way. But I don't understand . . ." she trails off.

"And now I've added one more layer to your worry. I'm sorry, Eva. You called me for support, and I made it worse."

"I needed the reality check. You really understand this stuff. Thanks, Camila." She dabs at her eyes. It's time to wrap it up. She has a lot of thinking to do.

The van and the Saab are not in the driveway when she gets home. Nobody is in the kitchen. A few bowls and spoons are stacked in the sink. She sees Lyman and Gabriel on the patio, each holding a mug. Their voices are barely audible through the open window. It's nice to see them in conversation; Lyman seems engaged.

Later, Eva takes a seltzer outside and finds Gabriel lounging in the hammock. "It was nice seeing you and Dad talking out there, earlier," she says.

"Yeah." Gabriel swings his legs down. "I ran my graduate school thoughts by him, and he was actually positive. Well, quietly positive. He had some good points to make, but he thought it was a good plan."

"I'm glad. Did he seem like—well—like his normal self?"

"I wouldn't quite say *that*. He was patient, and he was not angry. But he looks so *burdened*. None of his—his spark, you know . . ."

"I know," she sighs. She notices a weed between two patio tiles.

"So, I decided to ask him about it. About his mood. I asked whether something was going on."

"You did?" Gabe has always cared deeply; he and Lyman do have a special bond. "How did that go?" She studies his face. She moves to a recliner, and Gabe sits next to her.

"He actually told me about going off medication. I didn't ask, he just told me. He said he couldn't stand it anymore. He said something about side effects." His eyebrow is a question mark.

Eva nods. She sips her seltzer. "And?"

"I told him I've been worried about him lately. That he seems unhappy. I asked whether that's not worse than side effects."

"Wow, you said that? And then?"

"He said he was fine. He can handle it. And then . . . Mom . . ." Gabe looks pained.

"*What*?" she asks more abruptly than she means to.

"He said life isn't worth living if he has to be on medication all the time. I must have looked alarmed, because he held up his hand. He kind of smiled and said it was okay, that he just needed to figure out another way."

Eva tracks a trail of ants marching from the table toward the grass. She shakes her head. "There *are* other ways," she says. "But if he's found them, they're not working."

Gabriel touches her arm. "Yeah. I don't like how he sounds. Good thing I'll be around. Maybe he'll talk to me. Maybe I can help him, you know?"

"Thank you, Gabe, it is good of you to . . . but this is a burden you shouldn't have to carry."

"*Mom*! It's not a burden. He's my dad."

"Yes, of course." She considers. "You know, you have some of that quiet temperament of his. You could be right. He might talk to you more than to me. And maybe, seeing how you love him, and that you can tell what's going on . . . it just might persuade him to get help." She certainly hopes so.

"We'll see." Gabe stands up. "Got to go. I'm off to see Aviva. Can we come for dinner?"

"*Can* you? Of course! What time? Seven?"

"Sure."

She calls after him. "Gabe? Can you bring some salad stuff from the farm stand? We're almost out."

He gives her a thumbs-up through the open car window.

A few minutes before seven, the old Corolla crunches up the driveway. Olivia, Ezra, and Vicky are out with friends. Lyman is in the kitchen concocting an elaborate paella dish. Aviva cheerfully greets him and inhales the aroma of mussels and fish and . . . "Do I smell saffron, Lyman?"

"Yep," he smiles.

"Paella is one of my favorite foods, ever," she gushes.

Over dinner, Aviva shares her plans for the year, of spending it outdoors to get her head back into painting. They chat about skiing for a while.

"No better place than the mountains to get your head together," Lyman says.

"I remember the portraits you did in your Frida Kahlo phase," says Eva. "Powerful . . ."

"I framed that weird one that you did of me back then," Gabe says. "I took it to Colorado. I still have it."

"You do?" Aviva is surprised. "That wasn't exactly my best, you know . . ." She tells them about trying to paint snow and trying to catch all the subtle shades of color in it.

Gabe turns to Lyman. "So, Dad, Aviva and I are planning on a lot of backcountry skiing this winter." Lyman nods. "Why don't you join us? You and Mom. Like old times. Wouldn't that be great?"

Lyman goes rigid. "Nah, I'm too old," he says. He gets up and collects the plates. "I'm tired, folks. Going in."

"Already?" Gabe protests.

"Like I said, getting old." He walks away.

Eva follows him with the silverware and the salad bowl. "Be right back," she tells Gabriel and Aviva over her shoulder. "Don't go anywhere."

At the kitchen sink, she puts a hand on Lyman's back. "Are you okay?" she asks. "You got up so suddenly. Won't you stay for dessert?"

He shakes his head. "I'm fine. I'm tired, and I really don't have more to say."

She touches his shoulder. "See you upstairs then."

She brings out a fresh fruit tart. They talk for a while longer. After a while, Aviva touches Gabe's shoulder. "I ought to go home," she says. "Can you drive me?"

"Sure. Let's go."

"You two managed to pull Dad out of his shell a little tonight," Eva says as they leave. "Thank you."

Eva finds Lyman reading in bed, slides in next to him, and moves his nearest arm so she can nestle her head on his shoulder. His wrist and hand flop onto her pillow. She rolls on her side, puts her arm around his waist, and drapes a leg over his.

"Hi . . ." she says.

He rests his book face down onto his chest, open to the page he was reading. "Hi."

"Thanks for an amazing dinner, love," she says.

"*Hmm*. Sure."

Stars sparkle in the clear night sky; the moon is just coming up over the trees. "It was so nice to have you involved in the conversation, you know?" she says.

"Yeah," he shrugs.

She still has her arm over him and gently taps his chest. "And—well . . ."

"What?" he turns slightly toward her.

"Well, it's hard to explain, but it feels so—normal?—when you engage. No, *blessed* really. I get all knotted up when you withdraw . . ."

"Let's not go there again. I've told you, I can't always be chipper. Can you just let it be . . ."

She sighs, strokes his neck, and snuggles more deeply into the crook of his arm. "Do you have any idea . . ." Tears run onto his chest.

He looks at her with surprise. "It can't be *that* hard on you? When I'm a little somber?"

She pushes herself up on her elbow and looks at him. How can he not understand this, how it feels for others? It's not just "a little somber." It is so much more dense than that. How can he not see, that like a seagull caught in an oil slick, she cannot breathe under his dark moods, let alone fly?

"Yes, Lyman," she says simply. "It is. It feels like I'm . . ." She pauses, unsure how to convey that deeply lost feeling.

He nods uncertainly and stares off.

"Lyman?"

"*Hmm*?"

"You're in the very center of my life. But lately, it's been like watching you drown. I'm not strong enough to swim both of us to safety. I can't. We would both sink."

He reaches to turn the lamp off by the bed. "I didn't ask you to rescue me, did I?" he says flatly. "You've always tried to fix everything for everybody, Eva. Has it occurred to you that I might be tired of *that*?"

"But . . ." she begins and then stops herself.

"I'm sorry that it's so hard for you," he adds more gently.

"So, do you . . ." She almost asks him, again, whether he will do something about it. But she thinks better of it and kisses his cheek. "I love you, Lyman," she says. She rolls over to turn her own light off.

The moon faintly illuminates the room.

"Wouldn't you rather be on your own?" he asks out of the blue, without turning her way.

She bolts upright. They look at each other in the dim light. "Lyman, *no*. For heaven's sake, of course not." She sits cross-legged on the bed, her head in her hands.

She tries one more time. "No. But since June, I have been watching you unravel. And it terrifies me. It totally terrifies me, Lyman."

He clips his words. "I'm not unraveling, Eva—" She stifles a sob. He sits up. He swings his legs off the bed. "Eva, I'm sorry you were so—whatever it is—worried." He stands. "But I cannot handle you being so dramatic. I just need to do this my way. Your being anxious is *not* helping me . . ." *Gabe has told me something like that, too*, she thinks. He walks toward the bathroom. "And I'm sorry I am not meeting your expectations at the moment. Can we please get some sleep?" He slams the door shut.

How did this go so wrong? she wonders. Why couldn't she just end the evening on a positive note?

In the morning, Eva is up before anyone else stirs. She makes a cup of tea and sits on the window seat in the kitchen nook. All the windows are wide open. She leans her head back and breathes in the summer air. Everything smells wonderfully fresh. Drops sparkle on a leaf here and there, and the tall grasses in the field seem greener than yesterday. Was there a rain shower during the night?

She broods over last night. A gentle breeze ruffles her hair, like a consoling hand. How defensive she made him. He actually said, "Sorry I'm not living up to your expectations." She had only wanted to tell him how precious he is to her, how lovely it is when he emerges and engages the way he used to. And now he claims that being himself is something different. It's bewildering. Who is the real Lyman?

She always loved his introspective self too. She stares into her mug, at the lovely amber color of Assam tea. She did, didn't she? Or . . . deep down, did she secretly reject his full, true, complicated self? She is all knotted up with doubts. And yet she has a gut feeling that he is *not* himself these days. That he is lost in a darkness that *keeps* him from himself. He is so touchy, so ready to misinterpret her words, and she should be more careful.

The birds are busy outside. She imagines they love the rain-washed morning. Her eyes are blurry suddenly; she hadn't felt those tears coming. Too many tears, lately. She blinks and gets up to find a pencil on the counter and a piece of paper. She needs to organize her thoughts. She sits on a stool and draws three columns. She erases them and starts again, holding the paper the other way. Four columns. A double line separates the first two from the next.

Above the first, she writes in block print: *WHAT I SEE.*

Above the second column: *My assumptions and my fears.*

Third column: *WHAT LYMAN SAYS HE FEELS.*

Fourth: *What Lyman says he needs.*

She stares at the first column, writes *withdrawn*, then *irritable*. Then *shut down*. She erases that last. Too loaded, even if it's how it feels to her.

Disorganized images and memories crowd her mind, of being a child surrounded by unresponsive faces; told to hush, not to make a fuss. Her heart is in her throat. She gets restless. It's obvious what's in the second column. She is scared of becoming as invisible to her husband as she was in childhood.

She stands. In the third column, what should she write? She cannot know what he feels. He *says* it's just a dip. That he can handle it. Why is it so hard to believe him?

She walks back to the window. Is she truly afraid for him? Or is she being a needy partner? She hiccups a little sob. *Get a grip*, she tells herself. *Try to think. Check your assumptions, Eva, be a grownup!* She returns to the list. Is this really about him? Or is it about herself? She hates the messiness. That it is some of each. Why can't things be black and white just this once?

She looks at the fourth column. What does Lyman say he needs? She taps her teeth with the eraser end of the pencil. She writes *Space*. Has he also asked for support? To be heard? She sighs and puts the pencil away. He hasn't. If only he would accept support, let alone ask for it once in a while! But he has always preferred to hurt alone. *Damn* his need for space.

This isn't getting her anywhere. She crumples the paper, drops it on the table, and picks up her mug to go outside; then she turns around to grab the crumpled page again. She rummages through kitchen drawers until she finds matches. Once outside, she burns the paper and lets the ashes float on the breeze. She takes her mug and walks slowly toward the field. This field has been her place of belonging for all these many years. She tells herself, again and again, *Stop assuming the worst, Eva. Have a little faith.* Another voice answers, *And what if you're right to be alarmed?* And then *what would it mean to give him space?*

She walks toward the edge of the field where the woods begin, to the huge northern red oak with its sturdy, low-hanging branches. The kids loved climbing that tree. Before that, she and Lyman sometimes took a glass of wine out here at dusk. Spilling only half of her tea, she hoists herself onto their favorite branch, the biggest one. She remembers how he used to sit in the crook of this branch, leaning against the trunk. How it felt, sitting in front of him, leaning back against his chest. They could be silent together, with the songs of birds and the whisper of tall grasses.

They were so close then; their silence was filled with love. That kind of silence was a precious gift from nature, shared, and safe. It felt both grounded and joyful. There was a current running between them, and it needed no words. A look across the room; a shared task; an unspoken choreography. Is it still there, that connection? Could she still feel it if she sat still long enough and tuned into it?

She stretches herself out along the branch. Dangles the empty mug. *So, what got into me?* she wonders. It is not the first time Lyman has been withdrawn, working through something. She has never grasped *how* he did it, but he came through in his own way. So why would it *not* be true this time? Perhaps Camila was onto something when she said people often have an instinct when it's time to come off medication. A sense of being healed enough to stop.

She jumps off the branch. She might as well give him the space he asks for. *Well, old girl,* she tells herself, *you sure haven't helped so far, what do you have to lose?*

She finds Lyman brewing coffee in the kitchen. She walks up, ducks under his free arm, and hugs him. She stands on tiptoes to kiss his cheek.

"Lyman . . ."

"*Oh-oh*, now what?" he says, not exactly joking.

"I made a decision."

"What about?"

"It's just dawned on me—Well, I love you so much, and yet my worry must be boxing you in. And I'm sorry."

He puts the coffee filter in the sink. He glances at her and turns toward the refrigerator. "But?" he asks, taking out the milk. He sits on another bar stool. He holds his mug in both hands, inhaling his coffee's aroma.

"I realize that I don't have to understand *how* you pull through things, I just have to let you do it."

"That's progress," he says. He stands and walks to the window.

"Do you have any notion of . . . You asked for space. Do you know how much space?"

"I don't know," he sounds impatient already.

She looks at her hands, hesitates, and joins him by the window. "Bear with me, I have to ask. Don't shrug this off, it's a real question, and I need a real answer."

He turns his head to look at her. He has that tense expression he gets, of preparing for something he won't like to hear.

"Do you . . ." My, this is hard for her to say. "Did you . . ."

"Did I what?"

"Are you tired of—our life? Do you want out? Is that—?"

It takes him a moment. He shakes his head and turns back toward the window, sipping his coffee. "No."

She breathes out. "I just had to ask you straight out. Because if *that*'s—"

"Beats me, why you would want me to stick around," he mumbles. He takes out cereal, a bowl.

There is no use answering that. She shrugs. "Well then, keep me posted. And I'm here, any time you want to talk."

"Nothing to talk about. But yeah . . . sure." He pours milk into his cereal.

"Meanwhile," she says, "I will try to fret less." *All I can do is try*, she thinks.

Chapter 14
August 2004

They're having one of their "typical, happy" family nights. Lyman is quiet. All the young people are cheerful. Everyone helps. Plates are filled, bottles are taken out of the cooler, and wine is poured. Eva hardly listens to the conversations around her; she enjoys the smiles, the teasing, and the animated talk. Aviva and Vicky lean across the table, deep in discussion. They have trouble hearing each other above the general din; Aviva moves her chair closer. Ezra explains something to Lyman, who doesn't look at him. Gabriel turns toward Olivia. Eva hears her ask something about Boulder. His face lights up; Olivia is riveted.

When Ezra calls out, "Dessert, anyone?" the dinner plates disappear, and small plates and dessert forks materialize.

"I haven't had gooseberry pie in ages," Eva says. She tastes it with her finger. "It's delicious, not too sweet! Lyman, try some?"

They all know he doesn't have a sweet tooth. He declines. After a moment, he stands. "Going in," he says. "G'night, everyone."

There is a chorus of *good nights*, and then they fall silent. It is Ezra who speaks up.

"He sure was quiet again tonight," he says.

Olivia shrugs. "At least he wasn't irritable."

Gabe frowns at her, then turns to Eva. "Seriously, how do you think he *is* doing, Mom? I'm worried. Should we let him be, or do we need to try harder to draw him out?"

She is not sure. Not at all. "I wish I knew, Gabe. He is working through some stuff, but he says he's fine."

"Do you know *what* he's working through?" Olivia asks.

"I honestly can't say," Eva says. "I have no real answers. So why don't you just do what feels right, in your own way?" A thought occurs, and she turns to Ezra. "Have you played chess with him since you got back? I bet he'd love that."

"That's an idea," says Ezra.

He glances at Vicky. "Go ahead," she waves him on. "We don't need you to clean up, we have too many hands already."

Ezra bounds inside. "Dad? *Dad!*" he calls.

Soon, he is outside again with a puzzled frown, shoulders slumped. "He looked like a thundercloud, and he said *maybe another time*. It's, I don't know, it's getting scary. I just can't reach him." He sits next to Vicky; she nods and rubs his neck.

The next few days bring rain, and the air is full of heavy dampness. Dinners move inside. In the closer space, conversation is more subdued. Lyman, at the table, offers a comment here and there. No loud music is played. There are no irritable outbursts. Nobody protests when Lyman excuses himself as soon as a meal is over. Eva does not ask him whether something is bothering him. She does not hover—at least not visibly. She gives him space. She offers gentle affection and wishes him good night.

One evening, she snuggles up to him when she comes to bed. She lays her head on his shoulder; his outstretched arm holds her for a little while. Her bedside lamp is still lit. The window is open to the wet sounds outside. *Drip-drip*. Birds sing here and there. She pictures them shaking their feathers. Downstairs, there is laughter. She kisses his neck lightly, strokes his shoulder, his chest. There is a little spark of hope in her heart, a small, excited little spark. Her hand strokes his belly, still muscular, still lean. Her fingers play with the graying hair that runs from his neck, down, all the way down. She fondles him, tentatively at first. There is a small, encouraging response to her fingers. She strokes him more deliberately. "*Hmmm*," she murmurs into his neck.

He takes her hand, lifts it, and moves it aside. He simply moves it aside, away from him. She looks up, startled. He pulls his arm from under her head and rolls toward his side of the bed. "Good night," he says.

They have always responded honestly to each other's overtures. They have, she thought, an agreement about this. If one of them reaches out, and the other is not in the mood for sex, they hold each other for a while instead. They replace sex with affection. But this? Nothing? This has never happened.

"Good night, then." She turns her light off, lies on her back, and stares at the ceiling.

She sighs, finds a book light on her bedside table, and picks up the novel she started. She has recently discovered Dorothy Baker's classic, *Young Man with a Horn*. She slowly lets herself get lost in the story of a talented young man to whom music was everything. But the music world is a hard life. She thinks about Ezra. She reads until she is sleepy enough to turn her light off.

Within the week, Ezra and Vicky have moved into their friend's house. Their van leaves a large empty space in the driveway, and a matching emptiness in Eva's heart. Ezra's room has no amplifier crowding the carpet. There is no funky-shaped case for Vicky's bass. The space is colorless without Ezra's sparkling emerald-green saxophone case. The bed is carefully made, Vicky's work, surely not Ezra's. The door is ajar, and each time Eva walks by, the emptiness stares at her, like a black hole.

On the way to her room, she pauses at Gabe's closed door. Soon, he will be gone too. He and Aviva have signed a lease on the apartment in town and started moving some things there, bit by bit. Soon, another room will be tidied up, another door left ajar, and another bed made to remind her of the summer she had imagined—the summer that will not be. Of course, Olivia is still here, but not for much longer. Eva already dreads the empty nest. *Let them go . . . let them go . . . let them go . . .* She daydreams, weirdly and often, of dry milkweed stalks. Dried out and empty. Gone are the leaves. Gone are the bright green cocoons, gone are the monarchs. The seeds have blown away, like her children, to their own destinies. Or been eaten by birds . . . Only some white fluff spills out of the dry seed pods—white as her own hair will be, soon enough, until there is nothing left but stalks, turning to dust.

For the umpteenth time, she reminds herself to get a grip.

She shakes herself, looks at her watch. Six o'clock. Olivia is not home yet, and it's likely that Lyman will be late, again. She runs downstairs. There are probably leftovers; they can fend for themselves. She needs to get outside. She leaves a note on the counter, in large block print: *WENT OUT. DON'T WAIT.*

She drives off. Without planning it, she finds herself at the trail where Lyman took her on their first date. The hidden trail toward the river. They sat there in moonlight, didn't they, watching the gathering of birds. She follows the path, remembering. Early fall, it was. They sat there a long time, until dark. He had put his arm around her when she got cold, and wrapped her in his jacket . . .

Near the riverbank, she battles through the overgrown grasses and a patch of thorny blackberries. She gazes out toward the nests in the muddy bank opposite, remembering—what did he call those flocks gathering for migration? Ah yes, a *sussuration.* No, that wasn't it. *Hmm.* A *murmuration*! That was it. How lovely.

And now . . . she feels desolate, alone on that rock. She buries her face in her arms and cries until she is empty of tears, and her grief floats out like mist on the slow-moving river. Images of her future well up. Of her and Lyman, aging together, in immutable heavy silence. *No, not golden years*, she thinks. Instead, gray empty space. She feels cold dread at the prospect. Lonely. No children to care for. Nobody she matters to. Nobody she can love with abandon.

A few clouds travel past. The early evening light is uninspiring tonight. The air is silent. Heavy, like her increasingly quiet husband, focused on what is no more. An old fart, he said a few days ago. "I can't keep up anymore, skiing with you," he told Gabe. So he won't go out at all. *What about the rest of us? Can't you at least make an effort, Lyman?* She flings a handful of mud and pebbles into the river. He doesn't even like sex anymore. She flushes with shame and anger at his rejection the other night. How he moved her hand away, turned his back, and said good night. And went to sleep. She stares into the water, not seeing anything at all.

A small fish breaks the surface with a tiny splash. She lifts her head and tries to breathe. Swallows dart across the water's surface. A pair of coots meanders among the eelgrass, with a few little ones trailing behind. How amazing that these birds mate for life. How do they do it? Do they have marital fights? Do they work it out? Do they still enjoy each other's company? Or do they just build one nest after another, year after year, with more fledglings to take care of?

Slowly, she calms down and follows the heavy flight of a heron until it sails down onto a rock.

She sighs. Lyman asked for space. He doesn't want her care. On top of that, he recoils when she herself needs more connection. She can only stand by and get out of the way. Just as she had feared, it's like her childhood, all over again.

Dammit, she *will* get out of his way then, and take care of herself.

It's getting dark. She turns to make her way through the shrub, back to her car. Back home to face the silence. A wave of rage surprises her. She picks up a stick and swings it at a young birch. *Damn it, Lyman, damn you. You're abandoning me! Whack*, she swings the stick at an alder. A small branch yields, then whips back into her face. Furious, she whacks at it again. *Whack*!

The wave of anger crashes her onto the rocky shore of old history. Bruised and drained, she walks on. Sometimes, she simply hates herself.

Since Gabe and Ezra have moved into town, Eva often plans a dinner out with everyone. Tonight, they are in the beer garden, in back of the Farmhouse Grill. They push two outside tables together. Orders are sorted out. Ezra requests samples of various microbrewery beers. They comment on their favorites. Ginger beer? Blueberry? Dark ale?

"How about us all going backpacking for a weekend?" Ezra proposes. "Before Vicky and I return to New York. Just like in the old days?"

"Yes!" Vicky echoes. "That would be a great way to end our summer."

"A perfect beginning to my year outdoors," Aviva chimes in.

"Wow, that would be fun," says Gabe. He turns to his sister. "Livvie? Can you keep up with us?"

"Can *you* keep up with me, you mean? Yeah, dude!" She thumbs her nose at him.

"Mom, you and Dad will join us, right?" Gabriel asks.

"Join what?" comes Lyman's voice. He has just arrived.

"You're here!" Eva waves. "I'm glad, I was starting to think we wouldn't see you tonight. We're almost ready for desserts, but the burgers here are excellent."

"I ordered take-out. I can't stay. So, what did I hear about Mom and Dad coming? To what?"

Ezra explains his backpacking idea.

"Come on, please . . ." Olivia cajoles.

"I'll pass, thank you." Lyman shakes his head. "Sounds like a good thing for all you young people, though." His name is called. He turns toward the voice. "I guess my order is ready. I'm off, see you all later." And he is gone.

Ezra looks at Gabriel, who shrugs. "Can't get him interested in much, can we?"

Olivia turns to Eva. "Mom, I know you're worried about him. But dammit, can't he make a little effort once in a while? For us?"

"Well, he did say he needs some time," says Gabe.

Eva sighs. "He did. I suggested he take a few days for himself, but . . ." She bites a fingernail, a habit she had overcome years before. "Perhaps, if Dad won't go backpacking, I'll go visit Camila that weekend," she says to nobody in particular. "Dad might enjoy a few days to himself, maybe he'd take some long solo hikes. Go check out a river or a lake." She is only thinking out loud.

She figures she could fly to Arizona on a Friday and come back Monday if it works out on Camila's end. She'll check with Lyman, feel him out. She imagines he'll be pleased to be alone.

At the end of August, on a Thursday, Eva helps Olivia collect backpacking gear. Their trip starts the next day.

"Make sure you pack rain gear and a couple of warm layers."

"It's summer, Mom!" Olivia complains.

Eva reminds her that mountains are unpredictable. It can get bitterly cold at night, even in summer. "And anyway, your brothers won't let you come along without proper gear."

Olivia shrugs. It is a comfort to Eva that Ezra and Gabe are experienced outdoors, and so is Aviva. They'll be fine, and they'll keep Livvie safe.

She packs her own overnight bag for an early morning flight.

That night, Eva and Lyman are alone in the kitchen. "Before I forget," she says, "please ask one of the kids to leave their cell phone with you. That way, they can reach you in case they need to."

"I can ask, if it'd make you feel better."

She remembers her alarming discussion with Camila some weeks ago. She shivers. "You'll be okay while I'm gone, right?" she asks Lyman one more time.

"Why wouldn't I be?" He keeps scrubbing the pan.

"If you're teetering on the brink of something, then I need to know."

"Don't be ridiculous. What kind of brink?"

She will not get anything more out of him. "Well then," she says very gently, "I hope you have some lovely quiet days."

In Phoenix, Camila waits with wide-open arms. Her face is alive, a deeper shade of bronze than it was in Vermont. A turquoise ruffled dress shows off her muscular arms.

"Camila!" Eva waves as she runs toward her friend. "I am so glad to be here. You look radiant! Thanks for picking me up."

"Of course."

Eva feels sweaty and gross, as always after a plane trip. Her blue shirt and capris are wrinkled. She can't wait to take off the hiking boots she travelled in. They find Camila's car in the parking area and get onto the highway going north. Camila opens the moon roof. Eva unties her laces and rummages through her day pack for sandals.

"*Aah*. That feels better! I can't wait to see your new house."

"I forgot you'd never seen it. You can freshen up, and I have lunch waiting for us."

"That sounds great."

"Our house is only twenty minutes from the hospital. Better yet, it's really close to Echo Canyon and not far from the Phoenix Mountain Preserve. We can check them out when you're up for it."

"Yes! I might need a nap, or else some caffeine first. I had to be at the airport at six a.m."

"Did you leave your car there?"

"No, Lyman dropped me off and went to the lab early. He was glad to be out of the way while the kids got ready to go. Smart of him, avoiding that bit of chaos."

Camila's Spanish-mission-style house has two stories, adobe walls, and a terra cotta roof. Cool floor tiles and wooden shutters keep the heat out. Around the courtyard, curved archways support the veranda. Flowers grow in oversized clay urns. A swimming pool beckons with a shimmering mosaic of tiny tiles in every shade of blue and green.

"Wow," Eva sighs. "How lovely. Forget that nap! I'd rather float in the pool!"

Camila chuckles. "I hear you, girl. Lunch first?"

"Lunch sounds amazing," Eva says.

She changes into a fresh sun dress. They eat outside in the shade and sip tall glasses of limeade. Ice cubes and slices of lime float in the glass pitcher. They catch up as old friends do. They linger until the sun is no longer scorching hot above them.

"Do you want to get in the pool before or after we go for a walk?" Camila asks lazily.

"Tough choice . . . after? Okay with you?" Eva stands, bends to touch her toes, and moves around to loosen her back. "I'm so stiff, I could use a walk."

"Perfect," says Camila. She stacks their plates on a tray. "It's three already. There is a delightful trail near Shadow Mountain. It doesn't go to the top but has nice views and easy terrain. Sound good?"

"Sounds fantastic," Eva agrees. They carry dishes to the kitchen. "Are hiking sandals okay? Or do I need my boots?"

Camila looks at Eva's feet. "Those will be just fine," she says. "That's all I'm wearing."

After the walk, they get into bathing suits, and Camila brings out a couple of large flotation rings. They pour themselves fresh limeade and idly float around. They laugh and chat, their feet dangling in the water. By now, the sun is behind the bougainvillea. They are still floating when Camila's husband, Cesar, gets home. A cheerful man, his big smile lights up his copper face.

He opens his arms wide. "Eva," he says, "get yourself out of that pool and come hug me, right now, old friend!"

"Do you like wet hugs?" she laughs. "Careful what you ask for, Cesar." She jumps up, comes splashing out of the pool, and runs up to him.

He doesn't skip a beat and wraps her in his arms. His dress shirt is soaked. He grins and takes it off.

"Be right back," he announces. He comes out wearing swim trunks, and soon he, too, floats around with a glass of limeade.

"Hey," Camila teases, "I haven't had *my* hug."

"*Mi amor*!" In mock horror, he leans over and places an unhurried kiss on her lips.

"Better?" he asks, and he winks at Eva, who feels strangely moved.

It is time to think about dinner. Eva calls home first. She takes her cell phone to her room. Lyman picks up on the third ring.

"Lyman here," he says.

"Hi!

"You made it, then."

"Flights weren't bad. How about you? Kids are gone?"

"Yep. Gone before I got home."

"And you have one of their cell phones, right? Just in case?"

"*Yeeesss,*" he draws out, annoyed.

Why did she imagine he'd be excited to hear from her? "Camila and Cesar's new house is amazing," she offers. "It's perfect for this hot climate. There are shady verandas all around the courtyard."

"Nice."

"We should come back together, before too long."

"*Hmm.* Say hi to them."

"I will—and how was *your* day?"

"Just a day. Fine."

"Okay then." She waits a beat. "Keep me posted if there is any news from the kids, would you?"

"Sure. Talk later."

Click. She sighs. Why did she imagine they'd have an actual conversation? Isn't that why he needs to be alone, to figure himself out?

Cesar has lit the charcoal kettle grill outside. In the kitchen, Camila rotates skewers of colorful shish kebabs in a marinade. She looks up and scrutinizes Eva for a moment.

"Is everything alright? You look perturbed."

Eva hugs her friend. "Oh, it's just that I keep bumping up against Lyman's non-answers and his silence. It's like a granite wall . . . I suppose it was dumb of me to expect that he'd miss me so soon." She shrugs. "But the kids made it out on their trip, apparently." She inhales the spicy mix. "Do I smell cumin?" she asks.

"And fresh cilantro. Family recipe."

Eva looks around. "What can I do here?"

"Feel like making salad?" Camila points her chin toward a bowl of peppers and tomatoes. "There are salad greens in the refrigerator. And a jicama in the veggie drawer."

"I'm on it," says Eva.

"Silence can be hard to take, right? Especially when it's not how it used to be. I hear you. Let's hope some alone time helps."

"Yeah . . ."

"Are you still worried? I mean *really* worried?"

"I'm confused. And yes, worried too. I did ask him whether he felt bad enough to consider that life isn't worth it. I asked again last night. He brushed me off again." She leans against the refrigerator with the greens in her hand. "I just don't know what's right anymore."

"It's so hard to judge, with people we love. Much easier in our clinic."

"Sure is. The kids are all worried because they can't engage him. He has been like a dark cloud over the family, all summer."

"Maybe this *is* all about stopping a medication he still needs? Is there anything else that bothers him, do you think?"

"I have asked. He keeps saying 'nothing.' That I make too much of it. But honestly, I've even wondered whether he wants to leave the marriage." She pauses.

"Did you ask that?" Camila stops skewering kebabs and looks at Eva.

"Yeah, I did." She attacks the jicama. "He shrugged that off too. Maybe I need to ask *myself* that same question, Camila . . ."

Camila studies her carefully. "*Hmm*, maybe."

"You know, I understand that depression is an illness. That it's not his fault. I try to be supportive, but—" Eva pauses. "I feel like a bad person, you know? I've caught myself getting angry at him, more and more. The rage feels awful, I hate it. And I hate myself for it. But this summer was supposed to be so special. Then he stopped all of his treatment on his own. He won't talk to me, he won't let anybody help, and he pushes the kids away and it hurts them . . ."

Camila throws her hands up in exasperation. "I was starting to wonder why you *didn't* sound angrier, Eva. Like, what the hell would it take for you to get pissed?"

"Just trying to honor—"

"Yeah, I know," Camila interrupts. "He wants space, but for how long? It's been three months. And what is he doing with that space? And . . ." She interrupts herself and focuses on the kebabs. "I'm sorry, my friend. I hate to see you hurting. And it bothers me that he isn't paying attention to how it all affects you, or his kids."

"Yep. I imagine he hurts more than the family does, but he just won't let—well, I guess there is a reason you can't be a therapist to your partner."

"I'm sure he *is* hurting. But he doesn't even seem to be considering anybody else. I have nothing reassuring to tell you, Eva. That's a lot of withdrawal, coming right after he stopped Prozac—well, we've talked about that before."

"I know, not a good sign. Especially if he thinks this is his true self," Eva sighs. "Which brings me right back to where I started about three months ago, right? Going around in circles about the right thing to do." She trails off, noticing the scallions in her hand. "Can I use these?"

"Knock yourself out. Cesar *loves* scallions."

On Saturday morning, they go to the Uptown Farmer's Market. They load up on colorful fresh vegetables, artisanal goat's cheese, and several bottles of a local wine, Summer in a Bottle. At a craft stand, Eva picks up a mask of a bearded old man, carved from the knot of a tree.

"Do you *like* men with sad faces, then?" Camila elbows her. Eva looks up in surprise. Does she? Camila fingers a necklace of bright clay disks. Cesar admires tumblers made of greenish recycled glass, full of tiny bubbles. He waves them over.

"These are lovely," Camila says. "Except that we have glasses bursting out of every cabinet in the house." She shakes her head gently.

"Mi amor, there is always room for a few more . . ." he pleads. "These are, I don't know, there is just something about those bubbles . . ."

Camila crosses her arms and gives him a hard look. "We have boxes of glasses in the garage that you haven't even unpacked yet." It's a statement.

He tilts his head. "Please?"

Camila walks closer, takes the tumbler out of his hand, and sets it down firmly. "You promised," she says. "No hoarding. Not anymore."

Eva realizes she has never seen them argue in all the years they've been friends. They always seem so close.

"I know," Cesar mumbles, and he walks off to the next farm stand.

Camila turns to Eva. "Sorry about that. Old argument. It got really bad at one point. We were in therapy about it."

"Don't apologize! But wait, hoarding, bad enough for therapy?" Eva asks.

Camila picks up the tumbler she had slammed onto the table, turns it to check whether it is cracked. "Do you remember, at your wedding? Cesar didn't come."

"I do," says Eva. She admires a pitcher, made of the same bubbly glass. "Wasn't he in Mexico? What was it, taking care of his parents?"

"That is what we told people. But in fact, he had moved out of the house."

"What? And I didn't know?"

Camila looks down. "I was ashamed. And you were busy with wedding plans." She ambles over to another table. "You know we had been trying for a second baby for some time, right, without success? Well, he was upset, and he started drinking. His mother is an alcoholic. No way I was putting up with that," she says grimly.

"I'm so sorry. I thought you guys *never* had problems!"

Camila shrugs. "You ought to know better, my friend. Everyone has problems. Anyway, I made him leave the house. Told him he could come back if and when he was sober." She looks at Eva and idly fingers a colorful kitchen towel. "To his credit," she adds quietly, "he stopped. He came home after six months. It was hard on Isabella, but we made sure she got to visit him. And, he has never once relapsed."

"Pretty impressive. But what about the hoarding? Is it related in some way?" Eva asks. She joins Camila by the linens.

"Yes. For years afterward, whenever he felt an urge to drink, he would go to yard sales instead, or antique shops, craft fairs. He brought back mountains of stuff. Our house got more and more crammed with things."

"That's a novel coping strategy, I must say."

Camila laughs. "It seems funny now, but . . .Well, we wound up in therapy because I couldn't breathe anymore. There was no space to breathe at home. Now we have an agreement. I'm allowed to stop him whenever I think it's out of hand. Periodically, we hold a giant yard sale, and we go out to dinner with the proceeds."

"That's creative and upbeat," Eva smiles. "And preferable to drinking . . ." If only Lyman were willing to work on this rough patch together, the way they did. Perhaps he will, after he has had some time alone . . .

The rest of the visit thoroughly lifts Eva's spirits. On Sunday at dinner, Eva asks Cesar about his new training program for freshly graduated medical students in Chiapas. It's one of the poorest rural areas of Mexico. His colleagues on the faculty of Family Medicine spend time there to support the fledgling doctors and teach. Cesar speaks with obvious passion, underscored with hand gestures. Camila is just as excited. She will contribute psychiatry training there. They freely talk over each other with much teasing and laughter. A vibrant story unfolds, ideas from each of them weaving together.

Eva's head swivels from one to the other to follow the rapid-fire back-and-forth. The separate strands blend into a joint project. Their baby. She sits back, a grin on her face, and lets the animated talk wash over her. Their fun is infectious. Over dessert, the three of them discuss the health care issues of Malawi compared to Chiapas. Eva feels as if they might very well solve the problems of global health care, once and for all, here and now. Several new ideas emerge for her projects in Mangochi. With a nostalgic twinge, she remembers how she and Lyman used to debate things, how they looked at problems together, from every angle. Will that come back?

Later that night, she packs her bag. Then she calls Lyman.

"Lyman he-ere."

"Hi, how is everything? Any news from the kids?"

"N-no . . . All f-fine."

"I checked my flights for tomorrow. I should arrive late afternoon, as planned. I'll get myself to campus, and I'll meet you there, okay?"

"Sure—s-sure. Bye." He hangs up.

That sounded very strange, Eva thinks. She finds her friends outside.

"What's the matter?" Camila asks, ever perceptive.

"He sounded very odd," says Eva. "His speech was funny, sort of slurred—could he be drunk? No, that can't be, he never . . . I don't know *what* to make of it."

On Monday morning, Cesar leaves early for the hospital; Eva and Camila have a simple breakfast in the kitchen. Camila drains the last of her coffee. "It was lovely to have you," she says. "And maybe Lyman will be in a better headspace now." She carries her dishes to the sink.

"I hope so. But the way he sounded last night felt really weird. Maybe I woke him up, I don't know . . . we'll see." She picks up her bowl and mug. "The kids should be getting back before dark too."

"Just leave those in the sink," says Camila. "And call me tonight?"

"I will."

Eva's cell phone dings. Surprised, she flips it open and looks at Camila with a frown. "It's a message from Gabe's phone. But that's the phone the kids left with Lyman in case they needed to reach him. Strange." The text reads: *Check your email before you go.*

She tries calling back. No answer. She tries the landline. Nothing.

"Here," says Camila, "use my laptop."

Eva opens her account, reads the message, and screams. Camila rushes to look over her shoulder. They read the email, read it again. It is addressed to Eva, Ezra, Gabriel, and Olivia. Eva starts sobbing. Camila grabs the bags and runs to her car; Eva follows her, punching numbers into her phone.

I'm sorry, I cannot do this anymore.

I cannot go back to treatment, and I cannot find my way. You'll be better off without me.

Don't go looking for me. Send the sheriff to the old northern red oak.

Take good care of each other.

Love you all.

Lyman/Dad.

Part III
Aftermath

"... maybe I could go from the haunted to the ghost, from reader to writer, and I too could have the stars at my disposal, and their undeniable gravity."

—*Ta-Nehisi Coates*, from *The Message*

Chapter 15
August 2004

The next hours are a blur. Lyman's message runs through her mind on an endless loop. Frantic, she calls 911 on the way to the airport, hoping it might not be too late, that Lyman can be pulled back from the precipice. She almost yells at the operator, frustrated with her difficulty understanding about the old northern red oak and with her trouble spelling the address. She is aware of Camila's soothing hand on her arm, while she repeats it all one more time, slowly, to the sheriff.

At the airport, she waves, runs into the terminal, and sprints to her gate. She calls Ezra's cell phone twice, but there's no answer. Breathing hard, she tries Olivia's phone. What will she say if her youngest picks up? But there is no answer. She almost dials Gabriel's number, then remembers that's the phone they left at home. She supposes the kids could still be out of range, up in the hills. Finally, Vicky's phone connects briefly, then immediately breaks off. She notices people streaming toward the gate. It's time to board.

She looks for her seat, mind racing. She *has* to intercept them. She cannot let them get home before she does. They must not access their email and discover Lyman's message, not until she is with them. Another thought assails her: what if they drive straight to the house, and find—God, they'd find *what? The sheriff? Sirens wailing?* She cannot let that happen. Someone stares. Is she muttering to herself? She finds her seat on the aisle, shoves her carry-on in the bin, and sits down, phone still in hand. The person next to her looks over briefly, then turns away.

She buckles her seat belt, thinks of an even worse possibility. What if the boys drop Olivia off at the driveway and continue into town? What if they leave their sister alone, to discover—oh God, Eva cannot imagine. She cannot focus, she wants to jump up, do something. Do what?

Just before take-off, she sends Ezra a text. "IMPORTANT: Please pick me up at my office, in the hospital, before you go home. All of you together, please." Then she adds, trying not to sound alarmed. "See you soon. Love, Mom." She types: "Call me as soon as you can. I have a layover in Newark at 2 p.m." She erases that last. It sounds too urgent, too ominous.

An annoyed attendant stands over her. "Ma'am. *Ma'am*?" She declares that Eva *must* turn off her phone. Eva holds up a hand and whispers, "Just one minute, please." She types: "Arriving in Burlington at 4:30." She hits send, flips her phone shut, and powers it off.

As soon as the seat belt sign is off, she gets up to walk down the aisle. She spends a long time in the bathroom, crying. When she comes out—after how long?—other passengers look at her strangely. Her eyes are burning, her face is wet. It occurs to her that she might be a disturbing sight.

A stewardess approaches. "Ma'am, do you—may I—um, excuse me, can I get you anything?" She gently places a hand on Eva's arm.

Eva shakes her head. "No, no. There is nothing . . ."

The attendant is an older woman, kind and calm. She guides Eva toward the rear of the plane, the area reserved for personnel. She closes the curtain that separates this section. She sits next to Eva, hand still on her arm. "I can sit with you a bit. Or would you prefer privacy?"

Eva looks up. "Thank you. I just need to be alone for a bit . . ."

The woman stands.

"May I . . ." Eva asks, "would you mind bringing me my day pack?"

"Of course. Is it above your seat?"

* * *

Eva pulls out a small notebook and searches for her pen. Her hand hovers above the page. It's always easier to collect her thoughts by writing. But what is there to write? What is there to decide? What choices does she have? All she can do is wait . . .

Frustrated, she jabs the paper with her pen. That familiar burst of rage knocks her breath out. A black veil covers her mind; an inarticulate scream rises in her throat, but she traps it there, a hand on her mouth. Panicked, she drops the pen and reaches for that white paper bag; she is going to be sick, she knows it.

She retches and tastes bile, then the wave passes. It leaves white-hot, blinding anger in its wake. *How could he do this to them? How could he? How could he?* Her mind goes around and around, trying to escape the fury, falling back into it. She digs her fingernails into her palms. She ought to feel compassion for Lyman's suffering, not anger. "Do I feel compassion?" she asks herself. "I do, don't I? Certainly, I *did*." In the clinical part of her mind, she had known that this awful possibility existed. She and Camila had discussed it. But in her heart, she trusted Lyman, she believed he would never— She looks down at the notebook in her lap. She rummages under the seat for the pen she has dropped, finds it, and blindly scrawls *HOW COULD YOU DO THIS TO OUR CHILDREN?*

Useless, useless rage. She tries to focus on what she'll have to deal with, the practical things. She starts a list but quickly loses patience. She stares out at the vast, blank, empty cloudscape below her.

Will fiery Olivia conjure up her wise self, the strong one? Or will she rage and shout, act tough, and then lose it, fall apart? She is too young to have to cope with this. And too vulnerable: she has only just broken up with her volatile girlfriend. Eva can picture Carla pouting in the background. Outside the window, a snowy peak pokes through the cloud cover and floats past. Will Olivia turn back to Carla for comfort? Eva conjures up a teary reconciliation and a couple of weeks of dramatic, showy caretaking. She stares at a stain on the carpet in the aisle. Something sticky is there. Sticky like Carla herself. If she reaches down to touch that spot, will she find goo on her finger?

She blinks. She remembers Olivia sobbing about Carla's self-centered demands. Imagines her wondering what the point of love is. *Look where it got you, Mom*, she'd say. Eva breathes in. Her palms are clammy. She rubs her hands together. Breathe out.

Another mountain peak floats by above the clouds. And another, further to the north. And another. A jagged line of decapitated mountains, hazy wisps of cloud around their heads. *And what about Gabriel?* she thinks. Tender and quiet, his deepest feelings live below the surface. She can almost hear his calming voice, see his arms reaching for his sister. He will try to be their anchor. At only twenty-two, he will try to be their rock. He is just launching in the footsteps of his father's career, and now he will try to fill his father's vacated role in the family too. She mustn't let him carry that load.

Eva stands, agitated; the notebook drops from her lap. There is nothing she can do, nothing at all now. She reaches for the curtain in front of her. Should she go back to her own seat? She cannot face the stares. She sits again.

Should she worry more about Ezra, charming Ezra, so on top of the world? He can be impulsive, but he seems to be a man on his own path. He is building a life with smart and loving Vicky. Will this crush their hopes, twist their trust in the future? She puts her face in her hands and cries silently. She lets herself cry until she can lift her head, take another deep breath, and steel herself. She will do whatever has to be done.

During her layover in Newark, she mills around, looking for a quiet corner. There is no such thing. She gives up and dials the sheriff's office where she stands. Her heart beats so hard it drums in her ears.

"May I speak with the officer who answered my call earlier, about Lyman Willis, please?"

The receptionist asks, "Who?" and then, "Spell that, please."

Eva explodes. "Ma'am! I received a suicide note from my husband this morning. And I'm in New Jersey waiting for a flight home. I have only a few minutes. Please! Surely *someone* must have gone to our house? Please find them."

"Oh!" the woman says quickly. "I'm sorry, yes, of course. I will page Officer LaGrange. Please hold . . ."

Eva walks toward the food court. A moment later, a man's voice comes on the line. She sputters out her question. "Is he—? Did you . . ."

"Ma'am. We found your husband," the officer says, speaking slowly. He pauses, making sure she is listening. "We found him exactly where his message said we would. I am very, very sorry, ma'am."

"Then you weren't . . ." She turns and walks slowly back toward her gate. She cannot ask whether he lives. "Where is he?" she asks instead.

"We waited for the medical examiner, ma'am, before we transported him."

She does not want to take this in. "To the hospital?"

"No, ma'am. I am very sorry. To the coroner's office. You may come and see him whenever you are able."

"See him?"

"We will need you to identify the body, ma'am."

"My God . . ." She chokes down a sob. "And my children, officer? Have you seen them? Were they home?" She leans against the nearest wall.

"Your children? No, ma'am. We haven't heard from them."

Thank goodness, she thinks. They did not have to witness any of it. "Officer?" she hesitates. "May I ask how he—?"

"A firearm, ma'am. There was nothing the EMT team could do. I am so sorry for your loss."

"Thank you," she manages. She paces up and down the hallway near her gate. She has time yet. She finds a bathroom, sits there a moment. *Should she call Ezra again? Should she text? What will she say?*

She wipes her eyes, clears her throat, and stands. She finds a seat in the waiting area and dials. There is no answer. She sends him a text. Then she sends it again to Olivia. "Did you get my message? Meet me at my office, at the hospital, don't bother going home first. Okay? Love you." She hopes that sounds convincing, and yet casual enough. She doesn't want them to start imagining why she is asking. They will know all too soon.

Just as she boards for the short flight, there is an answer from Olivia's phone. "Got it, Mom. Just packing up the van. See you there, six or so. We'll text when we park." A small blessing . . .

She vaguely registers the bumpy flight from Newark to Burlington. A rough landing jolts her out of her stormy feelings and endless loop of useless thoughts. At 4:35 p.m., she is at the taxi stand. It will take less than fifteen minutes to get to the hospital, and she will have time before the kids arrive.

She gives the driver the address for her office in the psychiatry building. Then she calls the sheriff's department. The same woman answers and recognizes her immediately this time. "Excuse me," Eva asks, "is the medical examiner located near the hospital grounds?"

"Yes, ma'am, across from the Emergency Room."

That's only a minute's walk from her office. Eva's hand shakes. She dreads seeing Lyman, having to confirm his death, the brutal fact of it. But she will still dread it tomorrow, or the day after. It will not go away. She trembles. "I need to identify my husband's body. Can I do it now, in fifteen minutes?"

"Hold on a moment, please," says the woman.

Eva hears some voices, then Officer LaGrange comes on the line. "Ma'am, I understand that you'd like to see your husband in a few minutes?"

"Yes, please."

"Of course, I will meet you at the entrance. I would be glad to guide you."

"Thank you," she says. She updates the driver on the building she needs and texts the kids: "I will be at my office by 5:45 p.m. Text me, and I'll meet you at the entrance. Love, Mom."

When she exits the taxi, an officer approaches her and identifies himself. "Officer LaGrange. Let me take your bag, ma'am." He is a slight middle-aged man with penetrating, kind eyes. "This way, please."

She follows him through a hallway to an elevator, down to the second basement level. Away from everything, as far down as possible, she realizes. She shivers. They reach a steel door with a small window, too high for her to see anything. He pauses, his key in the lock, and turns to her. "Let me know when you're ready."

"I am," she says as steadily as she can.

He unlocks the steel door. "Nobody is here at this time," he explains.

He flips on the cruel fluorescent lights. They are in a large room, the walls are tiled white, and the floor is a nondescript beige. There are gleaming steel cabinets on three walls, and a double swinging steel door off to the left. At the far end, there are two narrow windows near the ceiling. A green slope blocks the view. It is cold in here. Three narrow stainless-steel tables stand in the middle of the room, seven feet long. The middle one has a white sheet covering what could be a body—what must be Lyman . . .

"Oh," she breathes, and she covers her mouth. She stares at the sheet. Is that *him*? Or is there another body in here?

The officer explains. "When you called me, I asked that the technician wheel him out, ma'am, before leaving."

"Out from there?" she points to the double doors.

"Yes, that is the cold room. I thought it might be easier for you if he were ready."

She nods, a little confused, and stands uncertainly near the entrance. "May I?"

"Yes, come in. And in case you need to sit, I'll bring a chair," he adds.

She imagines that people must faint sometimes, confronting what she is about to see. She slowly walks to the table. LaGrange gets there first, takes the top hem of the sheet in his hands, and waits for her. She just wants to get through this now. She gestures for him to go ahead.

At first, he folds the sheet down so only Lyman's head can be seen. He is terribly pale. There are blood spots on his chin, his cheek, and his neck. His mouth is slightly open, making him look gaunt. A hollow face. His eyes are closed. His head is intact. She looks up. Hadn't the officer said it was a firearm? Then, in a flash, she understands.

She reaches for the sheet and yanks it down, out of LaGrange's hands. She is not prepared for what she sees, for the bloody, ragged hole torn into his chest. "Oh my god," she cries out. She staggers to the chair near the wall. The officer quickly pulls the sheet back to Lyman's neck, then moves toward her, but she holds up a hand. "Give me just a moment, I'll be—" No, she will *not* be fine. She might *never* be fine. But she *will* get through this.

She takes deliberate, slow breaths until she can stand up. She looks at Lyman's face for a long while. "Why, why, why . . ." she whispers. Her eyes are dry. She is too devastated for tears. She reaches her fingers toward his face. Strokes his cheek. He is already cold. The cold penetrates deep into her bones.

LaGrange stands at a respectful distance, near the wall. When she finally turns away, he covers Lyman. He offers her a seat in the tiny adjacent office and pulls out a clipboard. He has some questions, obvious ones. Yes, she confirms, yes, this is Lyman Willis. There is paperwork to sign. They dispense with it quickly. LaGrange asks if she has any questions for him. She shakes her head. She has no coherent thoughts right now. He reaches into his breast pocket and gives her Lyman's ID card, which was placed in clear view by Lyman's side, at the foot of the tree. An unbearably practical touch, so very Lyman, so terribly meticulous.

LaGrange wheels her carry-on out for her, locks the door behind them, and asks where she is going. She points to her building. "I will walk you there," he says.

Eva unlocks her office door a little before six. She checks her phone: no text yet. She brings two additional chairs from the waiting area and rolls her desk chair into the circle. *That will do*, she thinks. She goes to wash her face, puts cold, wet paper towels on her eyes, and tries to make her mind go blank. And waits. She recites a mantra she learned once, but it's no help. She lets her mind wander to music. To the music she associates with their best memories. Oscar Peterson. Brad Mehldau.

She startles when her phone dings. "We're here, we just parked the van."

She hurries downstairs. At the entrance door, Gabriel looks at her closely and frowns. "What *is* the matter, Mom? What's wrong?"

"I'll tell you in a moment," she says and gestures for him to hold on. She waves them inside. She walks toward the elevator, fast, and they follow her. Vicky and Aviva tag behind.

"It's Dad, isn't it?" Olivia catches up with her. "Where is he?"

Eva reaches for her daughter's hand, presses the button for the third floor. In a few minutes, she gathers them in a circle around her and closes the office door. She looks at each of them, then down at her feet.

"It *is* about Dad, yes," she finally says. She reaches one hand toward Olivia, sitting on her left, the other toward Gabriel on her right, and asks them all to hold hands. "It's about Dad, and I'm sorry, it is not good news. I wanted to tell you in person." All three of them stare at her. Vicky and Aviva sit back awkwardly, concern on their faces. Eva gestures for them to join the circle.

"What happened? Did he have a heart attack?" Ezra asks. "Is he in the hospital?"

"No, sweetheart. He—he ended his life this morning. I'm so sorry. I don't know how to soften this. I'm sorry."

They look at her in shock. Olivia lets out a choking cry, a hand over her mouth; she stands, and Ezra moves quickly to wrap her in his arms. He rocks her a little.

Gabriel turns to Eva. Without a word, he puts his arms around her where she sits. She drops her head on his chest and leans into him. "Oh, Mom," he stammers. Then they are both crying, holding each other.

Vicky turns toward Aviva. "Should we wait outside?" she whispers.

Eva has heard and looks up. "No, please stay with us," she says. "I'm sure we will need time as a family at some point, but right now, please stay." Vicky moves to Ezra's side, where he is still rocking Olivia. They pull her into their hug. Gabriel crouches in front of his mother, Aviva joins him, and they each hold one of Eva's hands. Nobody asks how it happened. Perhaps they don't want to know. Or not yet. Then, of a common accord, they all sit in silence for a while. And it is somehow comforting.

* * *

They eventually make it to the van, in a daze, and Ezra drives them home. Nobody even mentions it, but they will all stay together at the house tonight. They gather around the dining table; Eva places Lyman's ID card in the middle, and she reads Lyman's email out loud. She needs a pause to catch her breath after the words *better off without me*. There is a gasp, a sob, then a dense silence descends on the house.

One by one, they go off to wash away the grime and sweat of backpacking and of air travel. Ezra orders pizza; they do have to eat something. They sit around the living room in pajamas for a long time.

Inevitably, someone asks a question that Eva dreads. "But why, Mom, why?"

And she has to shake her head. "I don't know, sweetie. I don't understand it either."

Olivia paces the room with clenched fists. "Why the fuck weren't we enough for him to want to *live*!" she bursts out. "Why didn't he *do* something about . . ." Her brothers look at her. There is an awkward silence. But she has said what they all feel.

Vicky and Aviva both stare at the rug, fighting tears. Three baffled faces turn to Eva.

"Because . . ." she tries. Her voice catches. "Because he came to feel so very badly about himself, I think," she offers uncertainly.

"But didn't he know we all loved him?" says Gabriel. "That we all wanted him to get better again. Wasn't that obvious?"

"I know every one of us tried to tell him." Eva's hands shake. "But even so, he thought we'd be better off without him . . ."

Olivia slams a fist on the counter. "Why didn't it occur to him that this was the worst thing he could ever do to us!" Then she drops onto the rug in front of Gabriel and Aviva, who are on the love seat. She cries into their knees. Gabe leans over and strokes her hair.

"Is it anything we did?" Ezra asks hoarsely. "Or anything we did *not* do? Could we—"

"*No! No, no,*" Eva interrupts him. "*Don't* think that way, please. I saw you try to reach him. I tried as hard as I could too. Maybe I did it the wrong way, I don't know. But we *all* tried." She prays that is true, because Ezra has just spoken her own darkest doubts. Should she have dragged him to a hospital? A ridiculous notion. Lyman would have told *them* he was fine, too.

"Why then was nothing helping?" Gabe asks.

Eva drops her head into her hands. When she looks up, she wipes her face with her sleeve. "His depression got hold of him this time, I think. I told him once, years ago, that depression can take over a life. It is just like an oil slick. It spreads over everything inside and around you, and it chokes out life. Back then, he heard me, and he did something about it. In fact, he did *everything* he could because he wanted to be the best dad he could be. He could see he was upsetting you. So, he got hold of it because he loved you. He did whatever he had to do. Remember that, always."

"Then why not this time?" Olivia frowns.

Eva has no good answer. "This time," she hesitates, "it got so much worse, so much faster than I realized . . . I'm so sorry I didn't . . ."

"Mom," Gabe holds up a hand to stop her. "You can't tell us it's not our fault, and then turn around and blame yourself," he says. "Please, don't."

She nods, looks down at her lap. Gabriel stands, reaches out, pulls her up, and hugs her. Ezra sits next to Vicky. She rubs his shoulder.

"Gabe is right," Ezra says. "But . . ." He looks toward Olivia before choking out his sister's earlier thought. "Still, why weren't we enough *this* time?"

Eva slumps back in her armchair, looking vaguely toward the windows. "I guess he was too lost in the dark to *love himself* anymore. And you know, if you can't love yourself, then you cannot take in anybody else's love for you. Their love makes no sense, and it can't get through." She looks at them. "I'm just guessing . . ."

Some time after midnight, Eva realizes she is spent. "I need to get some sleep, everybody," she says. "I'm falling apart . . . Sorry."

"Can I sleep in your bed, Mom?" Olivia asks quickly. "I can't face my room tonight."

"Of course you can, come on up."

Aviva turns to Gabe. "Shouldn't I leave? Can you drive me?"

"You don't have to, Aviva," says Eva over the banister. "You can stay if you want. It's up to you and Gabe . . ."

Gabriel casts a glance toward his mother, uncertain. "Could Aviva stay in your room tonight?" he asks Olivia. "Would that be okay with you?"

"Sure, I don't care." Olivia is already upstairs, grabs a nightshirt, and runs into her parents' room.

Nobody gets much sleep. Olivia finally drifts off toward dawn, her mouth slightly open, face down on her father's pillow. The sky has not yet lightened when Eva hears the earliest birds twitter and chirp. Slowly, the dawn chorus gathers, muted this late in summer. Eva quietly slips downstairs. She boils water and steeps her tea. She sets up the coffee machine but does not start it. Feeling heavy and disoriented, she takes her mug outside. She walks aimlessly through the field as the sun begins to rise. Without intending to, she wanders toward the old northern red oak.

She is startled to find herself here. She looks up at the thick, low branch where she and Lyman so often perched together, long ago. Perhaps the tree remembers too? Perhaps some sense of Lyman's presence might comfort her, sitting there? She takes a step forward. Suddenly, she imagines blood splattered on the ground, on the tree bark. She quickly turns away and retches. She cannot face seeing blood, and yet she cannot move away from the tree. She sinks into the tall grass at the edge of the field, draws up her legs, and lets her forehead fall onto her knees. She rocks herself, eyes closed. She tries not to think.

She feels hollowed out and unsteady. She allows herself to be scared: she cannot bear this burden. It's too much. An ant climbs up her leg. Several ants. She idly watches them, reminds herself that she has no choice. She *must* bear what lies ahead. There is nobody else. She is alone to see her family through this. She watches daylight paint the field and brighten the first purple splashes of asters. No, falling apart is not an option. She does not have that luxury.

An ant bites her; she jumps up. She brushes a dozen insects off her legs, realizing she was sitting right on their highway. Rage overtakes her again. She punches a nearby sapling, too hard; now her hand is sore. How could he do this to her? How could he make this awful mess, and leave her to mop it up? Leave her alone to hold their children's hands as they stumble through?

"Lyman, you asshole!" she yells up to the treetops. "You left us all, without consulting me! That was *not* the deal . . ." She sinks down and sobs, hugs herself. Obviously, he did not consult her. He didn't want her fixing his depression, did he? And he certainly didn't want her stopping him, at the end, when all he wanted was to give up.

After a while, she makes her way back to the house. The clock chimes seven thirty. She cannot put this off any longer. She must call Lyman's brother. She pours more water in the kettle, brews another cup of tea, and buys just a little more time. She listens for voices upstairs. Nothing stirs.

How will she break this news to Wilford? With the hot cup in her hand, Eva finds a chair at the furthest corner of the patio. At least, there is no need to tell Candace her son has died. Lyman's mother has late-stage Alzheimer's. In the long-term care facility, at every visit, the old woman frowns at Eva and asks the same question. "Who are you? Are you my sister?" That is followed by a glare. "Why do they keep me here?" The old woman's mind slipped away, bearing happy images of her sons and their families.

She'll have to tell Lyman's brother, though. When was Wilford's massive coronary infarct? Early April, wasn't it? She and Lyman had driven up to Montreal early the next day. Leaving Olivia—where? Oh right, with Carla . . .Wilford had looked awful in the ICU, tubes and monitors sprouting everywhere.

Finally, Eva takes a deep breath and dials Wilford's number. She hopes he is sturdy enough to handle the news.

After several rings, she hears the gravelly voice. “Hello there, stranger,” he says, slightly out of breath. He sounds much older than his fifty-nine years.

She skips the pleasantries. “Wilford, I have terrible, awful news. It’s Lyman—”

“What? What is it? Did he have a heart attack?” He immediately sounds agitated. Is there any way to tell him this without compromising his health?

“No, not that,” Eva says slowly. “He—he died yesterday. I am so sorry . . .”

“Yesterday? And you’re telling me now? Was he ill? What on earth? Why didn’t you call us sooner?”

Her heart races. She waits for a silence. “Wilford? It was—he committed suicide. We found out . . .”

He is practically shouting now. “Suicide? Did you see that coming? Why? Couldn’t you do something?”

“Wilford, listen, listen to me.” She tries to sound calmer than she feels. Her hands shake. “I know this is hard. He became very depressed again this summer. You knew he was taking medication, didn’t you? Well, he stopped in the spring, and—”

“Hold on, he stopped when? And you knew this? And *you let him*? But . . . what on earth, Eva!” Wilford’s voice is ragged.

Eva wishes she could hang up the phone. She wants to throw up. There is a muffled sound. “*Lillian? Lillian!*” Wilford calls out. A pause. “Come here. Yes! Right now.”

Footsteps. “What?” comes Lillian’s worried voice.

“I’ll go on speaker phone,” Wilford yells.

“Eva?” says Lillian. “What’s going on?”

“Hi, Lillian. It’s about Lyman. He . . . he ended his life yesterday.”

Lillian gasps. Eva starts crying. Wilford notices and softens.

“I’m sorry, Eva,” he says. “It’s just such a shock.” He takes a quick breath. “I’m sorry I ranted. How are *you* doing? And the kids, do they know?” His voice breaks. “Please . . . just tell us what happened?”

So, Eva tells them how she learned that Lyman had gone off treatment. And how the summer went. How she hadn’t wanted to worry them while Wilford was still in rehab. Dejected, she tells them Lyman had not wanted her help, nor anyone else's. How he had asked for space, to deal with the depression his own way . . .

"And then, the kids all went camping at the end of August. He didn't want to join. I tried to do what he asked, to give him space, so I went away for a few days too. He said he was fine, that he needed to be alone for a bit, that I should go. I—I believed him, Wilford!"

She cannot speak for some time. Then she whispers hoarsely. "I believed him, how could I believe him? I'm so sorry." She tries to catch her breath.

"Eva?" Lillian's soothing voice starts a steady stream of words, of comfort. "Eva, it is not your fault. Darling, breathe, would you? Breathe with me now, okay? Breathe in? Atta girl. Now, breathe out. I don't hear you, hon! Breathe in? There. Breathe out . . ."

Wilford stays quiet until both women are silent.

Eva collects herself. "Thank you, Lillian," she whispers.

Wilford clears his throat. "Did you know our uncle committed suicide?" he asks.

Eva startles. "Your uncle? No. Who? You mean your dad's—wait, your dad's brother? I never heard about that at all!"

"No," he sighs. "Depression ran on Dad's side of the family, for sure. You know, our father, our grandmother . . . Another relative somewhere."

"Wait, you mean on your mom's side?" She stands, trying to process.

"Yes, I mean our mother's side of the family," he says somberly. "She had a brother nobody ever talked about."

"She did?" This is startling. Lyman's mother never spoke about her family. She was private and proud, sometimes unapproachable.

Lillian reads her thoughts. "I tried to ask Candace about her brother once. Maybe ten years ago. While Lyman had that spell of depression. We were all *so* worried. Her mind was still all there, so I asked her because Wilford had mentioned something long ago."

Eva paces the edge of the patio, looks toward the field, toward the woods. The great old tree is not visible from here. She shudders and tracks a swallow. "And?"

"Well," Lillian continues. "You know how she is, right? How upright?"

"I certainly do!"

"She pulled herself up real tall, in that way she has, and changed the subject. She gave me a withering look that I won't ever forget."

Eva shakes her head, walks back to a chair. "So, how come I don't know anything about this, and how come Lyman never mentioned it?" She hesitates, frowning. "How can that be?"

Wilford answers quickly. "Oh, I talked about it with Lyman once, when he was in college. He didn't recall anything about the man at all. I almost think he didn't believe me."

"Why?"

"Well . . . you have to remember I am four years older. I was seven or eight when Mom's brother died. He was only three. I was old enough to know something very strange was going on. Old enough to eavesdrop. I heard Mom tell Dad 'We will not discuss this with the boys, do you hear me? Never!' She scared me, the way she said that."

"Oh, Wilford, that's awful," Eva groans.

"Later that night, after Lyman was asleep, I got up to ask her about it, told her she didn't have to tell my little brother, but that I was big enough to know. She looked at me very hard. 'Nothing you need to worry about. Somebody died whom you didn't know.' She turned away and said: 'He had been sick a long time. Those things happen. Go to sleep.' So, I pretended to go to sleep. Lyman was sucking his thumb in the little bed."

"Do you know anything more?" She grasps for anything that might make sense.

"Give me a sec," Wilford chokes out.

"Of course," she says, "sorry. No need to answer, I was just trying to understand."

Wilford blows his nose. "Our dad, in one of his kinder moods, took me aside the next day, and told me. He said that Mom's brother had been in and out of hospitals for years. Sometimes he'd be doing well, sometimes he was crazy and out of control, and sometimes too depressed to get out of bed."

"Oh . . ."

"He said Mom was ashamed of him, that I shouldn't upset her by asking about it. He said she saw her younger brother as trouble, nothing but trouble. She didn't want to think about him anymore."

Eva wants to scream. Why hadn't she known? Why hadn't Lyman? A family member with intense mood swings and a tortured life had ended his own life. And they knew nothing about this at all.

"I wish . . ." she says thickly and trails off. "I'm not sure I *could* have stopped what happened to Lyman, but I would have been more alert . . ." The words get stuck. She realizes this might sound like blaming. "I don't mean you *should* have told me, Wilford," she adds. "I just wish Lyman had looked into it and told his therapist. Maybe—Oh, Lord, I just wish I'd known."

"Yeah," Wilford grumbles. "I know. But chances are, it wouldn't have changed anything, would it? My brother is—was—even more stubborn than the rest of the family."

There is a long silence. "Eva, do you want me to come?" Lillian asks finally. "I can leave for a few days, couldn't I, Wilford?"

"No, no thanks, Lillian," Eva says before Wilford can respond. She is drained. She needs time to herself. "I just have to focus on the kids, on what they need." She starts toward the house, impatient to end the conversation.

"Okay, I hear you," says Lillian. "But any time, alright? I could help with logistics, Eva, or just be there. It's only a couple of hours' drive. Just reach out."

"I promise," Eva answers as she walks inside. "I will. Thank you. I'll be in touch."

She hears a noise upstairs and starts the coffee maker. Gabriel comes down a moment later. He looks awful. His eyes are red, and his shoulders are slumped. Aviva follows with a hand on his back. Eva looks from one to the other.

Without a word, Gabriel hugs his mother. She holds him until he stands straight. "How is Olivia?" he asks. "And you, Mom? Did you sleep?"

"Did *you*?" Eva deflects.

Aviva answers for him. “Not much. We were up talking.” She looks at Eva apologetically. “I was in his room . . . I hope you don’t mind?”

Eva shrugs. “Don’t be silly. I’m glad you’re here for him.”

Gabe grabs two mugs, pours some coffee. He asks Aviva, “Sugar today? Or not?”

“Yes, please. And lots of milk.”

They sit in the kitchen nook. Eva leaves them alone and goes upstairs to check on Olivia. She finds her daughter still lying face down on Lyman’s pillow, arms sprawled wide, eyes open. She does not move.

Eva sits next to her and rubs her shoulders. The muscles are hard and tense. “Morning, honey,” she says tentatively.

Olivia grunts. “Can you massage my head too, Mom?” she mumbles. “Please?”

Eva does. “Roll over, I’ll do your temples.” She straightens after a few minutes. “Come downstairs, alright? There’s coffee. Or shall I make you hot chocolate?”

“I don’t care.” Olivia gets up sluggishly and steps into her flip-flops. When they reach the kitchen, she changes her mind. “I can’t face coffee, actually.” She gives Eva a forlorn look. “Do you mind making hot chocolate?”

This is the easy part. Making coffee, rubbing shoulders, mixing cocoa. Offering comfort to people who are willing to accept her love. She finds another mug. She stirs cocoa into the milk. The tears come again. She has felt so helpless, all summer. So confused.

She needs a shower. She needs to call Camila.

When she comes back down after the call, Ezra and Vicky are in the kitchen. They look as worn out as everyone else. Ezra stands somberly flipping pancakes at the stove. Vicky silently mixes frozen raspberries and blueberries with a little maple syrup and puts them in the microwave. Gabriel has started another pot of coffee; he sets out milk and sugar in the kitchen nook and tells Eva there is more water in the kettle for her. Aviva concentrates on cutting up a very ripe pineapple. Olivia brings out plates and silverware.

Ezra puts a stack of pancakes on the table. “They don’t get better when they’re cold,” he says. He goes back to the stove to make more.

Gabe and Ezra are the only ones with any appetite. They eat in silence. When Gabriel gathers the dishes, Eva holds up her hand.

“Before you all get up,” she says, “I need your help. We need to make some calls. Can you help me decide who is a priority, and who can wait?” She brandishes her well-worn, handwritten book of contacts and puts it on the table. They look at her in alarm. “I already spoke with Uncle Wilford and Aunt Lillian.”

“Of course we can,” Ezra says finally. He looks sternly at his younger siblings. “There’s no reason Mom should make all these decisions, and all these calls. Let’s figure out who is a priority.”

“I can handle my cousins,” Olivia says haltingly, “but . . .”

Gabriel volunteers to call the head of Lyman’s department.

“I’ll go get some groceries,” says Vicky. She grabs the keys to the van.

It dawns on Eva that she’ll have to deal with the funeral home. And she has to write an announcement for the paper. She cannot think beyond that. She sits at the counter with a piece of paper. “With great sadness, the family of Lyman Willis . . .”

She can’t. Not now.

At the sink, Olivia and Ezra bicker while washing up. Nerves are frayed. Tempers will flare. That’s just the way it’s always been with these two. They love each other fiercely, and they can clash over nothing at all.

They all sit around listlessly in the evening. Eva rummages through their music collection. She finds the Schubert sonata Lyman always loved. They listen in silence for a while. “Remember when . . . ?” somebody says. Tentatively, they share a few memories. Gabriel mentions the summer of the Winnebago trip, how thoughtfully Lyman had planned it all. Ezra recalls a silly moment at a campsite that summer. “Remember how Dad—” he laughs, and instantly stops himself. Embarrassed, he looks down. Vicky pats his knee.

"I can't believe you think *any* of this is funny, Ezra!" Olivia snarls.

"Sorry, sis. I was only . . . Gosh, don't . . ." He stands and goes to the refrigerator.

Olivia starts sobbing and sinks into the armchair next to Eva, one leg draped over her mother's. She hides her face against Eva's shoulder. Eva holds her in both arms and remembers a much younger child leaning against her, a little girl crying. How can she possibly comfort any of them? They have lost the father they loved. He left them.

"I was so angry at him this summer," Olivia mutters, still hiding her face. "So mad at him for spreading his bad mood over all of us . . ." She hiccups.

"I know," Eva whispers. "I think we all were mad at one time or another. But . . ." She hesitates. "I kept hoping I could reach him, that we'd figure it out together. But he kept saying he could handle it, without me. I tried to believe him."

Ezra comes over to Olivia. "I wasn't making light, I really wasn't," he says gently. "Just remembering him at his best, you know? I'm sorry if . . ."

"I know," Olivia waves him off. "It wasn't about what you said, I'm just really jumpy. Sorry, Ezra."

A thought nags at Eva. She remembers that Lyman had Gabe's phone. Did he have it on him? And did LaGrange forget to give it to her? Did it fall where he was? Is she going to have to search for it and face the tree again? She shudders. Gabriel hasn't asked for it; maybe he doesn't want to think about it. She should just get Gabe a new phone.

On her way to bed, she stops at the door to Lyman's office. She pauses there a moment, blinks away some tears. His computer is off. Papers are in neat piles. And there, on the mouse pad, is Gabriel's phone. She runs upstairs to cry in peace.

They somehow make it through the rest of the week. Eva asks her secretary to inform her colleagues of the death. No details. Being psychiatrists, they call and offer sympathy as if it were rolling off a script. Eva lets it all go to voicemail. The funeral parlor sets a cremation date.

Just to get out of the house, Eva goes to the grocery store, where she carefully avoids any people that she might know. When she returns, Aviva helps her put things away and notices her drawn face. Without a word, from then on, Aviva gets all the shopping done before Eva has a chance. Gabriel posts a list of food requests on the refrigerator. He writes the obituary and shows it to Eva. Then the obituary elicits calls. Many calls. Gabe is the only one ever to pick up the phone, but most messages go to voicemail until the inbox is full.

Ezra is sweet and solicitous with his mother and his sister, unless, for no reason at all, he explodes at Olivia. He collects everyone's laundry without sorting it and adds bleach to the hot wash. Olivia screams that he has ruined her favorite shirt. She runs to her room and slams the door. She is heard sobbing. Eva knocks on her door after a bit. "Just fuck off, all of you," Olivia yells, "leave me alone!"

Vicky quietly goes about household chores, runs the vacuum, puts dishes away. One afternoon, Ezra and Vicky argue loudly upstairs, then Vicky storms out with the keys to the van. Olivia stomps toward her brother's room. "Now look what you've done!" she accuses him. "I don't know why Vicky puts up with you." Then she cries, hiccupping. "I'm sorry."

"Hush, sis. It's okay, it's okay," Ezra says softly. "Go ahead, have a good cry..." When they both come downstairs, they are looking at their feet.

Gabriel drops Eva's favorite bowl, the one Lyman loved most too. It breaks into a hundred pieces on the tile floor. Eva wants to howl, but she ends up comforting Gabe, who sinks to the floor. He sits for a long time amid the shards. She pats his back.

On Saturday morning, Eva gathers them all together. Nerves are frazzled. Dark grief hangs over everything. It's time for her to take charge before they all unravel. They need to do something, go out and do something meaningful.

"Listen up, everyone. We're going on an outing. Put on good shoes."

"Why?" Olivia needs to know. "Where are we going?"

"To a special place where Dad and I—well, you'll see. Can you be ready in twenty minutes?"

She turns to Ezra and Vicky. "Can we all pile into the van?"

Vicky looks at Aviva with a question in her eyes; Aviva nods.

"Eva," says Vicky, "perhaps this is a time for you to spend as a family. Aviva and I have wondered when that should be, and this seems perfect. Go ahead without us."

"Maybe you're right," says Eva. "Thank you."

They file out toward the van. Aviva asks Gabriel for his car keys, just in case, and Olivia offers hers to Vicky as well.

At the trailhead, Eva points to a stand of birches and asks each one to peel off a piece of bark. Olivia looks puzzled. She asks, "How big?"

Eva shows them with her hands. When they are ready, Eva leads them up the hidden trail to "their" small lake, the trail Lyman showed her long ago. She remembers the otter and hopes it will come today. Or, well, perhaps not *that* otter, a descendant maybe. Ezra, Gabriel, and Olivia follow in a single file, in silence. At the lake, Eva finds a rocky area at the water's edge, large enough for them to sit together. Birds sing in the trees; a frog hops into the water.

"This was one of my favorite places, even before I met Dad," Eva says. "Almost nobody knew about it. Well, it turned out to be one of his favorite hideouts too." She sits for a moment. "We came here often," she tells them.

They look around.

Eva pulls four pencils out of her pack and hands one to each of them.

"Let us each write a message to Dad," she says. "Whatever you want to say. Or maybe what you wished you had said?"

"Then what? Do we have to read them out loud?" says Gabriel. "Do we burn them?"

"And what if I want to write that he is a selfish asshole?" Olivia asks.

"Say whatever you want. No need to read them. We could send them floating on the lake when you're ready. To wherever they will go."

"Mom," says Ezra, "I'm not sure about this . . ."

Eva straightens. They are right, of course. She only wanted to make them feel better, but this is uselessly sentimental. "Sure, let's just sit together a bit. Thank you."

Chapter 16
October 2004

Eva stares at the notice in her hand. It's from the high school. Olivia has a Saturday detention for being late too many times. At first, the return to school had lifted Olivia's spirits. She was excited about Honors American History, which promised lively discussion and debate.

"I can't believe it, Mom," she had said. "You'll never guess what we'll be doing this year. We're reading a book that questions all the accepted teachings about American history. Amazing. It's written by a guy named Howard Zinn. Heard of him?"

"Of course, I have! The civil rights movement. I'm not totally out of touch, you know." She had taken in her daughter's enthusiasm, had wanted to believe it might focus her back on life, school, and friends.

But soon after the detention, there are more notices. A number of assignments are overdue. And then Eva learns that the book report on Howard Zinn's *A People's History of the United States* was due last week. Olivia will have an F in her favorite class unless she delivers it by tomorrow, Friday. She has fallen off the honor roll. Her highest grade is a B- in music, and that's only because of her lovely voice. Eva sees her daughter slip into a listless half-presence; she hardly hangs out with friends and hides in her room.

"Sweetie, how are you doing? Really?" Eva asks at dinner that evening, with just the two of them in the kitchen nook.

Olivia shrugs. "How do you *think* I'm doing, Mom? Stop asking."

"I know I've asked," Eva admits. "But I'm worried, it's my job to ask. So, how do *you* think you're doing?"

Olivia looks at her fingernails. "I miss Dad," she says in a low voice. "And I'm still furious at him too. I can't stop thinking about it. I can't focus on anything else."

Eva takes in her daughter's tight shoulders. "I know. It sucks," she sighs. "It really sucks, doesn't it?" She reaches across toward Olivia. "Can you . . . ? Oh, I don't know. Can you think of anything that might help? Some distraction, maybe? The dance center is launching a tango class, and you've always said . . ." Olivia turns away.

Eva tries again. "Please look at me, honey?" Olivia briefly glances her way. "I know you're sad. We all are. But we have to make it through somehow, don't we?" Shrug. "Would you want to try that grief group, maybe?"

Olivia shakes her head no and huffs in disgust. "Bunch of belly aching losers, Mom! I went once. Not my thing." She moves the pasta around her plate, reaches for a piece of garlic bread, and munches on the crust.

"Well, that's your call—but please don't call people losers." Eva reaches for the salad, offers some to Olivia, who declines, and puts some on her own plate. She waits, but Olivia only stares out of the window. Eva's feisty, outgoing daughter is now a sad, withdrawn teenager.

She tries another approach. "I honestly don't know whether you *want* us to talk about this, or whether it's off limits, sweetheart."

Olivia turns to her somberly. "There is nothing to talk about. It's just you and me at home, Mom. I hate it. Nothing personal. It's not about you. But everybody's gone, and I hate it."

"Yeah. Oh, Livvie, I miss him too. And I really wish your brothers could have stayed longer. Do look at me a minute, please?" Olivia does, briefly. "The summer was terrible, losing Dad is terrible. But we *have* to find a way . . . We can't just give up."

Olivia stands with her plate. "Well, *he* gave up," she mumbles. She scrapes most of her dinner into the trash, puts the dishes in the sink.

Eva fights a surge of anger. "Olivia, that's not a reason for you to—"

"Yeah, Mom, I know. You've said. But how can you expect everything to be hunky dory by now? It hasn't even been two months . . ."

"That is not what I mean!" Eva raises her voice in frustration. "And you know it."

Olivia crosses her arms, leans back against the sink, and looks hard at her mother.

Eva continues with practiced calm. "I hate to remind you, but this is your junior year in high school, Olivia. You know as well as I do that the pressure is on and that grades *really* matter this year. College applications and all that?"

Olivia snorts. "I *know*, Mom! I've noticed! Every teacher goes on and on about it . . ." She pauses and squints her eyes. "Oh, I get it," she explodes then. "It's about the history book report, I bet! So, they told you."

Eva is puzzled. "Well, of course they did. Parents get notices like that. But hold on, I'm not berating you. I'm trying to help. And—"

"And what?" Olivia interrupts. She stands tall and brittle. Her face is closed.

"Honey, you don't have to—well—if you want to take it easier for a while, or drop a class, that's okay, you know. But don't just limp along. It will only make you feel worse. Maybe you need an actual leave of absence?"

"That's ridiculous, Mom."

"Well," Eva persists, "then maybe some therapy would help." Olivia glares. Eva will not be deterred. "I'll give you two choices. You could go by yourself, or we can go together, but it's time to give it a try. A few sessions, and after that, you can decide. We have to do what it takes to get through. Dad would have wanted you to move on with your life."

"Yeah, right!" Olivia scoffs.

Eva ignores that. "When I see you hurt so much, I *have* to offer you everything I can do to help," she says calmly, relieved that she said it. "I just have to. So, think about which way you want to do this."

Olivia slumps back in the window seat. She leans against the frame and stretches her legs out. There are tears in her eyes. Eva fights back her own. She scoots over and pulls Olivia's feet onto her lap. "Foot rub?" she asks.

"Yes," says Olivia. After a while, she looks up. "Maybe, if you go, I'll go, but I'm not going to therapy by myself. Besides Mom, you're not doing so great yourself, you know . . ."

They are both silently crying. Olivia gets restless soon and goes upstairs. "Night, Mom," she says softly.

A couple of weeks later, on a Friday night, at 3 a.m., the phone wakes Eva up. It's a man's voice. "Mrs. Willis?"

"Dr. Bedard speaking," she bristles groggily. She has never been anybody's *Missus*. She's her own person. "Who's calling?"

"Ma'am, this is the Burlington Police Department. I am looking for the parents of Olivia Willis."

Eva bolts up, wildly alarmed. "I am her mother, officer. Is she alright? Where is she? Was there an accident? Oh my god, what time is it?"

The officer cuts in quickly. "She is fine, ma'am, she is not hurt," he articulates clearly. "There was no accident, but she is here at the police station."

"Why? What happened? Is she in trouble?"

"We stopped her for a breath test, ma'am. She was driving a bit—erratically. The breathalyzer was fine, but it turns out her license has expired. You'll need to pick her up at the station."

"Oh." She is already hopping into a pair of pants, her phone wedged against her ear, relieved that's all it is. "Of course, I will be right there!"

Darn, she had reminded Olivia about that license. Twice. And she assumed it got done.

At the station, she signs the necessary papers. They retrieve the key to the Saab and get into Eva's car, and Olivia immediately starts sobbing. She manages no coherent words; she just sobs. She is obviously in no shape to drive; no wonder they stopped her. At home, Olivia heads straight for her parents' bedroom and curls up on the bed on Lyman's side. Eva tucks her daughter in, rubs her shoulders a bit, and turns off the light.

"Good night, Olivia."

"Night, Mom," Olivia mumbles. "Thanks . . ."

They figure out what to do about the license. Meanwhile, Gabriel helps them retrieve Olivia's car. He stays for a while afterward. He looks closely at his sister and glances at his mother. "Game of Bocce, anybody? It's a mild day," he suggests.

Olivia shrugs it off. Eva waits.

"Wanna go for a walk then?"

"Leave me alone, Gabe," Olivia says morosely.

"Um, sis, no. I'm afraid leaving you alone is *not* in my plans. I want to spend some time with you. You can pick *what* we do, but I'm going to spend some time with my baby sister."

"I'm *not* your baby sister, you bozo!" She play-punches his shoulder, but a small smile plays on her lips.

He hugs her. "So, what's it gonna be?"

"Did you say anything I want?" Olivia asks. "You sure?"

"*Oh-oh*. Yeah, I guess I did say that. Shoot."

"Well, see, I have a book report due. It's on Howard Zinn. It's overdue, actually, but Mom helped me get an extension." She glances at Eva. "It has to be in on Friday, in less than a week."

"Ah," says Gabe. "And . . . ?"

"I can't figure out where to start," she says. "I'm stuck about what part to choose, or what to say about it . . ."

He waits, smiling, until she comes out with her request.

"Can you help?"

"*Now* we're talking," he laughs. "Of course. I'd love to. That was my favorite class. Is it still Mrs. Lebowitz?"

"Yeah, she's crazy, isn't she?" Olivia goes toward the stairs. Her step is a little lighter. "But I love her kind of crazy," she adds as she runs up. "Hang on, I'll be right back, getting my stuff."

"Has she been like this, I mean—" he asks as soon as his sister is out of earshot.

"If you mean somber, aloof, then yes. I'm getting worried about it. You just got the first smile out of her in weeks."

"Bozo here, that's me, always making my sister laugh," Gabe jokes. His grave face belies the playful words. "I should spend more time with her, shouldn't I?"

Chapter 17
Thanksgiving 2004

A traditional Thanksgiving meal would be unbearable this year. Eva doesn't feel terribly thankful. Gabriel and Aviva will bring dessert to the house, but Ezra and Vicky will be missed. Eva plans a Moroccan meal. With no loaded memories, it might feel new and different. Olivia slices a mound of tomatoes and peppers, while Eva's eyes water over the onions.

They hear the crunch of tires in the driveway and several voices. Eva looks up in surprise. Who else could be here? There is a loud mock-argument between Gabriel and another man, then a woman's laughter. The front door bursts open, and Ezra strides into the kitchen.

"Hi! Surprise! Happy Thanksgiving!" He leans down to hug Eva, picks her up, and whirls her around.

Olivia lets out a whoop and runs up to Ezra, tomato dripping from her fingers.

"Hey, don't knock me over," he laughs, picks her up too, and swings her around twice.

"How . . . ?" Eva stammers. "When . . . ?"

Vicky and Aviva walk in together, both smiling, each with a pie plate. Gabe comes in last, brandishing a bottle in a paper bag.

"Last-minute decision," Ezra grins. "Flew in this morning. Figured you guys can't survive this long weekend without us. Am I right?"

"You have no idea," Eva whispers. She hugs Vicky and then Aviva. She wipes at her wet eyes with her sleeve. "Sorry, it's just—I was slicing onions," she says, fooling no one.

Ezra surveys the kitchen, announces there are more than enough cooks in there, and pulls out the Charades game. "Who's playing?" he asks.

"Go, honey," Eva nudges Olivia.

"I'll take over the slicing," says Gabriel. He joins Eva at the counter.

She hugs him. "Thank you, Gabe, that was the best surprise you and Ezra could have cooked up. It makes my day, and it's just what Olivia needs."

"I know, and I wanted to talk to you about that."

"Oh?" *What now?* she thinks.

"I should live here," Gabe goes on. "This empty house is not good for Olivia right now." He picks up the knife and takes one of the peppers. "How big do you want these?"

"Oh, a half inch maybe. But . . ."

"Hold on. No buts," he stops her. "You know I'm right. You're a great mom, but you suck as a brother."

She snorts. "Can't argue with that." She goes back to crying over the onions.

"You see how she lights up, right? She'll get through this better if I live here. And I've already talked it over with Aviva."

"You have? What about your lease? Would she stay in the apartment by herself, and be okay with that?"

"Well, here is the thing. We've been careful about our friendship, you know? I've told you that, about how a romance could ruin it."

"Yes." She hopes that is not what's happened.

"We've been careful long enough. It's time to move ahead. So, we're giving it a go."

She drops her knife to plant a kiss on his cheek. "That's awesome, Gabe," she thrills. "You're so good together."

"Yep. And she's been my rock since . . . well, since the summer."

"Are you trying to ask me if she can live here too?"

He snorts. "Was I beating around the bush? Sorry. Yes, I was . . ."

"Well, of course she can. You know how much I care about her. She's wonderful to have around, and Olivia loves her too. It would be great to have her." She has a sobering thought. "What about that lease?" she asks.

He scrapes the peppers into a bowl and tackles the remaining tomatoes. "We talked to the landlord this week, just hypothetically, to see if he'd let us sublet the apartment."

"And would he?" She pours olive oil into the large clay dish on the stove.

"He read about Dad in the paper, apparently. I had no idea people still read the paper." He shrugs. "He is a nice guy. He said I was 'such a good boy' for wanting to help my family. He offered to let us off the hook about the lease, right away."

"That was nice of him. And Gabe—I would never *ask* you to come home, but you're right about Olivia. She is struggling with her grief. Thank you."

She stirs cinnamon and paprika into the pot and adds the onions. Gabe looks around at the food on the counter. "Anything else I can do here?"

"*Hmm*. Yes, can you open those two cans of chickpeas? And then off you go, play some Charades." She wipes some tears away and *really* gets onion juice into her eyes.

After Ezra's dramatic and buoyant arrival, he becomes subdued. He teases his sister, but his heart isn't in it. There is not much of their usual give and take, and he gets scratchy the minute *she* tries to tease *him*.

Gabriel brings out a pack of Table Talk cards, conversation starters. "Let's lighten things up," he says.

Ezra draws the first card. *If you could choose to be smarter, funnier, or more athletic, which would you pick?*

"How could I possibly be any *more* of those than I already am?" He tries to laugh, but his voice is dull.

Aviva draws. *What is the first thing you would do if you were president?*

"Yikes," she frowns, "jump off the pier, probably. On a cold winter night." She looks up, startled at what she just said. "Sorry," she mumbles.

It's Eva's turn. *If you could switch places with anybody in the world, who would that be?* How can she possibly answer that? Somebody whose husband didn't shoot himself?

"I'll pass," she says.

Then Olivia draws. *If you could change one thing about your family right now . . .*

She does not even finish the question, gets up, and runs to her room.

A day later, after lunch, Olivia loses her temper. "What the hell, Ezra?" she snarls. "Can you stop moping around? It's depressing me! As if any of us needed *that* just now."

"You're hardly a bundle of laughs yourself, Olivia!" he says, quickly angry. "Do you think you're the only one having a hard time?" He stomps off. Minutes later, he comes back to apologize. "Sis, I'm sorry for blowing up. Just let's go easy on each other, okay?"

Olivia nods. "I'm sorry too, Ezra. You're right, let's go easy. It's just . . . I really wish you weren't going away again in a couple of days."

He hugs her and she cries on his shoulder.

Before they all go off to do other things, Eva gathers them together. "Listen up," she says. "Can we all sit here for a few? It's been a hard summer, and it's going to be a hard year for each of us in our own way. Right?" Five faces turn to her. "We're going to need each other," she adds.

Olivia glances toward Ezra. He shrugs. Everyone looks at their feet. There are nods, and someone mumbles, "Yeah."

They all think I'm being sentimental again, Eva realizes. She probably is, but so it goes. "Can we have a moment of silence together?" The clock ticks. "Thank you all for being here together. And . . ." Before she can tear up, she goes off to busy herself in the kitchen.

On Saturday morning, Ezra and Vicky are still upstairs while the others have breakfast. Ezra's voice booms, something that Eva cannot understand. Then his door opens, and Vicky storms out.

"I know you're grieving, Ezra," she shouts. "And I am trying to support you. But that does *not* mean you get to be an asshole!"

The door slams. Vicky comes slowly down the stairs with red eyes. She mumbles "Morning . . ." and goes to the coffee maker without looking at anyone. "Sorry about that."

"It's okay," Gabriel shrugs. "None of us are at our best lately, to be honest . . ." Nobody speaks. He turns on the radio.

Ezra comes down well after everybody else has finished eating. Olivia is already in the shower. In the living room, Gabriel and Aviva discuss the move out of their apartment. Vicky helps Eva fill the dishwasher, and Ezra joins them in the kitchen. "Sorry about all that, Mom," he says. His eyes are red too. Eva looks at him and then at Vicky. She has an urge to comfort each of them, help them talk it through.

He puts a hand on Vicky's shoulder. "Can we talk, please?" he asks. "You're right, I can be such an asshole. I'll . . ."

"Let's go for a walk," says Vicky.

Eva hears the door close. She leans over the sink and cries. *Why can't I ever leave others' pain be?* she thinks. *I'm always jumping in and "fixing" it. I almost did it again, and it was none of my business. What the hell is wrong with me?*

After the outburst, and after they return from their walk, Vicky and Ezra tread lightly around each other. They hold hands; they sit at the bottom of the stairs, talking in low voices.

For the rest of the day, Ezra and Gabriel are unusually solicitous with Eva. "You okay, Mom?" they ask, again and again. The fourth time Ezra asks, while preparing her a cup of mint tea, Eva snaps. They all treat her as if she might break, and it sets her off suddenly.

"Why do you all keep asking?" she blurts out. "Do I have any choice? I *have* to be okay." She is not at all okay, but she regrets her words instantly. "I'm sorry, Ezra. Thank you for asking. Thanks for caring, and for being here. Really. I'm just exhausted, I didn't mean to . . ."

They stand side by side, his arm on her shoulder, watching the water boil. He hands her the mug with an impish crooked smile. "Well, I'm glad I'm not the only one who loses it, Mom." He gives her a little squeeze and turns to face her. "Maybe it's time to focus on whatever it is *you* need. Don't take this the wrong way, but you're on pins and needles, fussing over everybody else."

From the corner of her eye, she sees Gabriel nodding.

Aviva and Gabriel go into town and bring back lunch from the new take-out place on Main. In the afternoon, Gabriel suggests a Scrabble game by the fire. Later, Ezra draws Olivia out to sing with him and Vicky, and he asks Eva to accompany them on the piano. That evening, he and Vicky produce a simple dinner with fragrant garlic bread.

"I just hate that Vicky and Ezra have a morning flight," Olivia whispers when they sit around after the meal.

Gabriel breaks the stagnant silence. "Remember the year Grandma and Uncle Wilford's family came for Thanksgiving?" he asks.

"You mean that year the oven didn't work right?" says Ezra. "When the turkey never got cooked?"

"Yeah, that one," says Gabe.

"Boy, we were so hungry, and so crabby!" says Ezra. "Violet screamed at Jordan to stop being juvenile. And *you*, brother, you were bothering the heck out of me."

"For a change," Gabe quips. "You were maybe three," he tells Olivia.

"We were all turning into cannibals," says Ezra. "So why are you bringing this up?"

"Dad made us Thanksgiving peanut butter sandwiches, on little turkey napkins, remember?" Gabe smiles. "He used frosting to draw a little turkey on each one. He put on a silly apron to serve them. I don't even like peanut butter, but I inhaled mine."

"Me too," Ezra recalls. "And then Dad distracted us with a treasure hunt, outside, all over the yard. Cookies, peanut butter and cheese crackers, granola bars, Hershey's kisses . . . what a meal we had!"

"Oh," says Olivia, "yes, I sort of remember *that* part. It was dark, right? We each got a flashlight, and Violet took me onto her team."

These would be lovely stories to tell at his memorial service, thinks Eva, *when they are ready*. She glances at the urn on the mantelpiece. They are obviously not ready for *that* either. She might go up to the riverbank one of these days, by herself, and sprinkle some of the ashes where the birds gather. It might help her to sit there with her feelings, in the place where they began.

She'll need to figure out who she is now. On her own. With grown children who have their own lives. She stands before she starts crying again.

"I'm exhausted, y'all. Going to bed," she says without looking at anyone.

Chapter 18
December 2004

Gabriel and Aviva's presence in the house cheers Olivia a little. Eva figures out how to navigate Olivia's waves of emotion. How to offer her daughter support, without encroaching on her prickly need for independence. Taking care of herself can wait. It will have to.

They meet at the therapist's office every other Wednesday, directly after school. This week, when Olivia arrives, she is a storm cloud. Her mascara is streaked, and her eyes are red.

"Sweetie?" Eva stands to meet her. "What happened?"

The therapist, Jane, is ready for them. "I'll tell you in there," Olivia says.

The story soon rolls out. At lunch today, Olivia noticed a girl staring at her in the cafeteria. Someone she barely knows. The girl turned to the others at her table.

"See her?" she gestured toward Olivia. "That's the kid whose dad killed himself," the girl said, loud enough for Olivia to hear every word. "They all knew he was depressed, apparently. But they left him alone, like for a week. That's when he did it."

Olivia sobs as she recounts their eyes fixed on her. "I just dropped my tray. I ran out of the cafeteria and out of the school building. I sat in the park the rest of the afternoon by myself. They're so mean . . ."

Eva feels sucker punched. She never dreamt Olivia might get hints of blame too, like she does. There was such a cold look on that woman's face last week. Lyman's colleague.

"You know, people just don't understand," Eva says lamely. She turns away to collect herself.

Jane sits quietly until Olivia looks up. "Often," she says then, "when people cannot handle terrible news, it is easier to blame it on something." Olivia shrugs. "If a terrible thing happens and it's not anybody's fault, then it could happen to them too. If they can blame somebody, they feel safer, like they wouldn't let it happen to them. Does that make sense?"

"I guess . . ."

Eva touches Olivia's arm. "I ran into a woman from Dad's department last week, someone in another lab. 'I'm sorry for your loss,' she said, sort of down her nose. 'You must feel terrible about going away . . .' Sweetie, I couldn't believe it." Eva is quiet. Raw guilt had erupted at this woman's words, and burning rage. Olivia looks up.

"Even though, up in my head, I know better, it still made me feel awful," says Eva, "like it *was* my fault. You do know it's not our fault, don't you?" Olivia shrugs. "I know I was not perfect," Eva adds. "I also know I tried. That we all tried. But it will take a long time to let it go, to forgive ourselves. And . . ." a question enters her voice, "and to forgive each other too . . ."

They sit with that. *It will take* so *much time*, Eva thinks. A familiar wave of anger rolls in, at Lyman, at the pain he caused his children. At the pain of his abandonment.

When their time is up, Eva walks Olivia to her car. She is still chewing on the cafeteria debacle. "Oh, Livvie, I wish it didn't bother me when people blame me, you know? But I'm not immune to it either. People's comments, their looks? They are bloody hard to ignore."

"No kidding," Olivia says.

"See you later, right?"

"Yep, six or so. Love you, Mom."

Eva mentions the incident to Ezra the next time he calls home.

"Fucking ignorant idiots!" he shouts. He rants for a while. Then he calls Olivia regularly in the next few weeks.

Chapter 19
Christmas 2004

The old van rumbles into the driveway on December 22. Flurries of snow have started falling. Olivia runs out in her slippers, without a coat, to greet Ezra. "*Yayyy*! I'm so glad you're home! Promise not to annoy me more than once a day?"

Eva comes out right behind her. After Ezra's bear hug, she turns to welcome Vicky, expecting her to emerge from the van. But Vicky is not there. Eva looks at Ezra, surprised.

"I'll explain later," he says. "She can't make it."

How come? Eva almost asks. His tense expression stops her. "That's too bad. Come in then." He grabs his duffel and his saxophone case. Olivia carries his backpack and follows them inside. After dinner with Gabe and Aviva that evening, they all sit around the table chatting. Over bowls of ice cream, Ezra finally broaches the subject of Vicky.

"So, here's the scoop." He looks darkly into his dish. "No pun intended." He swallows. "Vicky announced yesterday that she wasn't coming up with me." He fiddles with his spoon. "I suppose I shouldn't be surprised."

Gabriel frowns. "Are you guys having trouble? You've been together forever. You seem so . . . solid, I guess. What's—"

Ezra sighs. "The thing is, I haven't been easy to live with. That's what she says. And I can't disagree with her, really."

Eva looks at him with alarm. Her son was always intense. He could be too much sometimes. But Vicky is so good for him . . .

"I know I've been brooding over Dad, a lot," says Ezra. "She tries to be supportive, but . . ." He runs the spoon around his empty bowl.

"But what?" Olivia asks. "Have you been an asshole again?"

He looks up. "*Huh.* Thanks a lot, Livvie. Yeah, I guess so. I don't always realize it, but when I'm down . . ." He leans his head on his fist, elbow on the table.

Gabe gets up for more seltzer. He walks behind his brother, puts a hand on Ezra's shoulder. "I'm really sorry, that totally sucks."

"Yeah," Ezra sighs.

"But you do know, right, that you can be a bear when you're upset?" Gabe adds. "You always were . . ."

"Rub it in, why don't you?" Ezra snaps. Eva bites her tongue to suppress that impulse to smooth things over.

"Wait, no, I'm not trying . . . sorry, Ezra. What I meant is, maybe this is an opportunity? Maybe you can work on that with her?"

Exasperated, Ezra shrugs his brother's hand off his shoulder. "Are you my therapist now?" Eva leans across the table and squeezes Ezra's free hand. He grimaces and tilts his chair back. "She said I get like my father when I'm down. That I get like he was last summer, when he was angry and irritable, when he got depressed, and nobody could reach him." He cries silently and hides behind his hand.

It hurts, seeing history repeat itself all over again. Lyman's dad. Lyman. Now Ezra too? Unruly and exuberant Ezra, could *he* be depressed too? Or is he just sad and angry? She doesn't trust herself to know what he needs. Her world is upside down.

Gabe sits next to Aviva, not sure what to say.

"So, wait," Olivia asks, alarmed, "she isn't actually breaking up with you, is she?"

"I don't know," he admits. "She says she wants me to pull it together. That she doesn't care *how* I do it, as long as I figure myself out. As long as I stop lashing out at everything. She's going to California for six months 'to give me space,' and she says that after that, we'll see where we are."

"California?" Eva asks. "And her master's program at Juilliard?"

Ezra shrugs. "She arranged to study with Larry Grenadier, who takes almost no students, ever. But he agreed to work with her."

"Well, that's great," Eva hesitates. "So, she is not actually leaving *because* of you?"

"Well, that's not exactly true either," Ezra goes on. "We had planned to go to California together, at the end of our programs next year. But we've constantly been at each other. Or—well—she's had to put me in my place a lot," he says. Eva's stomach lurches.

"We had another blow-up a few nights ago," he adds after a silence. "She said she was sick of my grief and my moods leaking all over everything, that she could hardly breathe anymore." That sounds awfully familiar to Eva. Only a few months ago, she couldn't breathe either.

"She said she has to get out of here before she is totally fed up with me. That—" Ezra's voice catches. "That she has to go before she stops loving me . . ."

"Ouch," Olivia whispers. Eva gets up, fills her glass at the faucet, and wipes at her face.

"Yeah. She called Grenadier two days ago and arranged to go out immediately. She got permission to take a leave at Juilliard. She told me yesterday." Ezra rubs his forehead. "I'll go out to see her in three months. Meanwhile, I promised her I'd get some help." He looks toward Eva, who stands at the counter. "Nothing makes any sense to me lately."

They ponder this. Lyman's last weeks hover over the room; their loss lies damp and heavy over everything. *See what you did to your kids?* Eva wants to scream.

"Ezra," Gabe says finally, "it sounds hard, I'm so sorry. But you know—and I don't mean to sound like your therapist again—I'm so damn proud of you. For listening to her, for tackling it." His voice breaks, and he leaves the table. "Dad might be proud of you too," he chokes out and sits down again next to Aviva, who hasn't said a word. Her eyes glisten.

"You know, he might," says Eva softly.

"Dad couldn't face his demons, in the end," says Gabe, almost to himself. "The least we can *all* do is learn from that . . ."

Olivia gets up to gather the empty bowls. "Love you, bro," she says hoarsely.

Epilogue
Summer of 2018

The afternoon sun has lost its heat. Eva brushes the onslaught of memories aside, as she has done countless times before. Her life goes on, it must. The seasons turn, and birds are singing. Her dreams are waiting. Interrupted projects clamor for her attention.

And, right now, she has to finish sorting these photographs. She wonders what Olivia plans to do, exactly, with all the old pictures. She has been awfully secretive about *the big party* that she and her wife, Jamila, are organizing for Eva's birthday next Saturday. It will be here, at home, but Eva doesn't even know who is coming.

"We'll arrive by three, Mom," Olivia said yesterday. "You only turn seventy once, so wear something outrageous." Then she refused to answer any more questions. "Mom, for once, you are not in control," she laughed, seeing Eva's frown.

Eva felt exasperated, until Olivia's little girl ran up and climbed into her lap.

"Grammy, don't frown," said Gabby. "It will be lots of fun, right, Mommy? And besides, Mama Jamila is cooking you the best . . ."

Olivia quickly put a finger on her daughter's lips. "*Shh*, no spoilers, remember?"

"Oops," Gabby giggled.

Then on Wednesday, Eva picked Gabriel's son up at school for their afternoon together. When she dropped him off, Luke whispered, very loudly, in her ear. "You're gonna love that chocolate cake, Grammy!"

"Lukie!" Aviva scolded. "Don't tell." She rolled her eyes. "I guess he's excited about your party, Eva!"

Ezra called last night. He and Vicky separated when their twins were five or so, but Vicky agreed to change the visitation schedule this week, so that he could bring them to Vermont. And Eva's mind turns back to Ezra's brooding over his father. In the end, there were just too many ups and downs for Vicky to cope with. Eva misses her; it has been hard for her to accept that she has no role in fixing this. It is time to focus on her own life and let her children lead theirs.

Eva is excited to have them all around soon. And she'd best sort through the last of the pictures before Olivia and Jamila arrive. She reaches for the tray next to her rocking chair. Here is a photo with a slightly ripped edge. A serious little girl walks unsteadily, grimly holding onto her father's hand. Or being pulled by the hand? He is slightly ahead, wearing a rumpled suit and tie, as always. He looks at the camera and is not smiling. *See: I'm doing what I'm supposed to*, Eva imagines him thinking.

In this next one, she is a toddler on her mother's lap. She is intently focused and reaches for the piano with a forefinger, her pudgy left hand flat on the keyboard. Her mother offers a thin-lipped smile, uncomfortable and self-conscious. Eva remembers that stiff smile only too well.

She rocks her chair gently and nibbles at a shortbread cookie. Her tea is nearly cold. She closes her eyes for a moment and leans back. She lifts the last picture from the tray, a lovely black-and-white print. She must be about three in this one. She sits in the sand at the edge of a moody gray sea, lazy waves under a cloudy sky. Her bubble romper has little hearts printed all over. It is soggy and limp at the bottom. A small wave laps at her legs. Her hands are covered in sand; she has dug a shallow canal and is bent over as the sea flows in.

Horses. Piano. The water's edge. They have comforted her all her life. They still do.

In just a few months, Eva will return to Mangochi to develop the network of peer support she and Clara conceived decades ago. The resilience project. Lyman's downward spiral brought it to a halt, interrupting all of their lives for a long time.

Now she has enough funding, finally, to make an old dream come true. And then, who knows? She might retire. Play more piano. A two-week trail ride in Iceland tempts her. She could ask for a white horse and secretly call it Tarot.

Book Group Discussion Questions

1. Did you have a favorite character in this novel? Someone you felt most connected to? Why?

2. While reading, were you annoyed or angry at any of the characters? Whom? Why?

3. How did each character change in the course of this novel? In what way did the events affect their evolution?

4. What was the central issue in this story? How was it handled by the different characters? Did they each see it the same way?

5. Could you imagine yourself living inside this story? As whom? If so, are there turning points where you would have done something different than what they did?

6. Eva is a psychiatrist. Does her professional knowledge help? Or hinder?

7. Did the book make you think of anybody you know? Did it offer you fresh perspectives on them? How?

8. Do you believe that people who grapple with deep depression are aware of how much their condition affects others? Might this make someone more motivated to seek help?

9. Does a person realize how their suicide will impact others, while deep in their darkness? Can they think about this with clarity? Would such insight make suicide less likely? Or more likely? Why? Or why not?

10. What did Eva learn about herself in the course of this novel? What did she realize about her childhood and its impact?

11. What do you imagine will happen for Eva after the ending of this book?

The author is open to questions and further discussion.
She can be contacted through her website
www.raedumontwriting.org

Acknowledgments

The support of family and friends was essential for me to turn a collection of random notes into a book. Your kindness, patience, and encouragement sustained me while the story colonized my thoughts and our conversations. Seth Harwood taught me all about "show, don't tell." Both of my writing groups are vibrant incubators of ideas. Thank you, Ami, Sara, Marissa, Dennis, Dan, Doug, Cil, Sylvia, Paul, John, and Wendy. You are amazing listeners.

My first readers gave generously of their time and feedback. My children, Laurel Dumont and Sylvan Herskowitz, offered their own unique insights. My friend Shirley Glubka, a writer and a poet, uprooted fuzzy thinking, poor grammar, and clumsy sentences, and she steadily encouraged me to keep writing.

I am grateful to my editors Caroline Leavitt, Donald Weise, Amber Hatch, and Heather Martin. From their different perspectives, they each helped the manuscript go through a transformation. Brooke Warner and the team at She Writes Press made the book a reality. Crystal Patriarche and SparkPoint Studio helped me to bring it to my readers' attention.

Finally, I owe a depth of gratitude to those who helped me discover who I am. My uncle, René Dumont, taught me to take risks and to always reach higher. My mentor David Kantor guided me, with the warmth of his spirit, as

I became a family therapist. My children were my motivation, and my partners, in creating the loving family that sustains us.

I wrote this novel for all who have experienced depression, their own or that of someone they love. Your courage and resilience are an inspiration. I hope that in return, my book may offer some insight and some comfort.

About the Author

photo credit to Mark Jaworski

Raymonde Dumont, MD, LMFT, is both a pediatrician and a family therapist. She practiced and taught for several years at Harvard Medical School, and at the Joslin Diabetes Center. She focused on the impact of one person's illness through their entire family, and showed that mental health and family function affect the medical outcome. She is currently a family therapist in private practice. She helps families to navigate difficulties by collaborating, rather than becoming divided.

She is also a mother, a widow, and a friend to many. She now turns her years of experience into words that speak of resilience, and of the flawed road that leads us to becoming good enough. She wrote this book because the story would not let her go, and because she hopes it will bring some insight and some comfort.

She has published many professional articles, but in fiction, she finds a more personal, intimate voice. Several of her short stories were published in Persimmon Tree and The Hemlock Journal.

She lives and practices in Montclair, New Jersey, within reach of New York City.

Looking for your next great read?

We can help!

Visit www.shewritespress.com/next-read
or scan the QR code below for a list
of our recommended titles.

She Writes Press is an award-winning
independent publishing company founded to
serve women writers everywhere.